The Path to
TAIWAN'S
Democracy

MEMORIES OF AN AMERICAN DIPLOMAT

AMBASSADOR NAT H. BELLOCCHI

Bellocchi & Company
白樂崎

ISBN: 145288384X
ISBN-13: 9781452883847

PROLOGUE

Starting in 1949, Taiwan was ruled by the Nationalist KMT party that had ruled most of China before World War II, and at the same time, mainland China came under the control of the communist People's Republic of China. Thereafter, Taiwan was ruled under martial law. Some political reforms began in the ailing days of President Chiang Ching-guo, and after his death, were completed by President Lee Teng-hui, when he became Taiwan's new head of state. During this time when democracy started to take hold there, Nat Bellocchi was Chairman of the American Institute in Taiwan (AIT), the organization set up by the Taiwan Relations Act (TRA) to handle unofficial relations with the government of Taiwan. Ambassador Bellocchi worked with the government of Taiwan to help the transition to democracy, but was often not in agreement with the U.S. State Department, which did not want to rock the diplomatic boat too much regarding mainland China.

Ambassador Bellocchi was at times the only American official grasping with the difficult but peaceful transition of what was often called a police state to a full-blown democracy, and dealt with the dangerous diplomatic dance with China during that period. In fact, in 1995 and 1996, China shot ballistic missiles into the Taiwan Straits as a warning against the will of the Taiwanese people to freely elect their President for the first time and to move away from the so-called "one-China policy." It was also in response to then President Lee-Teng-hui's visit to his *alma matter*, Cornell University. This was made possible only after the U.S. Congress had voted 396 to 0 in the House of Representatives, and 91 to 1 in the U.S. Senate, to grant the President a visa. Prior to that the U.S. State Department had confined his U.S. travel to refueling and would not even allow him to get off the airplane in Honolulu. When President Lee was finally able to visit Cornell, he was greeted by Ambassador Bellocchi at the airport.

These trials and tribulations are discussed in Ambassador Bellocchi's book in detailed fashion as they have never been revealed before. Previously classified and hidden conversations between foreign policy principals and senior officials are exposed and analyzed.

The book begins with a simple autobiography about his early life in a small town in New York State during the great depression, the loss of his father at young age, and his determination to complete his studies and become an engineer. It also chronicles his time in the Army serving in Korea during the war and his decision there to join the Foreign Service, first as a courier mainly in Eastern Europe behind the Iron Curtain, and then as an officer stationed in the Far East. His assignments include stations in Laos and Vietnam during the war, his Chinese language training in Taiwan, and his eventual climb up the diplomatic ranks in Japan, India, Hong Kong, to his appointment as Deputy Assistant Secretary of State for Intelligence & Research and then as U.S. Ambassador to Botswana. It was only when Ambassador Bellocchi was almost forced into retirement that he chose to take on the most difficult and historic journey of his entire life.

Ambassador Nat Bellocchi lives with his loving wife of over 40 years in Bethesda, Maryland, and has two children with interesting careers of their own.

INTRODUCTION

The book is written primarily for my family and friends. It has in it my life as I saw it in the world from my beginning in 1926 through 1995. The five chapters near the end is written about my five years as Chairman of the American Institute of Taiwan from 1990 – 95, at the beginning of Taiwan's democracy.

The first chapter: My father and mother were doing well in the 1920's – my father was an expert from Italy on the development of colors that could be used for leather shoes. The company was one of the biggest in the area, but in 1929, during the Great Depression, it went bankrupt as many companies did throughout the country. My father lost his job. He set up a small shoe repair shop, and Mom had to start working in one of the smaller shoe companies. I worked cutting grass in the summer, and in the winter cleared snow and checked cold furnaces in homes. In high school I worked at different companies part time.

The second chapter: When I went to college at Georgia Tech, I continued to work, this time on an ambulance, in the school in the register's office, in the cafeteria, and proctor in the dormitory. I completed the normal four years in a little over two years, and found a job in Pennsylvania. When the Korean War broke out I was called into the war. After two years as a rifle infantry Lieutenant there, it could never be forgotten. Thereafter, I spent a year in Georgetown University to get another degree at the School of Foreign Service.

The third chapter: Five years in the Diplomatic Courier system. I had no idea what it was, but it would permit me to see the world more than most people. The work was not exactly easy –flying in the aircraft of those days to some rather unusual countries almost continuously was dicey. What I saw then about the people in so many countries and what life was like in them, helped me to think about them in later years.

This work was interesting, but it also had problems. I was once in a U.S. military plane that crashed into the Mediterranean. Another time was on West Africa Airways, in a storm that flipped the plane over on its back but was righted by the Polish émigré pilot and landed in Monrovia. Another was a ride from British Palestine all the way to Kabul, and there were many others.

In the Courier days, the countries were still recovering from the Second World War. Some, mostly the European countries, were moving forward, though slowly, as at that time they did not have the money or the number of experts that could rebuild the country. Many others, including new countries that had been part of the European countries, were just beginning to developing their countries. Some were doing reasonably well, some were not.

And then there were those behind the Iron Curtain. At that time this meant going to Russia, Poland, Hungary, Romania, Czechoslovakia, and Yugoslavia. We always were tailed by police wherever we went, and people in those countries at that time would avoid foreigners. Without exception, we felt fresh air whenever we left these countries.

The fourth chapter, after becoming a Foreign Service Officer, much of my work during the earlier years was in commercial and administrative work. The short time, less than two years, was interesting to me as I came to know Hong Kong well. But I soon became a Foreign Service officer. I spent two years in Laos, and then went to the State Department Chinese language school in Taichung, Taiwan. Two years later I was assigned to the U.S. Embassy on Taiwan as commercial attaché, where I met my wife Lilan. Then I was transferred to Hong Kong for almost two years, and then to Washington. A year later we moved to Vietnam for two years.

The Fifth chapter: the request by the Commerce Department to have me promoted to senior status was important for me in Japan, and later it helped in attending the Senior Seminar at the Foreign Service Institute. A year later I made a study on winning bids for large projects abroad. I became economic counselor in New Delhi for three years, and then be assigned to Hong Kong again, this time as Deputy Consul General.

Thereafter, I was to work in the State Department for the first time as a Deputy Assistant Secretary in the Bureau of Intelligence and Research (INR). I was then asked by President Reagan to become his Ambassador to Botswana. After three years, I worked as an International Adviser in Fort McNair, Washington. Given my age, I finished my work as a Foreign Service Officer.

The last part of the book – largely the last five chapters – which carries within it the difficulties of changing Taiwan to a democracy, and the struggles between the relationship between the U.S. and Taiwan during that time. My views of it are based on my life from the early days, through the years of the Foreign Service to the difficult days of working with that Service and the people of Taiwan.

The first problem was how the relationship with Taiwan, after we had changed our relations to China, was to be arranged. The Executive Branch insisted it had the right to control this matter, while the Congress insisted it also had oversight on this policy. The result was the Taiwan Relations Act – the first and only domestic law of its kind.

There were some problems during the early days of this relationship (1979 to 1990), but they grew considerably after Taiwan became a democracy – the time I became the Chairman of the American Institute of Taiwan. The last five chapters include the problems that took place during that time (and continue even greater to the present). The impression that stayed with me is of the very fundamental change from an authoritarian system to a democracy that had taken place in Taiwan and its fragility with the U.S.

The opinions and characterizations in this book are those of the author, and do not necessarily represent official positions of the United States Government. The U.S. State Department has cleared the publication of the sections of this book dealing with the sensitive U.S. – Taiwan relationship.

CHAPTER ONE
Little Falls Years to 1945

At the time of my growing up, Little Falls was a town of about 12,000. One of a string of towns along the Mohawk Valley, in upstate New York, it was a mill town surrounded by dairy farms. The terrain is hilly with plenty of trees which turned beautiful colors in the fall, very hot in July-August, invigorating in the spring and fall, and piled high with snow during the winter. The Barge Canal and the Mohawk River separated as they flowed through the town, joining again at the eastern end of town at the world's highest lift lock for barges. The only public transportation was a trolley line that came into town from the west, circled on to the east end of town, and then westward all the way to Utica, through several small towns. It was replaced eventually by a bus system.

The Mohawk Valley narrows through town, with two railroads, the canal and the river, and the highway, all funneled through a narrow valley. The residential parts of town were hilly, with little community (often ethnic) stores spotted around, and people walked where-ever one wanted to go. The "down town" section had many square blocks of three or four story buildings, with the ground floor a store. Even chain stores like the A & P, or Woolworth's, were a double size store. The two bank buildings were the most impressive, and throughout the town there were fourteen churches, four public grammar schools and one high school. St Mary's, the largest Catholic Church (ethnically Irish), also had both a grammar and high school.

Though in the western part of town different ethnic groups coexisted because they were relatively small, (i.e., Polish, Ukrainian, German), other areas had a more clearly identifiable ethnic character. The Irish lived in the northeast with older Dutch-German and English families in the middle of town. The "southside", across the river and canal, was the Italian section. In that era, the Anglo-Saxon and early German-Dutch families were the establishment (some with money, some simply gentile). The Irish dominated local government, including the police, while the east and southern Europeans were the "new" immigrants who were largely mill hands. Ethnic grocery stores and community halls were located in their respective area.

Many of the children would quit school at 16 (the earliest age allowed). They would go to work in the factories, often bringing their entire paycheck home to the family. With the large families prevalent then, many of the family's standard of living improved rapidly. A minority of the families sent their children to college, and because opportunities for college graduates were so limited in such a small town, most emigrated elsewhere.

Unlike most Italian immigrant families, our house was located in an Anglo-Dutch area. It was, however, not like the surrounding, much larger homes, but one of four built close together in a dead-end alley. We were at the far end. The first house had previously belonged to an Italian family with whom we were not very close. The next two were Polish immigrant families. Our house was divided in two, with half belonging to our uncle, my father's brother, who lived there with his sister. Both my sister and I were born in that house, and grew up there until we left for college. When I was small, the biggest annual chores handled by the men were the stocking of coal and tending the furnace, getting and chopping wood for the kitchen stoves, buying grapes and making wine. My father had an extension built on our part of the house as we were growing up. A rarity in those days for an immigrant family, the house was paid for. Many years later, Mom had a picture window put in the family room, and shortly thereafter, the neighboring family built a garage in front of it, negating the charm of it. It was an old house, always needing repair, but it was all we had, and a great deal of sweat and work was put into it.

The small living room was used only for guests; the bedrooms only for sleeping. In the winter the beds were piled high with blankets as the furnace would be banked and the windows had to be slightly opened even in the dead of winter. I had my own small bedroom and once drew a map of the world on the wall, a bit of learning not much appreciated by my mother. The waking hours at home were always centered around the kitchen, and in winter, around the stove. For years we had an icebox, for which we bought ice occasionally in the summer. Eventually we got a refrigerator, and a washing machine. Storm windows had to be put on and taken off each year. For entertainment, on very rare occasions, we could go see a movie, and "Zio" (uncle) owned a small box radio, which we were allowed to listen to on Sunday evenings.

My father immigrated to America before World War 1, with his brother, later joined by a sister. They came from Viterbo, on a lake just north of Rome. The brother, "Zio", was drafted into the army in WW 1, shipped to France and was gassed during some battle. Thereafter he could only hold light jobs. The sister,

"Zia", never left the house, except once a year to see the doctor. Zio and Zia lived in their half of the house. While Zio was always helpful, Zia gave everyone a bad time. She didn't like my mother, and wouldn't permit us to play around the house because we were too noisy. Zio outlived my father by several years, and kept the house going in terms of heat, or fixing. After he died, Zia depended on my mother for some time before she died. By that time, both us kids were out of the house, so the house was made into a duplex, with Mom living upstairs and renting out the downstairs.

Father was a relatively well educated man. He had been to the seminary in Italy for two years, but then something happened and he broke with the Church. In Little Falls he worked for a tannery as their master dyer. It was considered a good job for an immigrant. Because he was better educated, he was voted the secretary of the local "Sons of Italy" chapter, and on rare occasions he or Zio would take me there, where I watched the men play cards, drink red wine, and smoke strong Italian cigars. He left the organization and was rather ostracized by most of the Italian immigrant men because he was strongly opposed to Mussolini.

When the depression closed down the tannery, he opened a shoe repair shop in the factory district of the city. It was a small shop between a barbershop and a saloon, where customers were mainly French Canadian lumberjacks down from Canada. Drunken fistfights were not uncommon. The shop was located near the railroad station. The trolley to Utica ran in front of it. It and all the factories were at the river and rail level, while we lived up the hill. In winter it could be a pretty rough climb. My father seemed to want to Americanize and change our last name to "Bell".

My mother was also brought to the States by her parents sometime before WW 1. After her mother died, her father took her back to Italy. He could not raise small children and work, so essentially he and his children went back to look for another wife. After he remarried, they could not return to America until after the war. Mother always remembered going to grammar school in America, then in Italy having little schooling, and how anxious she always was to return to America. After returning for some time, my mother met my father were married in the early twenties.

While father had no direct relatives in the U.S., just a few who came from the same area of Italy and one cousin, mother was one of five sisters, all living in Little Falls. There were also others who had come from Vagli Sopra, near Lucca in Tuscany. The origin of Italians was easy to distinguish by the dialect spoken, and by the food they made. As in most of America, the Italian community was dominated by southerners - people of the mezzogiorno - a poorer area of Italy. Their dialect was unintelligible to us, more emotional, stronger food, and among whom it was always suspected, the long arm of the "Black Hand" or Mafia, reached.

Before my father died, I would spend much of my time in the shoe repair shop. At noon, even when I was going to grammar school, I would walk down the hill to the shop to relieve him for lunch, and go there on weekends, etc. I would shine shoes but otherwise I was probably not very productive. At home, our diet favored my father's tastes, especially for seafood, but during the depression, and particularly after his death, meals had to become more austere. He shared in the men's work around the house, like chopping wood or making wine. But we always had to keep a wary eye on him, to detect quickly whenever he had an epileptic seizure. We knew what to do then, (use vinegar or smelling salt and put something hard between his teeth) but nonetheless, it was always traumatic for us.

Mother worked all day, often six days a week, in the silk mill, for very little pay. Wages were paid in cash then, and her whole pay was handed to her every Friday in a small envelope. How she was able to do all that had to be done at home at the same time, is now difficult for me to fully grasp. Meals had to be cooked, and once a week bread had to be made. There was no refrigerator, no frozen food, and canned goods were too expensive. Fresh food was then truly seasonal, each unavailable out of its own short season. Thus home canning was necessary to have food in the winter months, and it was done on a wood burning stove. Tomatoes, string beans, pears, lard, berries, and any number of other things were canned and stored in the cool cellar. The cellar also had a large coal bin, a place for ashes, stacked chopped wood, and a place where potatoes, apples, cabbage were stored during the winter months. Several large barrels of wine made in the present year would be fermenting, and bottled wine from the previous year stored.

When my father died, life changed rather drastically for us. I found him in the shop one noon when I had gone to relieve him for lunch. He had not unbuttoned his shirt collar and was strangled during a seizure. So my mother was left to raise us - I was 12 at the time, my sister was 16. It was in the midst of the depression. Mother had never handled the money before. The sale of the shop's equipment brought very little, and his insurance covered the funeral costs only. I will always remember Mother writing down every single expenditure - even for a few cents trying to make ends meet. We made it probably because the house was paid for, but our food and our life generally was very austere, and depended entirely on mother's very meager wages. Working people no matter how small the wages, were not eligible for the little food aid given by government, and there was no pensions or health insurance. As for Zio and Zia, on a few occasions during those times, Zio went for a relief package (welfare food) at city hall

4

for him and Zia, but like most people in those days, being "on relief" was shameful and to be avoided if at all possible. In those hard times, being able to survive on one's own was a matter of pride.

Without the need to go to the shop, I took on little part time jobs. At first it was cutting grass, or shoveling snow, or tending a furnace, or delivering newspapers. The pay was generally 25 cents per hour, and the work was for what I then considered well-to-do families near the house. In retrospect they were mostly middle managers of local companies. In junior high school I found a job in a jewelry-optometrist store, cleaning up and running errands. It was on the way to school, but the hours were limited and didn't pay much. Through one of my grass-cutting customers, I got a summer job as office boy in a local manufacturing company. That was extended to late afternoons after school started, and by senior year, I was working all my available time, even to the point of getting called out of school on occasion. The latter earned me the comment in the high school yearbook as the graduate with the most outside work.

Being a part of an immigrant family on the one hand, but living among the older established families on the other led to a sensitivity and reticence on my part that has stayed with me my whole life. During the week, my only free time was at home, and my playmates, then, were the kids in the neighborhood. Most were "establishment" kids and our "foreign" customs, including Church since it was a Protestant area, and our relative poverty, developed in me at the age an inferiority complex. On the weekends, when I was small, mother used to take us, walking of course, to the southside where "Nonno" (grandfather) lived in a small, rather ramshackle row house. My mother's sisters, with their kids, also went at that time. They would bring food, clean his house, wash, etc. while we played. Later, after Nonno died, I would go to the Church on Sunday afternoon and play cards with the other altar boys, some of whom were cousins but all immigrant children. This split loyalty to two different groups of friends lasted until I left for college. Anxious to assimilate, we would not speak Italian even at home. Getting a ride in a car from one of the more affluent neighbors was always a great treat. In my senior year in High School, a group of boys, myself included, were allowed to take a train ride to New York City. At that time the 225-mile trip was an incredible distance for us.

The Church was such a large part of our life, that it's influence has remained with me always. St. Joseph's was the "Italian" church, with sermons in English and Italian. The original church burned down, I was in grade school, and when the present one opened, I was one of the new altar boys. I served for nine years. These were the days when the service was in Latin (we had to learn responses in Latin). No meat on Fridays, fasting for Lent and the night before communion, catechism classes, and other disciplines that are now largely gone.

Catholics were a minority then. Despite the substantial Irish, Catholic population who had been there for at least a generation, Catholics and immigrants were synonymous to the Protestant majority. The parish priest at our church during my growing years was Irish and he loved to sing. He learned to speak Italian to the point where he even gave homilies in it. He butchered the language but the immigrants loved it.

So many of the values of those days have drastically changed, including duty to country. The atmosphere during World War II is hard to imagine now. It was an accepted duty to serve when the country was at war, and society looked down on those who did not. Thus I signed up, in my senior year, for the air corps reserve - the purpose being to go into that as soon as I graduated from high school rather than simply be drafted. All the male graduates during the World War II years would go off to war, and those for whatever reason that couldn't perceived themselves as having a social stigma. So it was that when I went for a physical prior to officially enter the air corps, I was found to have a heart murmur and rejected. That was like the end of the world. It was an enormous shock. It brought on my decision to go to a school far from home, simply to diminish my embarrassment.

After World War II, after I left home for school, the town went through an enormous change. The war had brought men from all ethnic backgrounds together. When they returned, inter-ethnic marriage became the rule rather than the exception. As a result, the ethnic distinction of the various areas of the town began to crumble, and the "immigrant" stigma began to disappear. These were trends that were sociologically easy to explain, and based on a variety of reasons. Still, one has to marvel that it all actually happened even in a community as small as ours.

The town was to go through yet another major change - urban renewal. With industry moving south or overseas, and the population shrinking, as was the case throughout upstate New York, there were calls to revitalize the town using federal and state help. The entire center of the town was demolished and converted into a shopping mall. Most of the old factories were leveled. The net result of urban renewal has been to destroy the character of the town, and to reduce its chances for reintroducing the economic activity that would stem the tide of emigration out of the area.

CHAPTER TWO
Georgia Tech, Army (Korea), Georgetown

After being rejected for the military, I more than ever wanted to get away. On top of my social sensitivity there was now the stigma of not having served the military. I was able to "sell" the idea of attending a distant college on the basis that it would be much cheaper than attending schools nearer home (all of which were private then - there was no State University of New York (SUNY). "Georgia Tech" (Georgia Institute of Technology) at that time charged $51.00 for tuition for a semester. As soon as the GI Bill came into effect and the campuses all over the country were flooded with returning servicemen, the tuition jumped to $450. Though that was a lot of money then, still, the cost was such that working one's way through college, though difficult nonetheless was possible.

So I journeyed by train the farthest I had ever been from home - some 36 hours. I remember only that I was struck by the poverty in the South, and the different kind of soil one saw everywhere. It was reddish - not black like the soil I was accustomed to, the result of overuse by cotton farming I was told. Also racial segregation was still prevalent and visible everywhere.

I registered at Georgia Tech and was assigned a room in a dorm with a fellow from Pennsylvania. It was an unfortunate beginning for me. I was in a very strange place far from home for the first time. I had gone only to public schools which ill prepares students for the self-discipline needed at college. And then with that to overcome I was also given a roommate who was crude, uninterested in school, and apparently sent there by his family to get him out of the house. That combination was almost fatal in terms of schooling for me.

In addition to that, I quickly had to find work. The school helped in finding a job at the Atlanta public library. It paid very little, and I simply could not understand the people. Their southern accent was incomprehensible. I soon ran out of money and at one point I remember I surviving one whole week on five hot dogs. Needless to say, my grades were terrible, and I almost flunked out. My mother gave me funds to buy a round trip train ticket to home for the Christmas vacation that first year, but I believe that was the last time I was to do that before graduation. The trip helped to settle me down, however, but my poor start meant I had an uphill struggle the rest of the time I was in college.

I had originally intended to take engineering, but my grades indicated industrial management was more realistic. I was driven always by the objective of getting through college quickly so I could earn a living. This meant I worked through any vacations, took as many credits - usually 17 to 20 per semester - as the school allowed, and took as full a schedule as permissible in summer school as well.

School was not fun. Still, I did join a fraternity, and made good friends while there. But invariably the other fellows were from different social strata, and from the south, so I could only partially really participate in the kind of social life they had. However, even in the dorm and elsewhere in school, I was simply too busy and too bent on hurrying through for me to have made any really permanent friends. In retrospect, that was a mistake. Also, it seems again, I had two different groups of friends. Perhaps, like before, one group (like me living in dorms and working) I felt comfortable with, and the other (more affluent students) is what I may have liked to be a part of.

As for jobs, after the first semester, I luckily found a much better paying job working on an ambulance. At that time in the south, ambulances were operated by private funeral homes. There were four of us students who lived in dormitory rooms that were private, clean, right in the funeral home that was a very beautiful, large place not far from the school. We were given free room and $10 a week. For that salary two of us were on duty every other night, and one was "first" on call every other time on duty. There were times when the night was very light. There were times when one got no sleep at all. I remember falling asleep in English class once and having to explain to the teacher why. One became hardened to bloody sights and death very quickly. Once a new student colleague got sick when he saw some of us dig into a hamburger just after returning from a very bloody accident.

I also had a job in the registrar's office filing transcripts. It didn't pay much, but added to the other jobs I had, it helped. I also was able to get a job in the dining hall. First it was serving at the cafeteria's hot table, then eventually graduating to the cash register. Working one meal a day at the cash register got me three free meals a day. I was able to quit the ambulance when I got to be a proctor in a dormitory (free room). With all the jobs and the heavy class schedule, my grades were very mediocre. I did not realize it at the time, of course, but in retrospect, I made no real lasting friends, and there was very little play. The only real accomplishment was completing a college degree in two and three quarter years, and using that to get a job.

Allentown 1948-50

In 1948, through the school's job placement office, I was hired by Burlington Mills. It was then one of the largest textile companies in the country, and considered a very progressive company. Most of their factories were in the south, but I was given a job as what they called "industrial engineering". In fact, it was a jazzy name for what is better known as efficiency experts. One disassembles a job into its smallest components, and then times the operations and develops ways to cut the time by making the operation more efficient. Obviously, labor out in the shop weren't excited when you zeroed in on their own job.

I was first sent for a training course at a plant in North Carolina. It was a typical southern textile town. There was only one company, very paternalistic, with a very docile labor force, and a well-run mill town. The company essentially managed the town, and though well done, obviously it was done in a way that most benefited the company.

Then to Allentown, Pa, the ribbon making division of Burlington Mills, and its most northern plant. Trolleys still ran then, with signs in Pennsylvania Dutch. I lived at the "Y", right in the center of town. I bought my first car, which I massaged, cleaned, and mothered as a matter of great pride. During that first year there, I got a very painful attack of what I assumed was appendicitis. There had been a pain on my right side for at least the last year in school. Having no money, I did not go to a doctor all that time. But in Allentown, the pain simply became too much. The manager of the "Y" got me to a hospital. After a couple of days of very excruciating testing, they operated. It was a kidney stone embedded in the tube between the kidney and the bladder. They had to take out the kidney, then put it back. I lost 60 pounds.

The ribbon division of Burlington Mills was different in character than the southern plants. It had been purchased from a New Yorker whose influence remained in the organization through many holdover people. It had a somewhat different market and was even more volatile than regular textiles. Labor management relations were adversarial, not the paternalism of the south. Eventually, after my time, Burlington sold it off. In late 1949 there was a recession in that industry, and the company had to begin layoffs. The company tried to keep the younger college grads by laying off older managers and foremen, and asking the young ones to take a step down. Most of my colleagues were married, had kids and mortgages, and had no choice but to take the step down. I sensed that would be the end of advancement in that company if I accepted. The company would surely hire young new managers when times got better, knowing that my colleagues had no choice but to continue at their lower tasks. As a bachelor, I simply said no and prepared to leave. It worked, and in fact they gave me a raise.

The highly repetitive high-speed jobs were in packaging. A few seconds shaved off each item saved considerable money. Having taken many time and motion studies on the various packaging operations, I became very familiar with them. I designed a machine that could put ribbon up in a different kind of package, a type the salesmen had long sought, at high speed. It was costed out, found very competitive in terms of price, and ahead of any in the industry in terms of the type of package. The company made a lot of money on that. Creating it was considered merely a part of my job, however, so the benefit was all to the company. It was this experience, and my interest in working abroad, that had much to do with my not wanting to return to working for a company when I left the military.

Socially, yet again, I had few friends. The people I worked with were all married, and most had always lived in that area. I dated some, worked on my car, and spent a lot of time aimlessly driving - or cruising - around the area. I did not realize it at the time, but nonetheless, I was not really fitting in to the life there.

U.S. Army 1950-53

I was, in fact, already exploring employment abroad when the Korean War broke out. My social reticence had persisted during my two plus years in Allentown. As a result, I had only a few friends and avoided partying. I had not really established any roots there or joined the community. Also, still carried some guilt for having been rejected for the military. So when the draft was resumed at the outbreak of the Korean Wan in 1950, I was early on called to take a pre-draft physical. I told no one of my previous rejection and simply prayed hard that somehow, this time, I would get through. I did much to my surprise. From this experience I assumed that a heart murmur was an on-and-off thing. Many years later a doctor told me that science had come to know much more about these murmurs, some of which were harmless and would not, say in the Vietnam War, have disqualified me.

So I was in the first draft group from Allentown after the outbreak of the war. We were sent to Fort Dix, New Jersey. I was put in infantry training, in a company that was about 65% college grads. It was pretty miserable. First I was unaccustomed to the physical exercise. Second, privacy was abolished. Ā Sleeping, showering, toilet-everything was open to full view. Third the platoon sergeant who was training us was crude and strict. In fact, he was excellent for the job, and in time we came to realize he had made soldiers out of us, and that in his own way and for what was needed of us, he was smarter than we were. Fourth it was very cold and we spent most of our time outdoors. Fifth, the officers were called up reservists who were very unhappy being back in service. Most of the officers and all the company that had not volunteered for Officers Candidate School went directly overseas after the fourteen week training - just in time to reach Korea as the Chinese began their push south. I suspect a great many did not survive.

There were a lot of experiences there, getting broken in and brainwashed. The bitter cold field exercises, wild dogs on the range, KP, uniforms, discipline, conformity, and a two-day pass to New York. As cold hearted as the city appears, the people can be good to servicemen. I remember three of us, sightseeing in Time Square, were invited in to a famous restaurant as we passed by. We were given a choice table up front, fed, and listened to the floorshow which featured Louis Armstrong. Toward the end of the fourteen weeks, I took another risk in signing up for OCS, knowing that another physical would be given. Once again I held my breath, but I got through. As far as I can remember, I did not get to go home before transferring to Fort Benning, Georgia for the three month OCS training at the Infantry School there.

It was a time when things were looking bleak in Korea. The US was in re-treat, men were getting frozen to death because both equipment and the right clothing wasn't available, etc. I was in the third OCS class, and the school was in a hurry to get us through and out to Korea. All those reservists lieutenants like the ones we were under at Fort Dix, were getting killed and replacements were badly needed. OCS was tough physically. They kept us on the run, liter-ally (one never walked in OCS, always jog). It was a factory, no doubt. Yet, I was never before, and probably never again, in such good physical shape. And I had acquired something very precious – self-confidence. Aside from all the infantry rules: "two up and one back, and head for the high ground", for example, one acquired the confidence to lead men. After two weeks leave, I was transferred to Camp Roberts, California. I spent about two months there, teaching in the "Leadership School", a training course for Non-commissioned Officers.

Then inevitably, the transfer to Korea. As second lieutenants, we were jammed into a charter DC-4 aircraft so tight that not only the seats but the aisles were used. In fact my "seat" was in the aisle. It was my first plane ride. It took 36 hours to fly to Tokyo, stopping in Honolulu and Wake Island for fuel. Tokyo was my first time out of the country and my first touch of the Orient. The Tokyo of 1951 was still very much recovering from the devastation of World War II. Every-thing was ridiculously cheap. We spent a few days there processing, and I got to have a meal at the famous general headquarters officers club. It was a Prince's residence, but being used as a club under the occupation. It had a fabulous atmosphere and unbelievable service. It was a never-never world which couldn't and shouldn't last, and didn't. Candy bars and cigarettes were still sought after items by the Japanese. There were no high rises in Tokyo, even on the Ginza.

We were shipped by train to Gifu for two weeks of CBR training. It was ridiculous, but it did give me a chance to see a little bit of Japan. Cormo-rant fishing, riding crowded trains, the countryside. I was fascinated by it even though it was just a glimpse. Then we were hustled on to a train and sent to

Sasebo, where we were put aboard a ship to Pusan, Korea. I was assigned to the 2nd Division, and with others put aboard a train to Division headquarters in central Korea. The devastation of the war was evident all the way, with people, especially children all along the rail side always with their hands out for food, candy or cigarettes. I was assigned to the 23rd Infantry Regiment and two of us were assigned to "A" Company.

We were dumped at rear headquarters, given a tent next to a veritable small mountain of Graves Registration rubber body bags, with the bodies of recent those KIA (Killed In Action) recently from the company we were going to. Then we were each assigned a group of raw recruits who had just arrived after their 14 weeks basic training. This group was to be my platoon. When I issued them weapons, they didn't even know how to assemble them. The atmosphere there, and the rumble of the artillery, made us all realize that the moment of truth had arrived. No more make-belief and no one of us had the immunity from death that the movie stars seem to have in their films.

We were trucked up some distance, then walked to the front lines. Each platoon was given a sector of the trenches to occupy. We were literally only about 50 yards from the Chinese forward positions. The first few days I lost several men from small mortar fire. The reason this is always the most dangerous time for new combatants is that one is not yet familiar with sounds. One's reaction to sounds has to be instantaneous. An incoming round from a 60mm mortar close by, for example, gives only a split second whoosh sound. One must hit the ground in that split second, or be a standing target for shrapnel. Direct fire from tanks gives even less time, artillery more. Then the sounds of movement, or a piece of equipment hitting against something. Each has a distinctive sound, and at night in the trench or out on patrol, one must recognize the sounds instantly as friend or foe. Even the buckle on the arm sling of a rifle, hitting against the top of a canteen, for example, has a distinctive sound.

There had just been a big battle on "Baldy" (from whence all the casualties we saw), and we had been assigned just to the left sector of that hill. To try to keep the Chinese from moving too close, a patrol had to go out every night, from each company, looking to ambush any Chinese patrol that may be probing our lines. The first time our company sent out a patrol after our arrival, Lt. Blohowiak, the fellow that had joined the company at the same time as I, was killed. The next night was my turn. About 50 yards out I encountered my first Chinese - he was dead, had been for some days, was all bloated up and smelled terribly. We got hopelessly lost, apparently wandered behind Chinese lines without knowing it, and somehow found our way back after a night of stealthy walking.

In returning to our lines and during my debriefing at battalion, headquarters to the rear, I discovered that the battalion the day before had erroneously sent my name in as being KIA instead of Blohowiak. Luckily, they were able to contact the divisions who were able to intercept the message before it had gone to the States. For the next several weeks Blohowiak and his replacement alternated every other night taking out a patrol. It's not something one can keep up too long, both in risk and in pressure. To add to the pressure, the army was in the process of desegregating. No problem there, but then they disbanded the Puerto Rican regiment, and I got several replacements from there. At the same time, it was decided to scatter Korean soldiers around frontline units to train them while fighting. So I would take maybe 10 or 12 men out on patrol, half of which couldn't speak English. In the pitch of night, relaying commands back and forth very quietly, became a problem. Especially when the command was "move out". Very conveniently, that message didn't get passed very far, and I would wind up setting up an ambush way out there with only a handful of men.

After a few weeks, we were pulled into reserve, not too far behind the lines. In fact we set up next to the MASH hospital, in Uijanbu. That is the one depicted in the long TV series. All officers received a bottle of whiskey presumably to help us relax. Two of us commandeered a can of grapefruit juice each, took our bottles to the tent, and proceeded to kill both. Got so sick from that, I have never been able to drink whiskey since. We went back up on the line in another sector - to the east of what was known as "Pork Chop Hill" and the "T-Bone. My platoon linked up on the right with the French Battalion (each regiment had an additional battalion from a UN member country, making it possible to call the war a UN action). We spent only 3-4 weeks there, but in that time the Chinese launched one of their human wave attacks, mainly against a ROK division to the right of the French, but also including the French. My platoon linked to the French, and though the waves of Chinese troops were hitting the Korean and French, we were under heavy artillery fire.

We were hit pretty hard, but fired cross fire across the French front. My platoon burned out nine machine gun barrels that night. The French held, but took heavy losses. I went over there the day after. The colonel and his men were all Foreign Legionnaires (who later went to Vietnam and were wiped out on "The Street Without Joy"). The French, typically, baked their own bread and carried their wine with them. They showed me the results of the night before. 485 bodies of what looked like young Chinese kids were strewn all over. Most had been killed by the French, but many from their own artillery. I had been under Chinese barrages, but not as concentrated as had the French.

Then the regiment was pulled back for a rest, and was assigned to guard Chinese prisoners on Cheju-do island. I was pulled back to Regiment headquarters, where I stayed the rest of my time in Korea. The commander was Col. Joe Stilwell, Jr. The son of "Vinegar Joe" Stilwell of China fame. My first task was to arrange the shipping of the regiment from Inchon, Seoul's seaport, to the island. Seoul was a bombed out city, but after the front, it looked like civilization. Soldiers did things like salute officers, shave, and not eat out of cans. I slept on a bed. When the troops arrived and began loading on the ships, we got into a big hassle with the navy. They cited Navy regs prohibiting soldiers from having any ammo. For frontline soldiers, weapons are pretty useless without ammo. It got resolved and then, en-route, we ran into a typhoon. I won't describe the mess aboard a troop ship in a typhoon. The navy may still be cleaning the ships. The one bright spot was the active trading that went on between the sailors and the troops. Unbelievably to us, the sailors wanted "C" rations (to make them feel like they were in a war, I guess). They traded things like butter, cookies, etc. To each his own.

The time on Cheju do was quiet. The Chinese prisoners policed themselves. They were the ones that in fact did not want to return to China, and eventually were turned over to Taiwan. We were shipped back up on the line, first to relieve the "Commonwealth" division, then over to the center sector. I remained at regiment headquarters as the assistant operations officer. We lived in tents, ate out of trays, and seldom got close to the front. For me, regiment headquarter was quiet, and division headquarters seemed half way back to the States. When my year was up I processed out near Inchon and boarded a troop ship for the States. About three days out, we were told that a peace agreement had been reached. Arriving in San Francisco was unbelievable. I was immediately struck by the color. No more khaki and camouflage. Buildings, cars, people, all in color.

After a train ride across the country, I was demobbed at Fort Dix and returned home by train. I was very tired. Without knowing it, all the strain of the last year was leaving me. I simply rested for a whole month, reading all the volumes of Churchill's history of World War II.

Georgetown 1953-54

I didn't want to go back to Allentown, or to work for that company. I decided to use the GI Bill, and enrolled in the School of Foreign Service at Georgetown. At that time it was the only school of its kind, and the one year course I took would (1) prepare me for the Foreign Service exam, and (2) give me a B.S. in Foreign Service.

I lived in a basement apartment on 5 Street with two other fellows. I worked in Kramer's book -store 20 hours a week. In addition, I carried 20 credit hours each semester and 5 in summer. In terms of gaining knowledge, I got much more at that more mature age, but the heavy load still limited what I could have gotten. I failed the first written exam for FSO by one point. At that time the exam was a long, essay type that favored the liberal arts majors. (When I took it again it was more a multiple-choice type). After graduation I returned home to fill out applications for work. I applied to several government agencies in particular. While I waited for results, I took a job with another fellow in New York changing Addressograph plates used to label mail to Stockholders. (General Motors had split their stock). We lived in a room in Brooklyn Heights.

Then I returned to Little Falls, waiting for some of my applications to come through. However, simply living at home without contributing was uncomfortable. I signed on as a temporary worker in our hometown bicycle factory and worked on the "bull gang", waiting for these responses, but at least earning my keep. The "bull gang" in the factories in that area simply meant being a common laborer who did the heavy work more experienced or technical people wouldn't do. In the meantime, I had applied to several places, overseas businesses and government agencies. USIA and CIA among them, but also the State Department. I read a brochure about State that included "Diplomatic Courier" and I applied without knowing what this really entailed.

(Clockwise from Top: Quang Tin province, Vietnam, 1971;
Afghanistan as a courier 1950's; Korean War 1952; speech in Taiwan 1960's)

(Nat Bellocchi, with wife Lilan, son Luke, and daughter, Jacqualine)

CHAPTER THREE
U.S. Diplomatic Courier 1955-60

I had written to my congressman to help in my job hunting. Out of the blue, after several persistent queries from me, an offer came from the Diplomatic Courier Service. I went for an interview where they showed me the enormous stack of applications for the courier job. I was accepted, and at the time I frankly did not know what a courier did except that he traveled a lot. In any event, in March of 1955 I began my Foreign Service career.

The Courier Service was established when wireless communications between Washington and its embassies abroad were less secure. It continued for classified material that couldn't or shouldn't use wireless for whatever reason. The couriers traveled alone (except behind the "iron curtain") with their pouches, either transferring pouches at airport stops, or entering the country and proceeding to the embassy. Schedules were established to cover all countries at specified dates so embassies could be prepared with return communications as needed.

The courier service then had about 70 men - all single, male over 25, past overseas experience, college grads. That's all changed now, but then being a courier has considered being a person of high integrity. Five had been killed in air crashes in recent years. A couple of couriers had turned themselves in for having lost control, even temporarily, of a pouch. There was a headquarters in Washington. One courier office covering Europe had just moved from Paris to Frankfurt. Another was in Cairo covering Africa and the Middle East. One in Panama covering Latin America, and another in Manila covering all of Asia. A courier spent two years at one location, then transferred to another. The average length of time a man stayed in that service was between two and three years. The turnover was brisk - most often a courier resigned when one got married, or switched to a different job in the Foreign Service. Occasionally one left rather quietly, and for us mysteriously. This was the McCarthy era, and the paranoia of the period even reached to the Courier level.

World traveling in the 50's was radically different than now. Commercial planes were props driven. Radar at airports was limited. Hotel accommodations were austere. High rise air-conditioned hotels were few. Flights were less frequent and less reliable. A courier often had to do innovative changes to maintain a semblance of his schedule. I have taken trips through the low countries, UK and Ireland without once having used my original tickets. Fog and bad weather continually disrupted airline schedules, causing us to switch to rail, boat or car. The planes could not fly as high so heavy turbulence was more common. Getting into cloud-bound airports often took several passes and often a landing at an alternate airport, causing havoc with the schedule. Being off schedule was the rule, meaning long agonizing waits at the airport.

Most of the planes we flew in were DC-3, 4,6, or versions of the Constellation, the Convair, and later the Viscount. Even the larger planes like the Constellation or DC-6 would get tossed about by the weather pretty harshly. The planes could not get above the weather as now, and the violent turbulence often had one wondering if the plane would hold together. Propeller planes are more difficult to maintain, and repair, as well. Weather, and mechanical breakdowns, therefore, were far more prevalent. Losing engines in flight, and near misses, were also quite common. In a great many countries without the tradition and discipline required in air operations, flights were especially risky. I've experienced forgetting to put the cowling back on in Madras, our plane going belly up in a storm off Monrovia, hitting an air pocket near Manila. Flying almost anytime into the old Kaitak airport in Hong Kong, or the harrows of flying into Katmandu, hitting a typhoon between Phnom Penh and Bangkok, and many, many more. Flying experiences of those days was an adventure.

So traveling was far more uncomfortable, and much riskier than now. The political atmosphere also was much different. Most especially in Eastern Europe, but elsewhere also, the cold war was in full swing. In traveling behind the "iron curtain", for example, we quickly developed a sense of knowing when we were being followed. Occasionally there were crude attempts at compromising. Security, therefore, was always upper most in our minds. On the other hand, there were advantages over the present. Our protection wherever we went was our diplomatic passport. That meant something then, as the fear of reciprocity assured our protection. Hijacking and terrorist bombing were unheard of.

Passports can have additional pages inserted. Our passports were usually bulging. Every country required a visa, some a new one for each trip. Finding the right visa was often a chore and thoroughly exasperated many immigration officials at airports. One of each courier office's major tasks was keeping up with our visas and our shots. Most countries then required a series of shots, and the shot record was always inspected at the airport.

Another chore, for us, was submitting travel vouchers. We theoretically were supposed to turn one in after every trip, detailing times arrived, depart, airlines, etc. However, given all the factors mentioned above, the always short handed couriers system seldom gave enough time off between trips to perform that chore. Perhaps once every three or four month we could do it, and then it would be a real chore. Given our constant travel, the voucher would be pages long. If we kept decent records enroute, it could be done. Some did not. Watching them trying to reconstruct trips from odd pieces of paper, matchbooks, etc. was a common in-house joke.

Money exchange was another chore. We could change money at the most advantageous rate in the most advantageous country provided it was for our own use only. Knowing where we would be traveling, we would know where it was best to change money into different currencies. We all lived in apartments in the city where our regional headquarters was located. Laundry would be done there, often on short notice, during the short time we had to spend there. Because of the unusual nature of the job, and because we would be running into each other in so many different cities, countries, and continents, there was a close camaraderie among us. It was often awkward joining parties or having dinner with embassy people because our experiences were so different, and their interest was so focused on the country of their assignment.

None of this was known to me when I started off from Washington on a Sabena flight to Europe. It was only my second airplane ride, and I was being assigned to Europe. The US dollar was so strong everywhere that we rode 1st class all the time. I learned very quickly, on that flight, that one doesn't over-eat, no matter how good the food. To this day, I feel uncomfortable flying on a full stomach, and I have never been able to really sleep on a flight. Arriving In Frankfurt, I was taken to my apartment. It was in a large apartment building complex, a part of which belonged to the Consulate General, of which our office was a part. Most apartments belonged to the U.S. military. It was all superbly built and maintained by the Germans as part of war reparations. There was also a huge PX and commissary there, and schools for children of the military. The office was in the Farben building. It formerly was the office building of the Farben chemical works, which had employed slave labor under Hitler and had therefore been dissolved by the occupation authorities.

The trips were structured by the office to provide service to the embassies against certain requirements. The schedules had to be changed often, because airline schedules changed often. The schedules we followed were not secret, and airport porters would come to know them. We wanted that because we needed porters readily available to help us through customs and immigration. As a matter of policy we always tipped well, for the same reason. The office communicated with the embassies to assure they knew the schedule, hotel requirements, etc. Once a courier started on his trip, however, it was up to us to keep the embassies ahead informed about any changes.

Although there were many places where we would simply have an airport exchange with someone from that city's embassy, and we would continue on to some other destination, the schedules changed often enough that eventually, we overnighted or spent one or two days in all the major cities of the region we covered. Our accommodations in the various cities also varied. In the fifties, with the dollar so strong, when we stayed in hotels, they were usually the best (though in the post war period always austere, no air conditioning, E conditioning, etc.). In some cities where couriers often transited on various trips, we might have a small apartment managed by the embassy. In others a hotel would simply set aside one room and we always used that one passing through.

Where we had "details", inevitably we had apartments. Details were temporary way stations from which, while on a larger trip, we would branch off on several side trips. Some details would last a month, some shorter, some longer. In most cases other couriers would pass through on other trips, so we often ran into each other all around the world. In the "Iron Curtain" countries, we always traveled in pairs. On the whole, however, we were most often on our own. That may have suited me, but contributed in fact to my natural lack of gregariousness.

There were also some very boring trips, such as the USAFE flights. These were DC-3 type planes with bucket seats that broke down almost invariably along the way, causing long waits at military terminals. One was the weekly flights, sometimes twice weekly, from Frankfurt through Marseille to Tripoli (to connect to the mail service the military provided between Washington and Tripoli - Wheelus Air Base. Another was Frankfurt through Rome to Athens (to feed the Athens "detail").

Just before leaving my first Helsinki detail, I received word that two of us were to be transferred to the Manila office immediately to cover a shortage of couriers in that area. Given the state of aircraft, radar and the climate, we were averaging about 185 hours a month in the air in the European area. There were times when we merely could change our laundry in Frankfurt before embarking on another trip. It was daunting to think we were going off to an area where conditions may be even worse. Thus my first two-year tour became a few months in Europe and most of the remaining year and a half in Asia.

I took a KLM airplane from Frankfurt to Manila, getting off in Bangkok enroute to get a visa for the Philippines. Don Maung airport was 22 kms from Bangkok – then - along a 1 and 1/2 lane road, through countryside (mostly rice paddies). The cobra population was legendary, and seldom over the next couple of years, did I ever ride in or out the airport where we would fail to see a run-over cobra on the road. The klongs, which ran on each side of the road, also ran throughout the city, making it almost a Venice of the orient. It also made it mosquito infested everywhere. Since hotels, restaurants or stores were at that time not air-conditioned, one was attacked by mosquitoes everywhere.

Still, it was this ride on a rickety bus into Bangkok, that decided for me what part of the world I wanted to study and work in. I had read Pearl Buck in early years, and then the two weeks and two R & R leaves in Japan (I saw little of Korean life as we were always in the combat zone area where civilians were not allowed). I also was interested in and taken some courses in Eastern Europe at Georgetown. It was a matter of deciding between these two areas of interest. Of all things, it was the smell of the open sewers, reminding me of the two weeks in Gifu, Japan, that convinced me my interest was in the Orient. It was a strange feeling, almost like coming home.

Manila, still recovering from the war, struck me as much Latin as Orient. Living with dollars was cheap, as it was in most places. We lived on the economy, with the embassy paying for quarters and utilities. At that time a new rule permitted the luxury of having an air conditioner in each occupied bedroom. Whatever couriers were in town spent much time at the Bayside Hotel, playing liar's dice and drinking cold San Miguel beer. The Filipino friends one made were always a delight - both because they spoke more English than most other countries, and because knowing Americans they saw no need to assume a feigned inferiority complex posture.

I first shared an apartment with another courier, but he turned out to have a drinking problem, and I soon found a small place of my own. Servants were available and cheap. She had a very easy job as the apartment was small and I was gone much of the time. I began during this tour to take Chinese lessons. Because I was not able to spend much time in Manila, and little opportunity to speak the language on trips, the focus of my lessons were on reading and writing. I could carry lists of characters on a trip, memorizing them to build my written vocabulary. This later helped me in getting into the much sought after formal language course given by the Foreign Service, but the method was the opposite of that used by the school and created a problem for me then.

There were far fewer couriers in this area, and the distances were enormous, much of it over water. The planes we normally used were the Constellation, the DC-6,Convairs, and of course the DC-3.Furthermore, much of the travel was in tropical areas. This was pre-commercial jet era, and these planes could not overfly the very turbulent cloud build-ups, or divert too far to avoid the typhoons. Some of the airports were still pretty primitive as well. In the 1950's, the big surge in tourism anywhere had not yet begun. The big airplanes, the glitzy first class hotels, sophisticated airports, communications, use of English were not yet there. This was true in Europe as well but to a lesser degree.

As in Frankfurt, we had special arrangements with the airport authorities to permit us unusual access to the airplanes we were to fly in. Before Hong Kong's new airport was built, Manila was used most frequently by through airlines as a stop between Bangkok and Tokyo. Nonetheless, like almost all the airports in the area, the facilities were at best about the size of small county airports in the U.S. - minus the electronic equipment. The courier offices were in the embassy, but the nature of our job inhibited close association with other embassy people. We were so infrequently, and erratically, in town. Then as was the case everywhere we went, working in an embassy requires getting involved in the host country. We on the other hand, found more in common with airline flight people (though we seldom associated with them), as our interest was both more broad and more superficial.

My second tour in the Courier Service took me back to Europe. Despite my greater interest in Asia, I was anxious to go because I had missed out on some of the trips in that area. In Frankfurt, the Courier office had been moved to the new Consulate general building, which was a little further, removed from the housing area. The housing was the same -very well maintained apartments built by the Germans as part of reparations. There were literally hundreds of apartments there, with a large school, PX, Commissary, and all the accouterments of the military.

The railroad station had been fixed to some extent - all the broken windows removed, etc. Stores and restaurants were beginning to open up, though the big building construction had not yet materialized. Rhein Main airport had expanded, and would continue to do so. Better planes were flying, such as the Viscount propjets, DC-7,etc., but not yet commercial jets. Not too long after my return, the courier "region" was expanded to take in both Africa and the Middle East (After the 1956 problem with Egypt, that office moved to Athens, but that was not satisfactory and the office was combined with ours).

For about a year we traveled on Aeroflot tickets, which most airlines did not like as they were denominated in rubles. The Russians had begun a two-tiered exchange rate system, giving tourists 11 rubles to the dollar while maintaining the official 4 Ruble rate for any other activity. Until they caught on to our scheme a year later, we purchased tickets at the tourist rate. Purchasing a ticket meant that we would review our trip schedule for the next month or two, which could well mean travel all over Europe and perhaps Africa or the Middle East as well, buying a ticket that took us to all these places in the right sequence. The savings to the Courier Service was about a million dollars that year. When the Soviets put a stop to it, we switched the practice to Yugoslavia for a time.

At the end of my full two-year tour out of our European office, I was reassigned to Asia at my request. There were changes there as well, but after a few months, I was assigned to Hong King in the regular Foreign Service. The end of my courier days was best remembered by my flying in my first commercial jet between Singapore and Bangkok. It was time to go. The continuous travel, being in a different country almost everyday, after 5 years eventually wore me down. But the experience of being a diplomatic courier at that time in history was so unique that I knew it was something that should be remembered. Relating these experience in the sequence they occurred would be confusing so they are divided by countries listed below.

Germany

Germany was the location of our largest overseas regional office, but with our large military presence there, courier services to our several Consulates General was not necessary. Most couriers saw a lot of Germany, but usually on a personal basis, in the rare opportunities we had for driving around the country. The exception was Berlin, still isolated behind the "iron curtain".

Our Mission in Berlin was serviced by a separate trip. We would take the train (trains in Germany were then still under the control of the U.S. military). When it got to the border with East Germany, all the windows were boarded up, and then the train would roll through East Germany into Berlin. We would not have much time there, especially in the mid-50's when we serviced Warsaw as a part of the trip as well. Later we spent time in Warsaw on regular trips, but then we flew in on a turnaround out of Berlin. Not on a scheduled airlines, but on a RAF Lancaster bomber. That type of plane, in taking off, would have to eat up almost all the runway. The Queen's messenger was aboard as well. This was part of an arrangement we had with the British. We got on this trip in their planes, they got to use our STEM (later Air America) contract planes in Indo-China. The Polish authorities always gave us a bad time, but at least we would get to buy some Polish vodka, and Polish ham at the airport, through some fancy footwork (with Polish Zlotys slipped to us in a surreptitious exchange with the embassy people who met us).

Spain and Portugal

My first trip out of Frankfurt was through Madrid to Lisbon, with a side trip to Oporto. I stayed at the old Hotel Florida, and had dinner at a restaurant that featured the mournful Portuguese singers. I got an upset stomach from the food on that trip, but it was probably tenseness. Throughout my five years as a courier, I very seldom had stomach problems, even when I would experiment with risky roadside hawkers in some pretty dirty places around the world. Later, out of Madrid, I eventually got to spend some time in each of the consulate cities (Vigo, Bilbao, Seville, Valencia, Barcelona). Of course there were many sights to see in both countries, though there usually was limited time. Both Spain and Portugal were then run by dictators, and the economies were anything but robust. British tourists came to Lisbon especially because living was so much lower than the rest of Europe.

Some of my recollections about traveling in the Iberian countries stand out. In riding trains, we always had a compartment to ourselves, but we couldn't leave our pouches to have meals. We always had to bring our own. Riding the train from Bilbao to Madrid, I would buy a bottle of wine, a loaf of bread, and a piece of cheese. It was a wonderful meal. I flew once on a converted Lancaster bomber on a commercial airline (in Franco's days that was a rarity), but they crashed several of them over time so we stuck to the train. The famous Prado in Madrid was always popular; the austere food, spicy yes, was always good but even in the best restaurants portions were small and watered down. We were never there long enough to get adjusted to the late evening meals (restaurants didn't open for dinner until 10 PM). In the earlier years, before the tourist business got too big, a Spanish policeman would take a picture of everyone coming off the airplane at Madrid airport. Here I had to get accustomed to the worldwide requirement that a foreigner had to deposit his passport with the hotel. Since that was such a vital document for us for protection as well as for travel, we were always uneasy about it.

France, Britain and the Low Countries

Paris had been the location of the courier European office before 1955, but whenever we were there, we had a room at a U.S. Government hotel on 22 Rue de la Opera. It wasn't much of a room but then, we seldom spent much time in it even though we had many stopovers in Paris. The sights were endless, and we could try restaurants of all kinds, go to nightclubs, or have the famous onion soup at Les Halle. There were then two airports in Paris, and the embassy people often had to drive us frantically through the streets of Paris from one to the other. I even once had the car driven right on the runway to stop an Air France plane so I could board it. We often also had to use the rail system, especially when the weather was bad in the low countries.

Servicing the low countries, the UK, and Ireland was always a frantic affair. We would over time get to see the major cities where we had embassies or consulates, but it was usually unplanned. The weather is always so bad that, in those days, cancelled or delayed flights was common. Trying to land in dense fog at busy airports with the relatively primitive radar of the 50's brought the sweat out. Then landing in some unscheduled airport raised havoc with your schedule.

As a consequence, we often, at the last minute, would switch to rail. On one occasion I even had to take the boat train from England to the Hook of Holland. We'd usually make a swing from Paris through the low countries, to London, Dublin, back to Paris. We'd do that twice during the course of a one-week trip, then go back to Frankfurt.

Some vignettes of that area: The differences in breakfast served at hotels in the different countries. France and Belgium were "Continental". Holland and the UK were full meals. Eating a meal in a London hotel in the 50's was an experience in frugality. Although I saw some of London in my later years, as a courier I managed a quick trip into Piccadilly only once, for about an hour. I was dropped off by an embassy car. When I wanted to return to the embassy by bus, a bobby told me to look for a bus marked "ITI". After some time I was getting uneasy (as usual, there was a schedule to meet), and I then realized it had been a cockney speaking Bobby who was saying 88. Riding back on the bus, I couldn't understand a word anyone was saying. I might as well have been in Bulgaria.

Switzerland

The Switzerland posts were covered almost entirely by rail, though we would also transit Zurich and Geneva by air. We had one side trip out of Zurich by air to Prague. At that time it was simply a turn around at the airport and back to Zurich. Later, we spent a day or two in town, but during the early years we would be met at the airport, and then we would have to wait there for the return trip. The only thing to do to kill time was to watch a free movie in the terminal. It was always the same movie, about the horrors of the Nazis in WW II. In Geneva, we stayed at the Du Rhone Hotel where American delegations to the many meetings held there would also stay.

For this reason, especially when there was U.S. - Soviet Foreign Minister level meetings, we would often have to make special trips there. In addition to the delightful city (then very affordable), I also once got into the same elevator with John Foster Dulles and Molotov. All I can remember is that both of them had very cold looks on their faces, looking like they were carved out of granite. That was during the height of the Cold War - maybe that was where the expression came from.

Moscow

Presumably as a reward for surviving the plane crash on the Athens detail, I was sent to the 2-month Helsinki detail. This was in 1955. Later, 1957-59, I was sent there several more times and it is sometimes difficult to separate incidents and experiences between the two periods. The purpose of the detail was to service Moscow twice a week. Because we traveled in pairs behind the "Curtain", it was a four man detail, with a lot of travel involved. Everyone liked Helsinki, both because people were friendly, and because it contrasted so well with the dreary atmosphere in Moscow. It was also because traveling to Moscow in the 1950's was hardly a tourist attraction.

Each time we came out of Moscow, one of us would continue on to Stockholm. After an overnight, we continued through Oslo, Copenhagen, Hamburg and Frankfurt. After two days we would return the same way, arriving in Helsinki just in time to go into Moscow with another courier. Though it was a continuous merry go round, we did spend two or three days at a time in both Moscow and Helsinki at least once a week. Once a month we would go into Moscow by train.

Once, coming out of Moscow by train, the other courier with me was a temporary "summer" replacement from the U.S. military's Russian language school at Oberamagau. He spoke excellent Russian. As usual on trains, we had our own compartment. At the end of each car there was a big samovar for chai (tea). At that time tea was still served in a glass put in a silver glass holder, real silver and much too nice for train service. The other courier kept regaling the Russian car porter with funny stories, and continually ordering more tea. By the time we got to Helsinki, there were many chai glasses on the table and we both helped ourselves to one as a souvenir. I always thought that poor fellow probably had quite a bad time accounting for the lost glasses.

That was serious business then. There was no tipping, and absolute accountability. Thus when I accidentally left a cheap cigarette lighter on a plane there, it was returned to me the following trip. That changed later, just as it did in China years later.

Behind the "Curtain", we were always "tailed" by security officers. They assumed couriers were spies and followed us everywhere. In the Soviet Union one could spot them fairly easily, usually about a block away. One developed a sixth sense after a while, knowing when one is being followed. In the Eastern European satellites a sixth sense was not necessary. The tail was always so close it would be impossible not to know. On special trips to Washington paid for by the CIA, we found that they were tailing us, presumably to verify our conduct. We were indignant, and they were no more subtle than their counterparts behind the "curtain".

We spent a lot of our time in Moscow playing the game of "losing our tail". In retrospect it was risky and foolish. But nothing pleased us more than taking the underground, getting off and immediately catching a bus, then again off, etc., trying to confuse our tail. We delighted, arriving back at the embassy, or the Amerikanski Dom, seeing the guard bolt for the telephone (to report our return our lost tail having already reported his loss).

The embassy drivers always claimed they spoke no English. Once, however, in being driven from the Amerikanski Dom to the embassy, I suddenly told my partner that I had forgotten my briefcase in the Dom. The driver immediately turned the car around and headed back to the Dom. His ears got quite red when he realized that no one had said anything to him.

The Amerikanski Dom was a building right across from Gorki Park. It had previously been a morgue. It at that time housed staff members of the embassy, and the couriers were required to stay there rather than in a hotel, presumably for security reasons. There was a large bar room which was open to all diplomats. Because Americans do not take well to such isolated conditions, a lot of heavy drinking took place there. Foreign diplomats doubtless found the place interesting as well. We spent little time there other than sleeping. Come to think of it, watching very drunk people leaving the place probably wasn't so unusual for the Soviets. We preferred eating in restaurants, and there were the Russians that always seemed to get very drunk indeed, all the time.

Since the detail was for 2 months, we knew our schedule well in advance. On trips where we would have two full days in Moscow, we could arrange for an out of town trip in advance (a requirement of the Soviet security). Through the embassy we could also get tickets for the Bolshoi ballets or other theatre performances. So in fact, despite the very constrained circumstances then in the USSR, and how closely they kept us under observation, we did get to see quite a bit.

In 1955, before Aeroflot began international service, they flew into Eastern Europe, Berlin, and Helsinki only. There was no built-in radar then, and no food service aboard. Thus, the unpressurized planes, the Russian version of the Dakota, would have to fly along the rail line between Helsinki - Leningrad - Moscow. They would have to fly low since weather usually limited visibility: in the frequent snow storms, that meant very low, like just off the tree tops. And the plane would have to stop in Leningrad to go through customs, and to feed the passengers. Very few passengers flew in or out of the Soviet Union then, and it would not be unusual for us to be the only passengers on board.

The airport stop in Leningrad was cumbersome and time consuming. As always, the Soviets were meticulous in being sure we and our bags were given very special treatment. We were permitted to have the bags within our sight at all times aboard the aircraft, in customs, and in any movement. At Leningrad a separate bus was always dispatched to the aircraft just to take care of us. We were transported along with our bags directly to the airport restaurant. Any other passengers had to go through a very thorough customs process. Then all foreign passengers were fed a full meal in the airport dining room.

The table was always set with a full set of silver and glasses. The silverware was clearly old Czarist silver, heavy and very ornate. Wines, mineral water, several courses, all were served while the authorities checked through the passports, and the customs people examined luggage in great detail. Never ours, however. The Soviets were intensely sensitive to reciprocity, and treating us this way in their view assured that their couriers entering the U. S. received similar treatment.

Eating in a Russian restaurant (there were not many open to foreigners then), and/or attending either the Bolshoi or Stanislavsky was our most frequent way to spend the evenings in Moscow. The doors to these performances always closed exactly on schedule, usually at 1930. If one was late, one simply missed the performance. We normally had an embassy ticket, but once I decided to go see something besides Swan Lake, or Giselle, and had no ticket. I stood out front of the Bolshoi beginning about 1900. I turned down offers of tickets (for sale) by scalpers until about 1925. Then, in those last few minutes, the prices would drop sharply, and I bought one. My seat, however, turned out to be in about the fourth balcony, in a section that was filled completely with Chinese soldiers. The Chinese were then on good terms with the Soviets, while we were not even permitted to shake hands with them. It was a rather uncomfortable evening at the ballet for me.

Foreigners were easily distinguishable simply by the clothes they wore. People generally avoided talking to a foreigner, probably because they had learned to sense the presence of the KGB (the "Tail"). The main streets were extremely wide but had very little traffic on them. In winter the days were short, lighting on the streets not all that bright, and the climate was damp. The appearance, in sum, was very drab and depressing. The people, in their very drab clothing added to the depressed feeling.

The underground (subway), by contrast, was very well lit, very ornate with marble construction, statues, and too many service people. (Old people were "employed" simply opening the door at the entrance. Relatively few hawkers were permitted on the streets, although elderly ones, under obviously strict rules, sold ice cream in the summer, and hot parushkis in the winter in a few places.

Driving to and from Vnukhova airport (it was then the international airport, later became only domestic), one passed collective farms. I witnessed potato pickers at work, and it was clear how little enthusiasm there was for the work, and how much of the product was clearly left behind. Service in the stores also reflected the lack of any incentive to do better. Construction was on the whole very shoddy. Buildings that were only a few years old, including the embassy, looked like very old buildings, with cracks, faulty wiring, etc. On one occasion on the way to the airport, we took along a VOA fellow who was surreptitiously testing the reception within the Soviet Union of their broadcasts. Passing the Lenin Heights apartment development, he suddenly asked us to stop while he went inside the building. He returned shortly thereafter, having been chased out of the building. He had spotted jamming antennae on the top of the building.

Whenever we wanted to leave the city of Moscow during the time we would be in the Soviet Union, one had to get permission from the government. Of course this would take several days. We would, therefore, have to arrange a journey out on the previous trip. I went to see Rosynia Polyanna, Tolstoy's home south of Moscow. The roads then were lined every half mile or so, with a soldier (I never knew whether it was for our "benefit" or whether the soldiers were always there). We did know that they were well aware where it is we were supposed to go. On one occasion a fellow from the embassy deliberately told the driver to turn onto another route, and within minutes another car caught up and had the car go back.

In 1955 Bulganin and Kruschev had taken over from Malenkov. Kruschev was not yet the sole leader, and Molotov was still foreign minister. I saw Molotov twice: once in Geneva, where I saw him and Dulles. The second time was at the Bolshoi, where he was hosting then foreign minister Pearson of Canada. Then too, the tomb in Red Square still housed both Lenin and Stalin. Stalin's appearance was far better than Lenin's (Newer technology I suppose).

On one occasion two of us decided to go to Leningrad to see the Hermitage museum. It was Christmas and we had made arrangements in advance. We flew from Moscow to Leningrad. It was bitter cold. We did not know then that the couriers who had left Moscow two days before were stranded in Leningrad because the weather was bad in Helsinki. The Soviets were apparently worried that we were up to something. Before we arrived, the security police had taken the two previous couriers from the hotel out to the airport (where they waited for hours) before leaving. The Russians apparently did not want us to meet. While were touring the Hermitage, our personal bags in the hotel had been searched. The Hermitage was spectacular and the city much more "European". Returning to the hotel, it was so cold I almost had a case of frostbite on one ear.

As we could not afford to miss our scheduled flight out of Moscow, we took the "Blue Arrow" train back to Moscow. The compartment had four bunks. Men and women would be assigned the same compartment indiscriminately, and ours seemed to have been especially orchestrated. We were two, one other passenger was a very friendly worker who eagerly shared his black bread and vodka. The other was a young girl who spoke some German (my partner spoke German), and, by chance, worked in a hotel in Moscow. She too was very friendly and anxious to have us visit her at the hotel whenever we were in Moscow. Doubtless the authorities knew this all was transparent and unlikely to succeed, but one can never tell....

In subsequent trips on my second tour in Europe, the apartment in Helsinki had changed for the better, and I got to see the northern lakes in the summer, which are very nice. We now usually flew Finnair convairs direct to Moscow's Vnukova airport. No more stops in Leningrad.

Although foreigners were still easily distinguishable by the clothes they wore, and constraints on dealing with foreigners persisted, still there was a difference in atmosphere. There were more restaurants, some even had small bands playing western music. But most of all, there was an air of confidence that hadn't existed before. I believe that was Sputnik. They were the first to put a satellite in orbit and that notion got very heavy play. It was typical, however, that while that first Sputnik was circling the globe, old, bent over ladies, warming themselves around oil cans burning something, by hand were patching potholes on the streets around Red Square.

On my previous detail there, I had gotten the embassy to arrange for us to be driven to Rosnya Polyanna, where Tolstoy's home still stands as a museum. Leaving Moscow and driving some distance to Tula was fascinating simply because so few people did it. The home was well kept and the curator himself took us through the whole place. He was very friendly. He later sent me a letter, which followed me to Manila. When I returned with another courier two years later, the curator had long since been transferred to Moscow, and who knows if he had been considered too friendly. The road to and from Rosnya Polyanna was somewhat less guarded than previously. Before, a soldier stood on the highway, all the way, about every hundred yards. When we made a wrong turn, we would be corrected almost immediately.

We also went up to Zagorsk to the monastery there. It was a depressing place, as they had made models and exhibits of all the bad events, the imprisonment and torture that allegedly had taken place there. Only old people were seen in the Church. We stopped in a little place en-route for some borscht soup, causing quite a commotion. The villagers simply were unaccustomed to foreigners. Wherever we went, even in Moscow, a crowd would gather to ogle around the car (they were Fords provided by the company for $1, and flown in to the embassy).

Somehow, Moscow was always just too interesting to spend time in the Amerikanski Dom. Even after many trips, and endless attendance at Swan Lake at the Bolshoi, or other performances at the Stanislavsky or other houses, it was just a place too few people got to see then, and so I always had the urge to see as much as I could.

Eastern Europe

Belgrade changed considerably between my first and second tour in Europe. In the mid-50's it was very austere. Cobblestone streets, very few cars, or people on the streets for that matter, long breadlines at the stores, and few stores of any kind. The airlines, unlike almost everything else in the country, were not equipped with Russia planes. They used early models of Convairs. Unfortunately, they were a little too complicated for them, so eventually they all crashed. One of the last had a courier in it when it crashed just outside Vienna. The courier (Frank Irwin) was badly burned. This was just days after my accident in the Mediterranean. Frank miraculously recovered (he stayed conscious at the accident site long enough to turn the pouch over to a U.S. military officer). Thereafter, the airlines used DC-3 type aircraft. Flying over the Alps into Vienna in an unpressurized and unheated plane was an adventure. The stewardess, who had been in the above accident and was still bandaged (but working), came down the aisle with one glass and a bottle of Slivovitz. We all eagerly had a slug.

Vienna then was still a divided city, like Berlin. We serviced Yugoslavia partly by plane (Belgrade) and partly by train (Zagreb). I saw Kruschev and Bulganin there as they drove through the main street in an open car. It was one of the few cars one could see in Belgrade at that time - horse and wagon still being the main mode of transport.

The trip by Orient Express from Vienna to Budapest and Bucharest (at that time we had no relations with Bulgaria) was a week long. In the past, couriers had gone to Vienna for a month, but in my time, we simply took the German train to Vienna, then switched to the Orient Express. It was still referred to as the "Vienna Detail" however. In those days of the cold war, it was a very interesting trip. The exchange rates were such that everything was very cheap. We tipped the wagon-lit people with packs of cigarettes and little jars of coffee. The same in the hotels.

First to describe the famous, "Orient Express". The foreign diplomatic couriers were always put in the same car. The Brits and the Italians, like us, traveled in pairs. The Swiss by himself. We always had the end compartment. Next to us the Italians. In the center was the Swiss, and toward the other end the "Queen's Messengers". We supplied the coffee, the Italians the wine, and the Brits the gin. We brought our own food as there was no dining car and we could not leave the train. (Except the Swiss, who during the long border crossing process between Hungary and Romania, had the wagon-lit man lock his compartment door while he went into the station to eat. So much for the security of the pouch!).

We would leave Vienna at night, pass the border into Hungary during the night (awakening us for inspection and passport) and then on to Budapest. Crossing the border between Hungary and Rumania was almost unbelievable. The train would stop on one side, soldiers would inspect everything, including under the seats, walking on the roof, and even taking all the coal out of the engine car. Then the train would chug across the border, and we would have to go through the whole exercise again (except then their own coal would be put on). The border had plowed fields on both sides of a barbed wire fence, with dog patrols, and wood towers stretched every 200 yards.

The affects of WW II were still evident in Eastern Europe. The standard of living was low, little infrastructure built, and repression of individual rights very evident. Budapest, in addition, had just had the failed revolution of 1956. A taxi driver in fact took us around and showed us where damage had been caused by the shooting.

Budapest was one of our favorite cities in the 50's, despite it being in Eastern Europe at a harsh time and in drab circumstances. We would disembark from the train there for a day, catching the following day's train to Bucharest. Some of the buildings, like the Emperor's palace that overlooked the city from the Buda side, was still in ruins from WW II, but the government was rebuilding it, stone by stone. Some of the damage at other sites was more recent - from the uprising of 1956. It was very much a police state, with people avoiding foreigners. We changed money at the Legation at a very favorable rate of exchange, so everything for us was very cheap. We tipped in either American cigarettes or small jars of instant coffee.

We would stay at the old Duna Hotel, at that time partially destroyed by WW II bombing, but still having the old Europe aura. The food was good, but that was the case in almost any restaurant (though there were only a few). There was the famous Grundel's restaurant, more like a palace, with gypsy musicians but only loud worker groups eating there. The food and service was suburb, but lost on the clientele. There was also a restaurant up the hill on the Buda side. One took a cable car up there from where one could see the whole city. It was always shrouded in smog, but one could see that it had once been a beautiful city.

The couriers were well known at the hotel, and always watched, as we were everywhere. There was a small bar, and whenever we were there, what passed for a sexy blonde gal would always try to stike up a conversation. We all knew of it, of course, and though it was obvious, on one occasion a fellow got caught up in the web (and lost his job because he missed the train the next morning).

In 1956 Cardinal Mindzenty was given asylum in the Legation, and he stayed there for 15 years. He became a symbol of resistance to the Russians. He said mass every day, and I once had a chat with him. He talked of the Church in the U.S. He was clearly a strong person, but also very political.

I most enjoyed the byzmontis (antique shops). I bought some good things there, but on reflecting in later years, if I had known more about antiques, there were incredible buys. Life was so harsh that people sold off heirlooms for a pittance (I have seen them actually crying to part with them), and with our exchange rate, and the lack of expertise among the clerks contributed to both the sorrow and the opportunities. One of the legation people showed us a small silver repair shop run by an old lady. In fact, she was surreptitiously selling silver-ware (a friend bought a set of Napoleon silver candelabra for $250). Another store sold cigarettes but under the counter sold stamps. I bought often, later trading them off for Philippine stamps. One other item I often bought was whole Hungarian salami, which was delicious but at that time, not seen in the west.

Bucharest was a city where repression was palpable. It almost seemed frozen in a prewar timeframe. Even the countryside, through Translyvania, one could see what the old world was like. The food was not good, and the hotel service poor. The stores had little. The only area of interest was the open food market where delicious white mountain cheese and pickles were available.

In the mid-fifties we serviced Warsaw by way of Berlin, merely turning around at the airport (after meeting the embassy people there). We would ride a train from West Germany through East Germany to Berlin. Once at the airport, we would fly in a WW II British Lancaster bomber to Warsaw. It was a weekly flight run by the British for the Queen's Messenger (we returned the favor in flying them through Indo-China on the Stem plane). At Warsaw airport the customs and immigration people were always frustratingly meticulous. Westerners were the enemy. We would swap bags with our embassy people who would slip us some zlotys to buy vodka and Polish ham in the airport shop.

Later we began flying on LOT, the Polish airlines, staying in town at the Bristol Hotel for a couple of days. There were only one or two restaurants, and stores were largely empty. We were tailed ridiculously close. Unlike other countries in Eastern Europe, Catholic Churches were crowded with young people.

Prague also was first serviced by an airport turnaround (from Zurich), but later we flew in for a couple of days. The turnaround period was very boring as the only activity was a small movie theater where the same film always showed - about the Nazi atrocities. That theme was played heavily though out Eastern Europe. Later, when we went into town, it was one of that country's "liberal" periods. Stores were better stocked, including their famous crystal (through most of the etchings showed factories).

We usually serviced the embassy and consulates in Zagreb and Sarejevo by plane, but on occasion we also used the southern leg of the Orient Express.

Italy and Greece

In Italy we rented an apartment on Via Tuscana, and operated out of there whenever we were in Rome. Many schedules put us through there, but the one servicing Italy would drop us there.

I remember having dinner one night in a good restaurant with a fellow courier who was very loud and came from Boston. He insisted on talking with the waiter, loudly, using what he took to be Italian. It was dialect that he obviously picked up from the fruit vendors in South Boston, and I was thoroughly embarrassed.

Among other memories was the Consul General in Milan who would meet us himself. He had an Italian name, and was clearly obsessed with assuring that all Italians there knew he was not Italian but American. He talked always about how they deserved all they got for siding with the Germans, and their manners, habits, etc. That experience made me notice how often an American of some ethnic background assigned to his family's "old country" overcompensated, by either exaggerating their differences, like the Milan fellow, or going native on the other extreme. Another memory was the excellent box lunch sold at the railroad station in Bologna (*en route* between Florence and Venice). In Venice, we would be met by a Consulate fellow who would take us by boat to the Consulate.

On my first trip to Rome, I had high expectations that at last I would be visiting a country where I could speak the language. It was late at night, and there was no embassy driver at the airport, so I hired a cab and we wheeled out of the airport heading for the embassy. A few hundred yards down the road, the embassy driver intercepted us (he had been at the airport, he said, but I had not looked for him). Of course, the taxi driver insisted on being paid the full fare to Rome (he had lost any chance of another fare at that hour, he said), so I wound up paying. Getting taken the first time I stepped onto a country where I expected to know a little was especially galling. The driver of the embassy car, in addition, spoke American English with a very heavy Texas accent. It turned out he had been a POW that had been interned in Texas during WW II.

The system permitted little opportunity for overnight stays (trains don't get fogged in) in the many cities we passed through. Someone from the consulate would come to the train station in Florence, in Bologna we had no consulate but the station was famous for its delicious box lunches. In Venice we detrained to take the consulate's speedboat to deliver their pouch, then returned to catch the next train. Trieste was a turnaround at the station, then on to Milan where we stayed overnight. The next day a stop at Turin and Genoa, and then back to Rome. The once a week flight to Palermo was just a turnaround.

The one-week detail gave some little time for sightseeing, but not anywhere near enough. The embassy was large, so we seldom knew anyone in it. Seeing Italy, or even Rome, simply couldn't be done as it should given our work and the time constraints. I was to see a little of Italy only on vacations in the future.

The Athens detail was one month long. Its purpose was to service Ankara, Izmir, Nicosia, and Tel Aviv. We did Tel Aviv this way as Arab countries would not permit entry for anyone having an Israeli visa. When we operated the mid- east out of Frankfurt, we began using separate passports. One could only remember the smog of our overnights in Ankara. The short stays in Israel did give me an opportunity to see some of the Holy Land. One had to cross the Allenby Bridge into Jordan occupied Jerusalem then which required a special pass.

The detail allowed us considerable time in Athens, however. Eating in outdoor restaurants, drinking Turkish coffee, it was a relatively restful detail. The Embassy driver, Manolis, was one of the best we had anywhere. On our offtime we could take a bus out to the seashore of Vuliagmaney (phonetic), which at that time was outside the city. It was a great beach, and there were stalls that cooked up freshly caught fish. It had a powerful tide, though, and once I almost got swept out to sea.

I believe it was once a week we would take an USAFE DC-3 flight to Wheelus base in Tripoli, Libya, to pick up Washington mail. It was an overnight at the BOQ there. On July 29, 1955 on the return flight I had quite an experience. On the plane there were several U.S. military officers, three Turkish officers, and I. The cargo strapped in the center of the plane was APO mail, and three footlockers belonging to the Turkish officers. They had been training in the States, were returning home, and as was customary, had loaded up on PX items to take back with them. The drill for them was to unload the loot in Izmir (on the following day's flight), where there was no customs. It was an important source of income for them.

About midway back to Athens, one of the two engines developed trouble. That was hardly a unique experience, especially with the old Air Force C-47s (the military version of the DC-3). But we were in the middle of the Mediterranean and it was risky trying to fly high with only the one engine. So the pilot dropped it down quickly to about 100 feet off the water. In the meantime the radio man was sending a distress signal, and another crew member was quickly briefing us on what to do to brace ourselves properly if we had to hit the water. He had us take off our shoes (I was later told that was the wrong thing to do). Then he jettisoned the door. In doing so he almost caused a disaster as the door flew past the stabilizer, nicking it but thankfully not damaging it.

Then the crew began jettisoning all the mail and even the Turkish officer's footlockers. Our suitcases went also. Fortunately, I had only two small pouches of mail, which I put under my seat. If I hadn't done so, in the frantic effort to lighten the plane, the pouches would have gone as well. As was our habit, couriers always sat in the rear of the plane for safety's sake. I sat right opposite the open door, facing it in our bucket seats arranged along the sides of the aircraft. Everyone was calm, no panic, but we all knew that if the one engine as much as coughed, we'd hit the water. As I recall, we flew this way for about 45 minutes, and then the engine coughed.

The pilot did a remarkable job in handling the plane. We hit the water much like a piece of flat slate that had been thrown in a way to have it skip along the surface of the water. We hit, bounced twice, and then settled in the water. The plane stayed afloat for 12 minutes. During that time the crew inflated one raft at a time, and we very orderly filed into one, then the next, until three had taken us all in. One raft paddled quickly over to the wing where the pilot and copilot were and they got in just in time before the plane went down, nose first. This relatively smooth landing and 12 minute float was possible because the sea was very calm.

The crew was already aware that the air force knew where we were, at least in general. Those of us in the rafts were, of course, pleased to be alive. One or two had cameras around their necks and took pictures, which were later published. As I had filed out of the plane, I threw the two pouches onto the water nearby. They floated nearby all the time we were in the water. The first plane we saw was a British bomber from Malta, who circled and dropped a flare to let us know we had been spotted. Eventually two air rescue SA -16 seaplanes landed nearby. A crew member from one of them inflated a raft and corralled our rafts along side the plane. He also picked up the two pouches and gave them to me inside the plane.

I do not know why the rescue people did not put some of us in each plane. As it was, we were all in one, and it was too heavy a load for the plane to take off from water. So the second plane returned to base empty, while we taxied some 95 miles on the water to a place on the Libyan coast called Miserata. It was certainly appropriately named. It was the poorest place I had ever seen, with people literally living in holes in the ground. A C-47 from Wheelus base landed at a temporary strip, and took us back to the base. As we filed off the plane, I handed the two pouches to the appropriate officer, and then went with the others for a check-up at the hospital. In the meantime, the pouch room at the embassy in Athens for some reason had word that I was lost and so were the pouches. The courier supervisor from Frankfurt immediately flew to Wheelus, arriving there the next morning.

We went to the base classified mailroom and inspected the pouches. The mail was water logged but all there. I was without shoes and my clothes had been soaked in seawater and now, dry, could almost stand by themselves. The supervisor and I boarded another C-47 to return to Frankfurt. It landed in Cagliari, Sardinia for fuel. In the process the plane blew a tire and there were no replacements at that airfield. So we had to take a scheduled military plane to Rome. We stayed at the apartment, and the courier on the Italy detail told me quietly that I should have thrown my passport in the water. That way I would have two or three weeks free while the office got me another one. The supervisor wanted to go to a good restaurant even though I was hardly dressed for it. Turns out he, who had done his WW II duty as a navy pilot in the Caribbean of all places, wanted me to tell him what it was like in the infantry at war. (He had a purpose in that he wanted me to take on a special assignment on my forthcoming detail out of Helsinki). I did not get back to Athens again until two plus years later.

To wrap up the ditching incident, I wrote to the Department asking for reimbursement of the things lost in my suitcase. The answer I got back was that insurance was available if I wanted it (at my expense), and therefore government would not reimburse. Some kind lady back in personnel in the State Department apparently saw how ridiculous that was, prepared a private bill which was approved by the Congress, and more than a year later, when I was back in Manila, I received a check for $120.

Middle East

Some thoughts that come to mind about the few times I covered northern Africa. I spent little time in Morocco, but I do remember flying Air Maroc. They used DC-4s, but their airports lacked starter equipment. So each time we took off from the various stops, the crew would fit a sleeve onto one blade of the propeller, and with a rope two or three men would try to yank the engine into starting.

Tangier was still an international city. Police, customs, other officials were mostly French and Spanish. We would fly over from Spain, spend the day there, and then return. Aside from looking at Gibraltar, the most interesting site was our Consulate. It is one of the first the U.S. built, and its halls, and the one story sections of the complex weaved all over, making it possible to get lost even in the building. It was like an indoor version of the Casbah.

Algiers was at war with the French. Little English was spoken anywhere, and it was dangerous to wander too far, so we saw little of the city. I did get to the Casbah, watched French soldiers patrolling the narrow street, wary of snipers. The Casbah was actually out-of-bounds for Americans, but the Consulate had failed to tell us. Our Consulate and library had been bombed on several occasions and looked like a fort.

Cairo was by far the most cosmopolitan city in the area. One could find almost anything. Pictures of Nasser were everywhere. The bazaar was fascinating as was the museums and the Pyramids. It was a place in which we spent little time, but one could use days just to sightsee.

Africa

The Cairo courier office closed and, after a brief stay in Athens, combined with ours in Frankfurt. During the transition, we in Frankfurt had to cover the enlarged area, going to places we had not been before. I came off a European trip (that included Berlin where I was instructed to get a yellow fever shot. The non-English speaking nurse, to my horror, shot me in the chest - a European practice), and was handed a set of tickets for Africa. It was a month long. Most of the countries were not yet independent. I knew none of them and simply followed my ticket. Flying between Freetown and Monrovia in a West Africa Airway DC-3, we hit a typhoon causing the plane to flip over on its back. The Polish emigre pilot miraculously righted the plane. The trip took us down the west coast to Pretoria, then up the east coast back to Europe. Flying "blind" that way in what was often pretty primitive settings, and sometimes having to search for the embassy or consulate was a taxing experience.

Subcontinent

The India detail was a month long, providing a weekly service to the posts in the sub-continent. Every week a courier left Manila for the detail, and every week another returned. This meant that at all times there were four couriers carrying out one part of the one-month trip. It began by flying up to Clark Air Base in a DC-3, transferring there to a U.S. Navy constellation or DC-6 cargo plane. The Navy called it "The Embassy Route". The plane flew from Clark, through Saigon to Bangkok for an overnight. Next day it flew through Calcutta to New Delhi for another overnight. Then through Karachi to Dhaharan for the overnight, (the mail connecting with another flight that came from the other, Atlantic, side). Then the plane returned by the same route. A courier would get on the plane at Clark, stay with it to Delhi. Another courier would take it to Dhaharan and back to Delhi. Still another would get on in Delhi and take it back to Clark.

While this was going on, one courier would be taking the trip to the south: Delhi, Bombay, Madras, Colombo, and return. Another would be doing the Katmandu run, and a third would be doing the trek to Kabul. Most weekends three couriers would be in Delhi at the same time. During my first tour out of Manila, the couriers were given one of the staff quarters at what was called "The Taj", a single story adobe type row apartments in a compound belonging to the embassy. The new embassy and living compound did not exist then. Though we had to eat and sleep on the economy when on the road, in Delhi we ate and slept in the apartment, this being one of the few times several couriers could be together swapping war stories.

Each incoming courier put a set amount of money into the apartment fund on arrival, and kept the book for that week. Since the accountant changed every week, the book was often rather difficult to decipher. That and the servants we had were the main topic of conversation not only in Delhi, but anywhere else two couriers might meet on the road. Comments in the book were studied with great care. For example, the late Jack Grover, always solicitous, noted he had taken some funds out to give the bearer's son to study tailoring (he said the boy spoke good English and was thus deserving). FXJ Sullivan, in an unusual sober moment, wrote that he knew a tailor in Boston who spoke Yiddish and clearly needed more training, but had not thought to dip into the fund to help.

We had three servants: Joseph the cook/ bearer; the sweeper (next level down), and the Dhobi - laundryman - just a cut above an untouchable. It was Joseph that dominated our conversation, however. He was fat, dirty, ruthless with the other servants, a bad cook, and he stole us blind. Yet because of the perpetual turnover, despite our continuous resolve to fire him, we never did. Even when it was discovered, after eight years, that the firewood (the only heat we had then), for which we had weekly given Joseph money to buy, was in fact furnished free by the embassy.

While the servants provided the topic of conversation, the trips out of Delhi provided the challenge. Even the "side" trip on the navy's plane to Dhaharan was not entirely without interest. The flights were long and boring (bucket seats and box lunches). We never went into the embassy which was then in Karachi because the plane only stopped there briefly, and embassy personnel would come out to exchange mail. We overnighted at the airbase in Dhaharan. An ex-courier was working with ARAMCO, the oil company, and we often went to his house (where he maintained an illegal still in his closet - liquor was banned in Saudi Arabia and even the officer's club served only soft stuff). Sunday mass was held surreptitiously in an empty hangar, with lookouts to warn of approaching Saudis. It was a pretty bleak place.

Indian Air Corporation flew Vikings (similar to the DC-3) to the south, and Dakotas (British made DC-3s) to the north. Flying in those days in those planes was always an experience. Flying was a new experience for most of the passengers, the rides over the rough terrain, and especially during the monsoons, were often turbulent. The plane would soon have a lot of used sick bags, remnants of box lunches, and betel juice liberally scattered around the floor.

The trip south took the better part of a week. A night flight to Bombay was always uncomfortable. The Consulate General driver who would meet us there to take us into town, was an expert at hiding while we carried bag and luggage to the car. After dropping the bag off, we'd stay at the Ambassador Hotel. Bombay can be hot and very humid. No air conditioning, of course, so windows had to be wide open. Since we had to leave early, breakfast was brought to the room. Once, one of the perennial blackbirds flew right into the room, grabbed my fried eggs off the plate, and flew out. Coming in at night and leaving at dawn, we always found the streets covered with people sleeping. One would literally have to step over people to get in and out of buildings.

The next leg was Colombo by way of Madras. The plane stopped at Madras where someone from the Consulate would meet us and pick up a bag (they would give us one on the return). Then the plane went to Trichinopoly (on the coast just opposite Ceylon), where customs and immigration was located. Passengers were fed on the ground there. It was always exactly the same - hot curry stew. In fact it was quite good, and I always ate it. Once on departing there, I was the last to get aboard and noticed the cowling of one of the engines on the ground. Presumably we would have left without it had I not asked.

The hop over to Colombo was short, and we would spend two days there, as it was the end of the line. The embassy had that time to respond to the mail in time for us to take it back. We stayed at the Galle Face Hotel, right on the coast with a beautiful surf. No air conditioning, so we could hear the surf all the time. It was very soothing, and given the heat, it was a great place simply to rest. There was sightseeing in Colombo, but the real attraction is Kandy up in the mountains. Unfortunately, it was too far for us to risk not being back to catch our plane, so I never went there.

We followed the same route back. Flying over India in those smallish, low-flying planes was tiring. Even during the clear weather time, the rough terrain below caused turbulence. During the monsoon it was even more so. And India Air Corporation, a government monopoly for domestic flights, was never easy to deal with.

The shortest detail trip we had out of Delhi was up to Katmandu. On my first tour there was only an AID office there, not an embassy. We took a Dakota IAC plane that stopped several times on its way to Calcutta. We would get off at Patna, transferring to another Dakota for Katmandu. The pilot was always the same Sikh. He clearly had the route completely memorized. He had to, as he would have to fly through the valleys below the mountain tops, through the clouds, with only an occasional glimpse of the side of the mountains often just off the wing tips. (He didn't make it once and was killed).

Then we would land on a dirt strip. We stayed overnight in a hotel featured in one of Han Suyin's books "And The Rain My Drink". Very old, very colonial. Hot water brought in buckets and poured in a bathtub. A huge grand piano in the lounge. Coat and tie for dinner. The same people sipping drinks in the lounge. The remarkable part is that the piano, bathtub, the very few cars in town - all must have had to be carried in by people along mountain paths. The road from India was still under construction.

In 1956 there were a lot of Tibetan refugees just coming out to Katmandu, and eventually moving on to India. The skin on their faces was like leather. They lived up to their tradition of only bathing once a year - the smell was overpowering. Yet they were completely without complexes. They would talk to you and

42

laugh, slap you on the back - even when you didn't understand a word they were saying. They brought skins down from the mountains, largely to trade for salt.

One of the legendary trips in the courier service was the trip to Kabul. Before regular plane service began, going to Kabul was done by road - or more accurately, on the ground as much of the road in the Afghan portion had not been built. We would take a flight up to Amritsar, take a taxi to the border, carry the bag and luggage through customs, walk across into Pakistan, then taxi into Lahore. At the Consulate General in Lahore we would pick up our bedding and after a meal go to the train station.

The station was always bedlam, with thousands trying to get on trains. Porters would carry the bags on their head, and we would have to strain to keep them together through the crowd. We always had a compartment to ourselves with a wooden bed on which we laid out our bedding. Getting in and then closing the door was always an experience. First to haggle with the porters, then to keep out the ferocious efforts by would-be passengers to get into the compartment. The train would have people everywhere, on the top, hanging from the sides, underneath. Naturally, a compartment for one person was viewed as an extravagance. With some help the door would get closed and locked, and the blinds put down.

The "Northwest Khyber Mail" went from Lahore through Rawalpindi to Peshawar, leaving in the evening, and arriving in the morning. In Peshawar, the embassy driver from Kabul with his jeep, would meet us and take us to the Dean's Hotel for food and cleaning up. Dean's was an old colonial hotel, requiring coat and tie and all the rest, even though it was pretty dusty and austere. Servants in brightly colored uniforms, like everywhere in the subcontinent, waited on guests. Rooms were first checked out to assure no cobras were about (an American had been bitten by one some years before).

We did not have a consulate in Peslawarthere then, but a consular agent, who was an Indian named Mr. Gai, who owned a dry goods store. When time permitted, we rode around the town, and especially the well-known bazaar, in a horse drawn tonga. As this route was the only way to get in and out of Kabul, we often found someone either going to or visiting the embassy waiting for us. Then when ready we would head for the border.

Heading north, we first traveled through the famous Khyber Pass. The blacktop road was well paved. Lookouts, mujahaddin type fellows with crossed bandaliers, were posted all along the route. One could see them on the cliffs edge way up above us. One could see why it had been impossible for the British to take it during their military campaigns in the last century. Once through the pass, the land leveled off into a desert at the border.

On the Pakistan side, immigration and customs were located in two small houses. The officials were not uniformed and clearly the discipline of the military was not there. Two things remain on my mind with regard to this border. One is that we always brought with us cheap ballpoint pens, because the officials never seemed to have a pen to write with, and without fail, they always kept the one which they "borrowed" from you. The other was the color of the official's tongue. It was deep purple, always, because the stamp pad was always too dry, so when they stamped your visa, they used their tongue on the stamp.

When this process was done, we'd get back in the jeep, the border guard would let down the chain across as the road, and we entered Afghanistan. Customs was haphazard at best on this side. It was somewhat similar with the Pakistan side. But the immigration office was well inside the country, as I recall perhaps a mile or two. It was a house located in a gulch that was not even visible until one was there. Only the driver could possibly know where it was. Another ritual we always performed at this point was to hand our passport, open to the page with the current Afghan visa (remember the passport had dozens of added pages, was bulging with visas), to the raggedly looking official - upside down. He would study it very seriously, grunt, nod, and hand it back. That was immigration, and it was clear he couldn't read a word of the visa, even though it was in Afghan.

Then we headed across the desert. This was flat desert land, with the Hindu Kush mountains off in the far distance. There was discernible wheel tracks to follow so long as there had not been any rainfall. I can only guess that the driver knew what direction to move by the far off mountain outline. During the summer months we would be the only moving thing during the day. The camel "Koochie" caravans that carried rugs and handicrafts to market would stop. A Blanket would be put up on sticks, and everyone would stay underneath to avoid the hot sun.

Our first touch point would be Jalalabad, a small settlement in the middle of the desert, where we would get a Nan or two (Afghan type bread), a couple of melons perhaps, but there wasn't much else. Then across the desert again to the base of the mountains at a place called Sorobi. Again, the driver had to know where Sorobi was by the outline of the mountains, certainly not by the road, which often didn't exist. The Germans were building a dam there, so a bottle of beer was always available.

Then the highpoint of the trip: we would begin the climb up the mountains to about 9000ft. We used the Laudabon Pass. It is no longer used since the Russians built a paved road through another pass - now called the Kabul Pass, but that was well past my time. The Laudabon was a rather frightening undertaking. Not much wider than one lane, sheer drops of 1 or 2 thousand feet straight down, icy and slippery during the winter months, and the need to avoid or pass the colorful Afghan busses that used the road as well. Colorful in that they were brightly painted with intricate designs. They were incredibly overloaded, and goods and people stacked so high that they would weave back and forth as they turned on the hairpin turns.

To make matters worse, the Afghan driver (inevitably named Mohammed) was a wild man who looked on any obstacle in his way as the enemy. He once broke the chain at the border when the border guards wanted to check his papers. Once in passing a bus on the Laudabon, he tooted so furiously, shouting at the top of his voice, going around sharp turns way up the mountains. This made the bus driver frazzled and eased the bus too close to the ditch, which the whole thing slid in and against the mountain. It likely took hours for them to unload everything, get all the passengers together and right the bus. In fact they were lucky, as the bus had veered to the mountainside, not the cliff side of the road.

At the top of the highest point on the road lived a holy man. At 9000 ft it was always windy there. He lived in a hut, with a lot of "flags" (solid color squares, light colors, like Buddhist flags) blowing in the wind. Every driver, going up to Kabul or down to Peshawar, always stopped there and gave a few coins. It was to thank the gods for the safe journey up, or pray for the one going down. Needless to say, we always gave. From there the road wound down into Kabul, whose elevation is 6000 ft.

Kabul was then a village, one-story buildings, erratic and very limited electricity. Only three or four streets had been paved by the Russians. There was no hotel so we stayed with the Marines. Winters were cold, summers cool. There was little to do – the bazaar was small, but one could buy sheepskin jackets and old coins. The sheepskin jacket, lasted me for several years. The old coins seem to be very good ones. In fact we had little energy to do much during the two days we would spend there. The trip was tiring, and we were unaccustomed to the altitude, so one slept a lot. Then the hazardous trip back followed exactly the same route. The jeep trip between Peshawar and Kabul took about ten hours. The train trip between Peshawar and Lahore overnight, and Lahore to Delhi about a half day.

Southeast Asia

Most of the flying we did around Southeast Asia in the mid50's was done in DC-3 type aircraft. The area is tropical, and the cloud build-ups, especially in the afternoon/evening were very formidable. Schedules were erratic and seldom on time. The planes, on the ground, were like ovens, and in the air cold. The flights were long, and usually very turbulent. The weather hot, and only in Singapore were there air-conditioned hotels (window units in the rooms only). There were two main trips - one covering Indo-China, the other Malaysia/Indonesia. Bangkok even then was already an air center, so most of our trips centered there. Later the courier office was to move to Bangkok from Manila, but that was well beyond my time.

Burma was covered by a side overnight trip out of Bangkok, usually coming and going in the middle of the night. We stayed in the Strand Hotel, which was a typical British colonial era hotel. Pie dogs roamed everywhere. The city was deteriorating, and years later, unlike almost all the rest of Asia, very little had changed. Besides the dogs, memories are of the cheroots that men and women smoked, and the betel juice, which people spit everywhere. One had to take off shoes when visiting the famous Schwerdagon Buddhist temple. It was very uncomfortable trying to avoid stepping on recently spit out betel juice with one's bare feet.

The old airport at Rangoon was just two or three small wooden buildings. Since we spent much time there in the middle of the night, it seemed even worse. We would use European or Pan Am flights, and since there was no long range communications or radar, we often had to wait long hours without knowing when the plane would arrive. At night huge rats would come out, so we had to keep our feet up on other chairs. I am told that when the "new" airport terminal was completed (it now looks as bad as the old one), the Burmese had enlisted a couple of British jet fighters from their base in Malaysia to make a low level fly by as part of the opening ceremony. No one, apparently, thought of the sonic boom, and every window in the building was busted.

There were two separate trips into Southeast Asia: one using a government chartered DC-3, the other commercial DC-3s. Both started out of Manila on a Pan Am Stratocruiser however, one flying to Saigon from where we would pick up our plane for Indo-China service, the other direct to Singapore to start the trip around Malaysia and Indonesia on commercial planes. The stratocruiser was considered a luxury plane, especially if one flew first class as we did then. It was double-decker, with a lounge downstairs. The first class seats seemed miles apart. The interior was either wood paneled or imitation wood, and the service was quite good. The plane was slow, however, and flying in turbulence, which was most of the time, it would creak and groan so much, one had to wonder if it would hold together.

The Indo China trip used a contract plane based in Saigon. It was then called the "STEM" plane, but later Air America. We would make two round trips from Saigon, Phnom Penh, Bangkok, Vientiane and back to Saigon each week. The plane had bucket seats and carried cargo for the missions in those countries. It was flown by Alan Pope, one of the Air America cowboys, somewhat younger than the old China types like earthquake Magoon and others that operated first out of China, and then out of Hong Kong. He was a character, however. He later switched to another job, and got shot down over Indonesia during an unsuccessful coup attempt against Sukarno. He spent six years in jail there before being sprung by the USG.

Saigon was still largely French. Some of the troops still remained. The stores and restaurants were French, as were the street names. It was a pretty tree-lined city, very few cars. People lived in walled off houses, and there were peddlers on bikes everywhere. Each made his own distinctive sound, depending on what he was selling. Behind the wall in a house, one would know what it was also, just by the sound. It was a lazy, quiet existence, though this was the time of the rival militias vying to take power as the French left. Up north, the French battalion that I had known in Korea was annihilated on the" Street Without Joy", the same road I was later to live on.

The plane would take off from Tan Son Nhut, land in Phnom Penh for a short time, then on to SimRiep (where Angkor Wat is located), and Bangkok for an overnight. The ride was seldom smooth - Pope had a knack for hitting any cloud, wherever it was and during the monsoons the trip was pretty rough. On one occasion we flew through a typhoon on that particular segment. Ambassador Reinhardt (Saigon) and his very pregnant wife and one or two others were aboard. By the time we were nearing Bangkok it was dark, and the rain and wind was so fierce that rain was coming in through the door.

We were being tossed about very roughly as the plane was going in for the landing at Don Muang airport. Even close in one could barely see the landing lights, when suddenly all the lights went out. Pope had to pull the plane back up into the storm and begin circling. The controller could only say that the lights had gone out (which we knew), but not how long it would take to put them back on. Just as Pope was preparing to head back to Phnom Penh - gas was getting low - the lights reappeared. Everyone was pretty shaken up by the time we landed.

The tourist area of Bangkok in the mid-50s was down near the Oriental Hotel on the river. Small shops and restaurants, mostly open air as air conditioning was almost non-existent then, was where tourists shopped. Bangkok has gotten even hotter now, covered as it is with high buildings and wide streets. The klongs are largely gone. Then mosquitoes were everywhere, breeding in the klongs, and taking refuge it seemed, in restaurants and hotels. And with no air conditioning, one simply perspired all the time.

We stayed then at the Princess Hotel, one of several in that area where westerners tended to stay. Not air conditioned, they were none the less in those days considered first class. In the rooms, the windows had no glass, only shutters. One used a sheet for cover against the mosquitoes, and the ceiling fan to stir the air. The Buddhist bonzes, who were everywhere, did more than pray and beg, it seemed. They also told time. Every hour they would pass through the alleys behind the hotel, hitting a gong and singing the hour. That in turn would awaken the dogs, which were second only to the mosquitoes in number. They would begin to howl, and of course wake everyone up. One did not sleep very soundly in Bangkok.

We got to know Don Muang airport very well. Bangkok was and still is on the main route between Europe and Japan. All major airlines, and many regional ones stop there. In the days of the prop planes and no radar, flights were seldom on schedule, engines needed constant care, and loading passengers aboard seemed like a new experience each time, for the ground crews. All of that translated into many hours sitting around the airport, eating the only thing edible: cowpot - a fried rice concoction topped by a fried egg - and swatting mosquitoes.

Sitting in the plane on the tarmac, waiting to take off, was always a draining experience. Ones clothes became soaked before the trip even began. On our trip to Vientiane, would not stay over, but return to Bangkok the same day. Wattay airport in Laos, had not yet been built. The "airport" was in fact simply a field where water buffalo grazed. The Queen's messenger usually joined us on this leg (reciprocating our use of the Lancaster into Warsaw). An enraged buffalo once charged a Stem plane, damaging it severely.

The Indochina trip, all told, meant two nights in Saigon, four in Bangkok, and a lot of DC3 flying in between. Some of the couriers managed to get some time off occasionally in Saigon, where Al Pope would take them tiger hunting not too far out of town.

Once a week there was another trip to Southeast Asia, sometimes via Bangkok, sometimes via Singapore. Bangkok to Djakarta took a full day of flying, with one stop. No food, just peanuts and bananas on the Garuda Airlines flight. Djakarta then looked very pretty from the air. A city of bungalows with red tile roofs, neat streets and canals running through it. That was so Dutch, and probably what it used to be like, and still looked like from the air. But when one walked around on the ground, it was quite a different story.

The canals were filthy, with people bathing, washing clothes, brushing teeth, all in the same water. The buildings and bungalows were run down. Law and order was whatever the soldiers wanted. But the markets were lush the tropical climate with plenty of rain caused everything to grow, and grow large. Street vendors sold things off the streets, including delicious satays. No English was spoken (and Dutch, even if one knew it, was not a healthy language to speak). There were no livable hotels so we lived in embassy staff quarters. The chief means of transport were the three wheeled "bechas". We memorized four words in Indonesian - "Kramat lima pula tuju". That was the address of the small compound where we were put up by the embassy.

AntiDutch feelings were still running high. Clearly the personnel that had been running the physical structure of the country had all been told to go, and that was why the country seemed so rundown. Some people simply could not be let go, however. The pilots for Garuda Airlines, for example. Once when I was at the small airport waiting for my flight, a domestic Garuda plane was having a problem getting the landing gear down. The plane had to continue to circle for some time, and since the city wasn't all that big, word got around and a crowd started to gather. Finally, the landing gear was down, and the plane landed. After the passengers got out, the crew came out of the plane. First the two Dutchmen, covered with sweat and grease-they had had to hand crank the mechanism themselves. No reaction from the crowd. Then two Indonesian crew, clean as a whistle, emerged, and the crowd erupted with cheers.

Djakarta was always a hot sweaty place, and flying through the huge tropical clouds was always teeth shattering. Singapore, only an hour away then, was hot also, but the hotels already had air conditioning. Under British rule, it was like a tropical Hong Kong. For those days, the hotels were good, the restaurants good, and plenty of duty free things in the shops. It was always great to get back to Singapore after either Djakarta, or the grasshopper trip up the peninsula.

The "grasshopper" was a Malayan Airway DC3 that was a steam box whenever it was on the ground. It would fly up the peninsula stopping at Malacca, Kuala Lumpur, Taiping, and Penang. In Penang we would change to another DC3 for a roundtrip ride across the Malacca Straits to Medan in Sumatra where we had a consulate. Penang was also a free port, and the plane to Medan was always crowded. Aside from the chickens, ducks, green vegetables and salted eggs, the plane was full of fat women with gold teeth, and a lot of jewelry. It was a smugglers run, with Chinese merchants on the Sumatra side "arranging" the imports. The jewels were glass on the trip from Medan to Penang, and miraculously real on the reverse run. This round trip started early in the morning from Singapore, and returned that evening. One regained the pounds lost with cold beer, a Chinese meal, and air conditioning.

Singapore was, and is, very much a Chinese city. But in the 50's, for a short time, Singapore was a part of the newly independent Malaysia. It was then pretty much a south China-type city. Later, when it became independent itself, it began changing very much. It became one of the cleanest places on earth. Too much, and clearly there were unfortunate reasons for it.

Australia and New Zealand

The longest flights we had were to Australia and New Zealand. The Qantas plane was one of the early Constellations. We would leave at midnight from Manila, land the next morning at Darwin, then land in Sydney that evening. Flying during the night over tropical areas with their large cloud build-ups, could sometimes be a very uncomfortable experience. It was always a long sleepless night to go through before landing in Darwin for fuel and immigration. As our loads were large, we were permitted to stay near the aircraft and breakfast was brought to us.

Then a long day's flight over the nothingness of Australia, until we reached Sydney. In the mid-fifties, Australia was still very English. Immigration from elsewhere was extremely limited. One could still find something to do in Sydney with a little effort, but other places like Melbourne, and even more in Auckland/ Wellington in New Zealand, it was staid and austere to an extreme. Sundays were simply non-days. Everything - restaurants, movies, newspapers, nothing opened. One ate at the hotels where meals were barely served.

The stay was enjoyable in a sense, in that one was in a more familiar setting: familiar but not interesting and certainly not exciting. One could really sense being in a new, wide open country, but reined in by an old system that seemed out of place. Labor unions, strict "blue laws", 9 to 5 mentality in a place that should have been bursting with activity. It was soon to change, but at that time the long trip to that area was a chore, not an adventure.

Hong Kong

The Hong Kong Consul General (Congen) was then the China watching center. We serviced the Congen from Manila 5 days a week. Every weekday we would catch the Philippine Airlines Convair around noon, arriving at Kai Tak mid afternoon. The courier would proceed into town while the courier of the previous day would catch the return flight to Manila. Couriers performed this function while they were between regular trips and supposedly resting.

At that time, the one Convair was the only one PAL had. It flew every morning around the islands, then in the afternoon to Hong Kong and back. Not surprisingly, it often had engine trouble, either delaying departure, or losing one of its two engines *en route*. Going to Hong Kong was less of a problem than returning to Manila. Going was during daylight with alternate airfields at Clark in the northern Luzon, or Tainan in southern Taiwan (none in China, of course, which was then forbidden territory). These alternates were available after dark, but at night with the state of radar then, not the safest.

The problem on the return flight was both the temptations for the crew, and Kai Tak airport. The crew wanted to do its buying during the layover, and exchanging money (the Peso rate was double the official rate). Thus, almost invariably and no matter what time arrival took place, it would be close to 6 PM before take off to Manila. There were no night operations at Kai Tak. The airport shut down completely at 6 PM. Losing an engine shortly after take off meant a longish flight on one engine over water to an alternate.

Arriving at Hong Kong was also an exciting experience: No radar. The clouds often sat on the water or close to it. So the plane would have to descend out over the water sometimes just barely higher than the fishing sampans, look for Lyemun Pass, go through it into Kai Tak on the Kowloon side. The runway was then rather short, running into the mountain behind the peninsula. Several roads crossed it, so all traffic had to be stopped each time a plane landed or took off.

The terminal was a very small wooden building, with a small customs and immigration area and a small snack bar that served sandwiches, noodles, tea and coffee. For us it also had something else: Lo On. He was a money changer whose office was in his hat. He was important to us as we changed our dollars into all kinds of currencies, depending on the countries we expected to visit over the next few weeks. Lo On would take our check and our order on arrival. He would show up the next day at the hotel with all the monies. He once took a rubber check from an American businessman, and for weeks he was accompanied everywhere by two thugs who took his profits on the spot until the check was paid off. He grew rather thin during that time, but somehow managed to keep his gold teeth.

We were always met at the airport by the Congen driver, driven in a jeep to Star Ferry (the jeep was caged in the rear, a result of a close call during the little heard about 1956 riots). We would take the bag on the passenger ferry while the driver deposited our suitcase at the nearby hotel. The Star Ferry pier on the Hong Kong side was then very close to the old Hong Kong-Shanghai Bank Building. We would turn over the bag to the Consulate General which then occupied the 3rd and 4th floor of that building, then head back to the hotel.

We had an arrangement with the Peninsula Hotel, always occupying the same room. It was the best hotel even then, but our dollars could easily afford it. The lobby of that hotel was where anyone who knew Hong Kong would meet. The service was superb, and many of the staff remained for years (I saw some even on my last assignment there almost thirty years later).

Nathan Road, the main street of Kowloon and about three miles long, was then lined by the typical southern Chinese 3 or 4 story buildings. The ground floor was always shops or restaurants, and the upper floors living quarters. The roof was occupied as well. In those days so were the streets. The upper floors of these buildings all arched over the sidewalk. It was handy when it rained. But hawkers always positioned themselves to present the greatest possible obstruction for pedestrians (hoping of course that this would produce customers). Also, the streets contained literally hundreds of refugees from China, sleeping, eating, washing, whatever. Competition among the small shops and hawkers was so intense that bargains for everything were available. Antiques, tailored clothing, a wide variety of imported goods (Hong Kong is a free port) from cloth to electronics. And the dollar was strong.

A foreigner was also perfectly safe any time of the day or night. It was no wonder then, that Hong Kong was a favorite place for us to go.

In Europe I had taken the Foreign Service officer exam and passed. By the time I got to Washington to take the oral exams, everyone was rejected because the Department had over-recruited. It was a great disappointment and in fact the written exam was not even offered the following year for that reason. By the time it was offered again I had just returned for my second tour in Manila. I passed the exam again, but had to wait almost two years before returning to Washington. I traveled the Manila courier circuit again, but asked for a regular assignment while I waited to take the oral exam again.

There were great changes in the area. For one thing, after flying prop planes for so long, flying my first commercial jet (Qanta from Singapore to Bangkok) was a notable event for me. It took one and a half-hour compared to the almost full day it had taken before. One other notable event was flying into a typhoon in an Air France constellation en-route back to Manila. We got badly tossed about and then hit an air pocket, sending food, dishes, glassware and whatever all about, and some people were injured. Ambulances were waiting at Manila to take us all to the hospital for observation. I was clearly ready for a more normal life by the time the offer came to transfer to Hong Kong, and I took it.

CHAPTER FOUR
Foreign Service Early Years

Hong, Kong, Laos, Taichung, Taipei, Washington, Vietnam

Leaving the courier service after five years was to mean a complete change in life style. I looked forward to it, however, especially since it was to be Hong Kong, where I had been so many times and knew it reasonably well. Since I had to wait until my return to Washington before taking the oral exam again, it was an ideal place to do so. Hong Kong was beginning to change rapidly. I had flown over here dozens of times so I knew Hong Kong well. My recollections cover the period from 1955 to the end of this assignment in 1961.

The Consulate General put me in the Astor Hotel temporarily until I found quarters of my own. An old-time Consul who had been rehired from retirement to help the Consulate General visa section, also lived there and we had dinner together many times. I remember it clearly because although his stories of the Foreign Service in China in pre-war days (he had lived for twenty years in Tsing-tao - home leave was not provided in those days) was fascinating, his mannerisms were embarrassing in 1960. He always would bellow out "boy" whenever he wanted a waiter, and they clearly resented it. I would also often eat out in the small Cantonese noodle stalls, or in the fast disappearing White Russian restaurants for western food.

My first apartment was in a new building in Causeway Bay that was built more for middle class local people at that time. It was a far cry from the more lavish ones that came later. It was pretty Spartan, no air conditioning, few electrical fixtures, and all locally produced water fixtures. The water supply was a serious problem. With no air conditioning and hot, sultry weather, bath water was even more necessary. At times, Hong Kong was divided into water sectors, with water opened for the specified sector every fourth day. Bath tubs, GI cans, and any other containers were filled on that day, and carefully used until the next supply was available.

Though the Hong Kong Government, with great reluctance, departed from its strict laissez affairs philosophy out of sheer necessity, it began building houses for the great many refugees that lived on the streets or the hillsides. Refugees living in big wooden boxes (for which they paid rent to the one who had obtained the box), still covered the hillsides, or if they couldn't afford the rent, slept on the streets. Through my apartment's landlord, I gave a small grant from the American Women's Association to one of his cleaning employees. According to the landlord, the family had five children, and all lived in one wooden box on the hillside next to the apartment. One of the children was chosen by them to receive the grant ($50) for tuition at an elementary school (he was the only child to go to school).

A Maryknoll missionary, Monsignor Romaniello, (from New Rochelle, N.Y.) was called "the noodle king". He had brought in a spaghetti machine from Italy and used PL480) wheat flour to make noodles which he passed out to the needy. The more entrepreneurial refugees started small businesses of all kinds on the streets. Unhappily, one established himself on the street below my apartment. He made fried "cho dou-fu" (fermented bean curd cakes with a very strong odor), the smell of which wafted up into my apartment every day.

The visa operation, for the local people, was by far the most important section of the Consulate General. Lines formed every day outside the building and winding down the hill, by refugees hoping to get a visa to the U.S. A great many of the refugees who applied for emigration were from Toi Shan County between Hong Kong and Guangzhou. At that time about 85 percent of the Chinese Americans living in the U.S. had originated from that county. The consular officers, though none had ever been to that county, knew the villages and the family names in them very well. Many of the refugees falsely claimed either relatives in the States or residence in that county and were often rejected.

Inevitably, where there is a need, business will flourish. The not so reputable lawyers of Hong Kong did a thriving business fashioning false documents for which they were well paid. Some were so badly done that even the newest consular officer could detect the blatant counterfeiting. Others were less easy. For these a special consular unit, with the cooperation of the Hong Kong police, would conduct illegal operations such as searching an applicants home, or gathering evidence in other illegal ways that verified the applicants papers were fraudulent. The unit operated for several years but the new Consul General who arrived at that time immediately saw the implications if this were discovered and dismantled the operation.

My job was a staff (as opposed to officer) position, and involved work on housing, car pool, and visitors. In those days, the latter kept us very busy. Codels (Congressional delegations) were very frequent. Any member of Congress who took a trip to Asia inevitably wanted to stop in Hong Kong. Handling them - the rascals as well as the serious ones - was always sensitive. Then Vice-President Lyndon Johnson roared in once, buying up a lifetime's supply of shirts. They stayed at a newly built, but still not open, hotel - the only one that could accommodate the group. We had a stroke of luck in finding and buying the only supply of Cutty Sark scotch - his favorite - just before someone from the embassy in Taipei (his next stop) showed up to buy the same thing.

The Consulate General had only recently moved into its own new building on Garden Road from the old Hong Kong & Shanghai Bank building (where I had delivered the pouch so often in my courier days). It was known as America's China-watching center, and indeed it had an impressive operation for this purpose. Refugees were interviewed, and books, magazines, newspapers obtained, many of which were scavenged from people leaving China. This operation became one of the principle sources of information worldwide on what was going on in "Red China".

The Consulate General rented a floor in the BAT (British-American Tobacco) warehouse in Wanchai, where many translators worked to put all this information into English. Another group typed up the result, mimeographed, collated, and mailed out to literally hundreds of universities, news organizations, U.S. and foreign government organizations (including some even to Eastern Europe). One problem with the latter was that these countries were also considered sources of information on what was then their fellow friendly communist country. It became difficult to determine how much of their news was original and therefore verified our own, or how much was simply repeating reports they had received from us.

Other parts of the Consulate General also conducted unique activities. The Treasury Department had an office there whose main purpose was to monitor business transactions with "Red China", all of which were illegal. This included American tourists buying handicrafts in the very few Chinese Government owned stores in the colony.

The individual who did all this looked the part - high starched collar, and a serious and strong sense of mission. It was at times difficult even for us in government to toe the line, setting aside most of the food we ate came from there. In putting some new partitions in the Consulate General, for example, we had to use brick. The only bricks available came from China. So we had to do our work on a weekend when the Treasury representative didn't come to work. (We were luckier than the American Club, who did some similar renovation and got caught).

Mentioned above was the managing of the unusually high number of Codels (Congressional Delegations), as well as the large number of military brass, which required considerable logistical support. Hong Kong was a favorite tourist stop with wide open facilities and a wide variety of goods to buy at very low prices. Members of Congress could find any number of reasons why their travels in Asia should include Hong Kong. They often flew in military transports, and were given "counterpart" funds to spend (local currency generated by our Aid programs which could be converted into Hong Kong dollars in the colony's open exchange market). Everything from radios to furniture was bought, and transported in their own aircraft .

Though I was in an administrative position, I was permitted to sit in on a Chinese language class used by the China watchers. It was on this tour that I came to know many of the Foreign Service Officer China-watchers. Knowing my interest, they were very supportive of my sharing in lessons. As I went on in my career, however, first becoming an FSO (Foreign Service Officer), then formal language training, then a rapid rise in rank, I found some of them less friendly. But, in any event, it was to help me later in getting more formal training.

When my assignment in Hong Kong was completed, my next job was slated to be another administrative position in the embassy in Laos. The Navy office in the Consulate General at that time was to get a new vehicle, and as required, it auctioned off the old World War II jeep they had been using. It was a special jeep, and I won the bid. The jeep had been completely refurbished by the Hollywood company that had filmed "Love is a Many Splendored Thing". It had been used by the leading star in the film, and since the Navy office couldn't take the money offered for its use, it was returned in first class condition.

I took the President Cleveland liner back to San Francisco, and then on to Washington to once again take the Foreign Service Officer oral exam. The journey from Hong Kong to San Francisco on the liner was a great and restful experience. It took 21 days, and one is continually offered delicious food for meals and for in-between snacks. My weight soared, and it was to take a long time to bring it back under control.

Laos 1961-63

The oral exam proved totally different than my previous one. I breezed through it very quickly and passed with the recommendation that I receive language training to meet the requirements for Foreign Service Officer. Naturally I was delighted after such a long wait, and immediately asked for Chinese language training. It wasn't going to be easy, however. Personnel decided my assignment to Laos, which they had made before knowing the results of my exam, would have to be done first - language training would follow.

After home leave, I took the President Cleveland back from Hawaii to Hong Kong. On the previous trip I had gained many pounds eating far too much of the delicious food. This time, I ate less and daily jogged on the deck. The result was that by the time of arrival at Hong Kong, my right foot had become very swollen. In jogging around the deck my foot would hit the deck too hard too often as the ship swayed. I arrived in Laos on crutches.

In 1961, when I arrived in Laos on assignment, the country was in the headlines. President Kennedy often spoke about it (he pronounced it Lay-ous) and remained very familiar with what was going on there. The leftist guerrillas, called the Pathet Lao, controlled the countryside, whereas the government only controlled the capital Vientiane, Luang Prabang the royal capital, and a few other villages most of which hugged the Thai border. The government was headed by a rightist general supported by us. Eventually, we negotiated an agreement that brought a neutralist government into power. It didn't work very long. Soon the neutralist government was in exactly the same position, with the leftist still out in the countryside.

One problem has always been that Laos is not really a country. Along the Mekong River are the Lao, who are really country Thai. The rest of the country is made up of various hill people. The government in Vientiane did not exercise authority over this disparate area. Vientiane, the capital, sits on the Mekong, right across from Thailand. During the rainy season, the river is a raging torrent; during the dry season it is a little stream. The Lao had not yet entered the twentieth century. The city did not have running water, nor electricity. The taxis were samlors (three wheeled pedicabs) and even these were driven by Thai from across the river. When I arrived there was a small US military advisory group stationed there. After the Geneva peace agreement was signed, they left and US Aid people began returning. We in the embassy needed another agency, any agency, that could pay for our services just to keep our own embassy operation running. (We charged them enough to pay for embassy operations as well).

My job there was General Services Officer. That is the position that maintains the embassy, housing, inventory, procurement, etc. .In a place like that where one has to provide all the services normally done by either government or service companies, the job kept me fully occupied. When I was given the assignment in Washington, I was not very pleased. But as so often happens, at least for me, the work became a challenge and It turned out to be a fun one as well.

When I first arrived, families were not permitted there (after the agreement they were), so I lived with several other officers in a house. We had a Vietnamese cook (male) who had been the former cook of the French Director General in Hanoi. He was really superb, so good that we never told the Ambassador. If he had known, we would have lost him. Once families were allowed to come, however, everyone lived in separate houses. We had several leased houses around the city for the officers, and everyone else lived in "Silver City". That was a compound with about twenty small houses, all built by the US Government. We had a water tank and generator, telephones, etc. It was a small self— sustaining little community. The officers living in the city had much larger houses, but no electricity until we started to build little generators sheds around town that supplied electricity on a part time basis. Likewise, water had to be provided by tank truck that pumped water into a couple of GI cans usually located high enough at each house to provide the needed pressure.

The tank truck was very critical, of course. It was old, however, and we had scrounged it from another USG agency. It ran on baling wire and hope. Once I wrote to Washington to get funds to buy spare parts for it in Bangkok. Washington wrote back saying I should get the money from wherever I had gotten the truck, as it was not on the State Department inventory. Another time I got an urgent radio call that the truck had hit a Lao parachutist. I dashed out only to find that it was the parachutist that had hit the truck. His parachute had failed to open (or just as possible he didn't know he had to pull the chord). He was dead, of course, but the truck was not badly damaged.

The GSO crew was made up of Third Country Nationals (TCN) because skilled Lao were not available. The maintenance crew chief was a Thai, the plumber a Vietnamese, the electrician a Japanese, the carpenter a Filippino, the motor mechanic was a Frenchman, the inventory was handled by a Chinese, and the labor contractor, who provided all the manual laborers, was a Thai/Japanese named Haruki. In later years, when the communists eventually took over, Haruki was grabbed, sent to a labor camp in northern Laos, and presumably died there. This crew was so good that in addition to maintaining all the U.S. Government houses and the embassy, they rehabilitated every house we had to lease, and we even built an addition on to the embassy ourselves. We rehabilitated air conditioners, put in whole water systems, and built water cooled generator operations in several places.

We often had to shop in Thailand, in a place called Nongkai. It was a small village with thatched houses and the one or two small stores there were the same. To get over there required a short drive which was as far as we ever could go out of Vientiane. Then we would have to cross the river in a very narrow shallow water boat, which were commonly used as ferries. When the river was high it had to struggle to fight the current. A Philippine medical group had a much bigger boat which we used sometime for outings. Once, when the river was high the motor conked out. We started drifting downstream pretty fast. After many attempts we were able to lasso a tree and pull the boat out of the current.

There were other sources of supply besides what could be trucked up from Bangkok. The Canadian small military unit would buy our scotch for which we asked to be paid with British cigarettes. We then took the cigarettes to the larger French unit to pay for large jugs of Algerian red table wine.

Only once, just after the Geneva Peace Agreement was signed, was I ever able to get out into the countryside. It was unsafe because of guerrillas. We went on a picnic, almost running over a snake that was at least eight feet long. I also lost the spare tire of my jeep. The jeep was the one I had bought in Hong Kong. Though it was of World War II vintage, it was in excellent shape and never gave trouble. That was fortunate because repairing a car in Laos took more ingenuity than skill. (A new economic officer, after arriving in Laos, had to wait several months before his car arrived. When he did he ordered it cleaned thoroughly. It was – with soap and water. Engine, spark plugs, anything removable – all got a thorough soap and water cleaning. I do not believe the car ever ran again). This foray out of Vientiane was also the only time I would get to see "Kilometer 6". It was like a small American subdivision in the suburbs, nice newly built brick houses, just like home. It had been built by USAID years before to house its personnel (as compared to the Quonset huts of Silver City). USAID personnel had been evacuated some years before, but the location had become too far out of town for safety in any event. What I saw was like a modern Ankor Wat, with trees growing in, through, and around the houses. The ban on traveling outside Vientiane was lifted for only a few days, and then resumed.

After the Geneva agreement, the Russians and Chinese opened embassies in Vientiane. I had people out checking where they were leasing their housing. Whenever one of them leased one, I would try to lease one close by for those among us who were in that business. After a while we realized we were all doing the same thing. It was like catch 22. All three embassies were leasing houses all over town to get close to the others . We all wound up with a lot of houses we really didn't need.

When the AID people started to come back into the country (post agreement), they had a lot of air conditioners and refrigerators, that had been stashed away. With the money they always seem to have, they soon started buying new ones. They didn't know the situation too well. I would go over to them and scrounge old air conditioners or other appliances, then I'd have an auction. Because of exchange rates, I would get very inflated prices, almost the same as a new one. Then I'd take the money and buy new ones in Bangkok and ship them up.

The last project I managed was the largest one. The Silver City compound was only half occupied with twenty or so small houses. The other half was swampy during the rainy season. Furthermore, all the repair shops were in makeshift buildings across from the embassy. I decided to build some warehouses and repair shops in our compound at Silver City. For one thing it would be safer there, and could be made attractive. Also the generators that supplied electricity to the compound had been put right across from the Philippine hospital. I wanted to build a good water cooled system with new generators and in a building that would make it much quieter. During my last dry season there I employed several trucks for several weeks, getting sand from the dry river bed and filling in the swampy area at the compound. Then we began construction of all these things. During my two years in Laos we did so much that when I met a fellow who had been posted there years later, he said stories about my work were still being told.

Thanks to USAID, we weren't the only builders in Vientiane. A hotel was badly needed and someone (probablyThai), with USAID help, built a small one called the Lan Xang. When completed, the new Thai manager was brought to Vientiane and he conducted an inspection. All seemed fine, including a large dining room nicely furnished. Unfortunately, when he looked for the kitchen it was not to be found. They had forgotten to build one.

USIA also had a unique program in Laos (and perhaps elsewhere). This was several groups of Lao village singers. They would be briefed on the recent news that would be of interest to villagers, then sent out to the villages to sing the news in Lao.

When an inspection of the embassy was scheduled, we had the inspectors from Washington take the rackety train up from Bangkok and cross the river in one of these small boats, just to impress them. The heavens cooperated as it rained heavily while they were there. The streets, and our offices were all flooded. We all kept on working as if it was an everyday occurrence. Needless to say, the inspectors were mightily impressed. Sufficiently at least for them to recommend that I be assigned to Chinese language training for my next assignment.

Much of what has been described above is doubtless gone now. But it was a very satisfying time because one could actually see accomplishment, something rarely possible in our business.

Taichung 1963-65

With the much coveted assignment to the Chinese language school in Taichung, I landed at Sungshan Airport in Taipei and met by a student and teacher from the school. We drove south half way to Taichung, and spent that night in a hostel run by Buddhist nuns, high in the mountains east of Taoyuan. Our only meal there was breakfast - several courses of bean curd made to look like shrimp, chicken, or pork chops. Thereafter we drove on to Taichung where the school's administrative assistant helped me locate a small Japanese house to rent.

It was typical of the school and what made it unique. Adults could learn a difficult language like Chinese better and much more quickly by being totally emersed in the culture we were studying. Only Chinese could be spoken in the school, even for rank beginners. Aside from attending class - all of which were one student, one teacher, with the teachers rotating every hour - a student (and family if that was the case) was on his own. If the plumbing needed fixing, we would have to cope with a plumber who knew no English. Groceries were purchased in the local market.

As a Courier, I had been taking Chinese lessons in Manila. Since I was out of town most of the time, my teacher would prepare characters to have me memorize while I was on trips. I would add my own phonetics to each character and learned words and phrases that way. Unfortuantely, at the school romanization (Yale) was used, with character reading beginning only about halfway through the course. The two systems of learning clashed and it took some time to reorient myself and build up my confidence using the new method. The level of competence reached by the end of the course was useful, but it took another six months at work in Taipei actually using the language for real, that I felt confident and comfortable using it on most any occasion. The system for language training, nonetheless, is very effective, but very costly - only government could do it. It is a valuable asset for government and for the individual. Surprisingly, however, it was not unusual for officers with this skill to leave the service not long after obtaining it. The reason was often family related - not comfortable living abroad, for example. The opportunity to earn more money in the private sector was not a factor in those days. In the mid-1960's it was a language few outside of government had a need for.

One of the experiences of the program is getting out to the villages, managing the transport and accommodations, and casual conversations with the local people. On one occasion the whole class with a few teachers took a round-island trip. One stop was at the Taiwan Pineapple Corporation (government-owned) in Taichung, in southeast Taiwan. We stayed at the company hostel and were fed a big meal that evening. After endless courses, we were thoroughly stuffed, but they then wheeled out huge platters of dumplings and steamed breads just to be sure. Then when we thought the bounds of courtesy in stuffing ourselves beyond limits was sufficient, out came a large roasted turkey (it being Thanksgiving day), covered with sweet-sour sauce.

On another trip with just me and a teacher, we passed through Taipei on the way back to the school. I invited the teacher to dinner at the U.S. Officers Club. We both had steaks, and then continued our trip back to school. About halfway there, the teacher wanted to stop for noodles. He said he enjoyed the steak, but whenever he ate a western meal, he quickly felt stuffed, but not too long thereafter would be hungry - the opposite of what we say!

I was always struck by the lack of attention paid the language officers by the Ministry of Foreign Affairs. The future of U.S. relations with China and Taiwan would to some extent be in the hands of some of the students, but the seemed to pay no mind. The school was later moved to Yangmingshan, where it continues to this day. In my judgement it loses much of its effectiveness being located out-side the city, north of Taipei, in what amounts to an American ghetto. Further, AIT provides them with all the services they would have on a regular foreign assignment. The advantages of being submerged in a Chinese community are greatly diminished.`

Taipei 1965-67

From Taichung I was assigned to the embassy in Taipei as assistant commer-cial attache. The commciasl services function at that time was done by foreign service officers who were not necessarily experienced or interested in this work. Assignment to a commercial "slot" in an embassy was not sought after because it was felt to be outside the mainstream of foreign service "substantive" tasks (i.e. economic or especially political work). I was no more excited by it, but as was the case time and again, the work was taken as a challenge, and an opportunity to stand out, and this turned out ot be the case yet again.

Taipei was (and is) considerably different than Taichung. I moved into a small Japanese style house on Jen Ai Rd, section 4, which was then on the out-skirts of the city. To expand contacts, I joined the Lion's Club - English speaking, but as the only foreigner it was voted that I had to use Mandarin. I also produced the musical "Fantastiks". But the size of the challenges I saw at work soon oc-cupied most of my time.

The challenges came first by the visit of a Los Angeles lawyer immediately after my arrival in Taipei, and much more broadly the changing economic cli-mate in Taiwan. The lawyer came pursuing a trade complaint by his client. The problem was a shipment of scrap metal from Taiwan that did or did not reach Los Angeles, and the payment of U.S. $100,000 that was or was not made. After a week of negotiating in which I was the interpreter, it was resolved by the lawyer getting $40,000. Who actually won is not clear, but I surely gained confidence in my language capability. The lawyer sent a very commendatory letter to the am-bassador, who passed it on with a note saying he did not believe in commending an officer just for doing his duty!

The economy was changing. The U. S. AID program, which had been used so effectively by the authorities, closed its operations there. Taiwan was clearly capable of taking off on its own. We now had to learn how to sell to Taiwan, not give. The shift of embassy priorities was from economic to commercial. This had demographic implications as well. 70 percent of Taiwan's industry was then government owned. As mainlanders controlled government, these companies were headed by, and senior positions given to, mainlanders. Students who were given exit visas to attend American universities, also tended to be mainlanders.

But small businesses, now expanding into larger ones, and family conglomerates, were largely Taiwanese. The percentage of private sector industries began to grow. U.S. exports to Taiwan increasingly were going to go to the private sector, i.e. the Taiwanese. The Commerce Department, rightly, put its priority on exports to Taiwan generally, and for this a strategy was developed at that level. In addition, on the "local" level, I developed a strategy for getting to know the private sector.

The larger strategy began with my working with a Commerce Department expert making an island-wide market survey. This lasted a month during which time we visited most of the major companies on the island. This helped to hone my language skills even more, but importantly, I met people useful to both strategies. It took several months to publish the survey, but then it was effectively used to solicit and then put on the first large machinery exhibition Taiwan had ever had.

This was all done professionally by Commerce Department experts who eventually came to Taiwan for several weeks. There were many problems to overcome, including helping Taiwan authorities develop laws and regulations for such events. Taipei's only enclosed circular sports arena was renovated completely and was made into the exhibition site.

To exclude what we called the "ladies with babies and popcorn eaters", we required people entering the exhibition to deposit their business cards (for later use in follow-up). One noontime, I happened to be in a spot where I could view the entrance. I noticed a short, plump fellow obviously searching for a business card. I rushed to the entrance and let him through-it was the then Defense Minister Chiang, Ching-kuo, son of Chiang Kai-shek and future president. The exhibition was a great success.

To pursue my own strategy to learn more about the private sector, through a colleague I met with Jeffrey Koo, then a mid-level employee in a bank-China Trust Co. -owned by the Koo family, which was headed by his uncle Koo, Cheng-fu. He agreed to help and invited me into the Wednesday luncheon club, a group of scions of large, well off Taiwanese families. It was the beginning of my getting to know the Taiwanese business community (later I produced a directory of them), almost all of whom had seldom or never met U.S. Embassy personnel).

At the same time, I made a survey of all the food processing industry, this time alone. It was a growing industry than, and in need of new processing machinery. It also had few people who spoke any English. Many were jolted by a foreigner speaking Chinese knocking on their factory door. That was something they expected of ministers of foreign churches looking for funds.

With the support of my boss, I organized the first catalog show (which was later adopted by the Commerce Department worldwide). First soliciting catalogs from hundreds of American manufacturers of food-processing equipment, then setting up an exhibit of them, inviting hundreds of Taiwan food processors to see it, then following up with those who showed interest.

Through the Lions Club, I had met and began dating Lilan, and as my assignment was nearing its end, we decided to get married. The rules then for Foreign Service officers to marry a foreigner, the officer had to submit a letter of resignation. It would be held by the State Department while a security check was made. This took some time, and in the meantime, I was transferred to Hong Kong.

Hong Kong 1968-69

My assignment in Hong Kong was to be in the China/economics section. Since we had no relations with China, the best assignment for Chinese language officers was China-watching in Hong Kong. I was eagerly looking forward to it. I moved into an apartment at mid-level above the Consulate General. There were many changes since my last posting to the colony-mostly in many more high-rise buildings, but even more in the growth of industry there. Refugees were no longer on the streets or hillsides, but working in the many factories. Labor was needed, and illegal entrants (now no longer called refugees) could become legal residents by making it south of Boundary Street in: Kowloon. But the China - watching function in the Consulate General was still operating.

To my very great disappointment, almost immediately after starting my new job, Washington insisted one position had to be cut, and as the newest entrant, that was me. Washington offered me the soon to be vacated deputy chief of the Consulate's commercial unit. It was a position below my rank, and as I knew the chief's position was also soon-to-be vacated, I insisted it should be that. Once again for me, being given a Commercial assignment was disappointing for a language officer.

In that position I soon found a challenge, but I also had other things on my mind. As I had sent in a letter of resignation, and there was no certainty what the State Department security officers would decide, I was busy writing letters and sending out my resumes. At the same time I had already started writing a book on Chinese food: the variety, the ingredients, the etiquette, and how to order. With thousands of U.S. soldiers taking R&Rfrom Vietnam, there was a market. I had many colorful photos and the draft was soon completed. Jimmy Wu, a long-time friend and owner of the Maxims and Jade Garden chains of restaurants, would offer the book in his restaurants,. An American publishing house with an office in Hong Kong had agreed to publish. Unfortunately, it decided to sell off its Hong Kong operation to a Singapore firm, who promptly lost all photos and only published a black and white paper back. Under those conditions it was hardly a success, and took so long the market had shrunk considerably before it ever hit the bookstores.

The challenge I found for my assignment as chief of the commercial unit of the Consulate however turned out differently. Sometime after our assignment to Hong Kong was completed, I wrote a paper describing the process of encouraging the establishment of an American Chamber of Commerce, for my own files.The growing number of U.S. firms in Hong Kong, and the need to communicate with them effectively for a variety of reasons caused us in the commercial unit of the Consulate General to begin an analysis of our problem and to recommend a solution.

Changes in the way Americans did business overseas, especially in the Pacific area, had much to do with the growth of U.S. firms in the colony. In the immediate postwar period and on into the 50's, American companies largely picked up where they had left off-selling through trading houses. Most of these trading companies were given exclusive rights for specified markets (sometimes covering several countries). Though there were some American trading houses as well, the largest ones in Hong Kong were not to.

As American multinationals began to expand both production and marketing overseas, increasingly they established their own personnel abroad and eschewed trading houses. Hong Kong with both its favorable location, and it's free port tax haven status became very attractive first as an East Asia branch headquarters, and then, for many, as a production site as well.

Thus in the 1960's, the character of the American business community in Hong Kong was changing, as were the numbers of them. The managers of the American trading houses and shipping companies, many of whom had moved from Shanghai after the change in government in China, were becoming a minority among the American business community. Their way of doing business, mainly through personal relationships, was being replaced by organization managers following modern management techniques with well established and often worldwide policies.

There had become, in 1960's, a marked increase in the number of branch headquarters operations, attracted by the entrepot function and tax incentives offered in Hong Kong, and production facilities mainly in the electronics industry, attracted by cheap and productive labor. The need for Service's (tax experts, consultants, accountants, executive search, etc.) also added to the numbers of U.S. firms.

Pre-war, China had been a much smaller entrepot than Shanghai. The new revolutionary government in China, however, triggered an exodus of (a) successful people who could buy their way south, mainly from Shanghai, and (b) tens of thousands of peasants, workers, and small entrepreneurs who could walk largely from Guangzhou province. The hills of Hong Kong became covered with refugees looking for work, and the business districts, rich with experienced business talent, scratching to begin again the climb to wealth and power. Hong Kong was desperately short of water, and largely cut off from performing it's entrepot function for South China.

By the mid 60's, the world had witnessed a transformation. The former Shanghai textile interests had begun putting people to work. Hong Kong was becoming an important regional entrepot and a major financial center. By the late 1960's, high-rise buildings were going up everywhere, electronics and other labor intensive industries were setting up plants, banks and other service industries were moving in rapidly. From the gloom of the 1950's, the atmosphere had changed almost completely to a can-do optimism. Even relations with China had improved, bringing in critical food and water, and providing services to such a degree that Hong Kong became, and remains, China's principal source of foreign exchange. The atmosphere generated more interest by U.S. firms in Hong Kong, contributing to the factors that caused the number to increase and that made the U.S. business community an increasingly important element in Hong Kong's economy.

There was one serious, but fortunately in Hong Kong a relatively short lived shock-China's Cultural Revolution. Government was greatly concerned that business confidence - the sine-quo-non of Hong Kong's of viability - would be damaged when riots and protests occurred in the colony. Business generally and most importantly the American electronics companies, did not leave -a factor that was instrumental in bolstering critical business confidence in the colony at a crucial time.

In the 1950's, and into the 60's, a major focus of U.S. Government commercial objectives in Hong Kong was enforcing trade restraints with China. The U.S. Treasury Department officer (Foreign Assets Control) was the scourge of the business community, including most especially the American businessmen. It was then illegal for an American entity to do any kind of business with China, no matter how indirect, while foreign businessmen who did so were classed as " designated nationals ". Americans could not do business with the latter, nor could they be issued U.S. visas. Strictly observing these U.S. regulations bordered on the impossible and often had farcical (though costly) results.

With the opportunities in Hong Kong growing, the character of the American business community changing, and commercial relations in the region becoming of major importance to the U.S., U.S. Government commercial objectives began to focus more on trade facilitation and promotion, and less on trade controls. In 1968, while the former had grown in importance and the Consul

General was devoting more resources to it, the Foreign Assets Control regulations were still in place, still a major irritant, and still an important constraint to participating in the growing commercial activity of the region.

Thus, while the Consulate General focused on a means to improve communications with the growing business community, largely with trade facilitation in mind, we were also aware - and the U.S. businessmen were even more so - that U.S. trade restraint problems also needed addressing.

In 1968 both the U.S. Government and the Hong Kong Government continued to share a common concern about the American business presence in Hong Kong. It was encouraged by one and welcomed by the other, but it should not be seen to raise too high a profile for political reasons (China). An American Chamber of Commerce, it was commonly believed, would do just that. Furthermore, the Hong Kong General Chamber of Commerce had always been the voice of business in the colony. It wielded a powerful influence, and in addition was open to foreign business membership. A competitive chamber would not be well-received by an indigenous one that had for so long ruled the roost.

These concerns weighed heavily on the American business community as well. Relationships between the government and the expatriate community was very important for most American businesses and businessmen. The entrepreneurs, especially those who had been in Hong Kong for many years, had well-established relationships and saw a competitive chamber as disruptive.

On the other side, the professional managers saw the advantages of an organization that could surface concerns and problems with government (Hong Kong as well as the U.S.), without an individual company taking the heat. The growth of the American business community and the greater emphasis on business facilitation by the U.S. government also favored an established channel of communications between U.S, business and U.S. government. Even the Hong Kong Government, based on its experience during the time of the Cultural Revolution, realized the value of some channel to communicate with the increasingly important U.S. community. (At the height of the troubles during the Cultural Revolution, there had been problems with communicating, but to the relief of the Hong Kong Government, U.S. business, through informal channels, passed the word that they were sticking it out). This was the general atmosphere, and with this situation as a basis, the possibility of an American Chamber of Commerce began to be explored

Our first step, once convinced that an American Chamber or similar organization was needed to help the commercial unit do its job, was to convince the Consul General and through him Washington. The arguments already posited above were made, adding to it two more: we were reluctant to raise the highest profile in Hong Kong on the business side even though almost daily one could see elements of the U.S. 7th fleet anchored in the harbor (at that time Hong Kong was a liberty port for the 7th Fleet). Secondly, the business community itself did not wish to become a political target and could be relied on to maintain a low profile. Once these arguments were accepted, the commercial unit compiled a mailing list of all the American businesses in the colony. Then a questionnaire was sent out, polling them on the desirability of forming an American Chamber. The results were heavily in favor

Next we approached the director of Commerce and Industry of the Hong Kong Government. He clearly was not enthusiastic but after hearing the arguments, reluctantly agreed on condition the chamber did not raise a high-profile. At this point, having the clearances from the two governments involved and the expressed desire by a large segment of the American business community for such an organization, we had gone as far as appropriate for government. A breakfast meeting was organized pegged on the visit of a vice president of the U.S. Chamber of Commerce to the colony. Invitations were sent out to a representative spectrum of U.S. businessmen, including some who would had responded negatively. That breakfast meeting was held in the Hilton Hotel on November 18th, 1968. The process used to poll the wishes of the community was explained and it was made clear that as government, we could go no further. An AmCham was a business organization which could on occasion be in an adversarial relationship with our government. The thrust of the discussion that followed was clearly negative. The concern that an American Chamber would sour U.S. business relationships in the colony seemed to prevail. Just before breaking up, however, Jack Wolf (Caltex) stood up and volunteered to form a committee to explore the issue further. Bill Mortson and Al Bart (Chase) joined him, and that, for all practical purposes, was the real beginning of the American Chamber of Commerce in Hong Kong.

Thereafter, the Consul General's role was purely one of support although we participated in meetings held in the Cal tax conference room, chaired by Jack Wolf. Different aspects of getting the American Chamber organized were farmed out to several who had now joined in the process.

The grand opening of the American Chamber of Commerce in Hong Kong was held at a dinner in the Eagle's Nest in the Hilton Hotel. Maurice Stans, then Secretary of Commerce, gave the keynote speech. The very first action taken by the American Chamber happened then when the Secretary was handed a letter complaining about the Foreign Assets Control system and the loss of American business because of it. It was reassuring to the Hong Kong Government and the Hong Kong business establishments that the new American Chamber was in fact to be a positive asset to Hong Kong.

The decisive meeting (for AmCham) that was held on November 18, 1968, described above, has been easy to remember. The meeting was held in the morning, and our wedding took place at St Josephs Church very close by, in the afternoon. It was the beginning of a different lifestyle, but along with added rersponsibilities also came much help in pursuing my career in the foreign service. We had about a year left in this assignment. With the AmCham project now in the hands of the business community, I focussed on making the commercial unit more useful for the many companies that had established regional operations in Hong Kong. I wrote a detailed report for the Department of Commerce on the benefits of using Hong kong for such operations. At the same time, I solicited publications, reports, and other information useful to businesses for a regional library in the Consulate General.

Several months later, I had to be rushed to the hospital to remove my appendix. My wife, then about seven months pregnant, came with me. The Italian nuns who ran the hospital, and spoke no English, immediately took her toward the maternity ward. It took a lot of hand waving but it finally got things turned around. A couple of months later my wife was back, giving birth to our son, Luke. Shortly thereafter, while he was still a very small bundle, we returned to Washington on assignment to the Foreign Service Institute economic course.

Washington 1970

After 15 years overseas, this was to be my first assignment to Washington. It was both appropriate and needed. The family should be Americanized (and in any event my wife had to become an American citizen). I also needed to learn more about the bureaucratic process at the home office. Still, I had become a Foreign Service Officer later than most, and I was anxious to catch up. Opportunities to shine, and therefore get promoted, were better overseas than in Washington. In retrospect, not being familiar with the bureaucratic process-and politics-in the State Department while I was working overseas was probably not a good idea. It's certainly was a shortcoming when I reached more senior levels.

I was assigned to a six months course in economics. It was a fairly new thing then, and in my judgment had too much theory. One would have to do a great deal more formal study to become expert enough to accurately and usefully be able to report on economic matters unless one already had an economic background. On completion, the Department wanted to assign me to the " E " (economic) Bureau. I have always considered that to be a dead end in terms of career, I wrestled hard to get out of that assignment, and finally found the one way to do it.

Foreign Service Officers were being assigned regularly to the pacification program in Vietnam. There was extra money in it, which we needed, it was in

Asia where my interest is, and so we signed up. First was another six months of studying about Vietnam. The language training part was a waste of time - one could not learn a language like that in such a short time to any to any degree that would make it useful. For me the rest of the course was not much better, but perhaps it was better for people who were not familiar with the area.

While the year was not very productive from a career standpoint, it did make it possible to buy a house, get a little acclimated to Washington.

Vietnam 1971-72

The Foreign Service Officers assigned to Vietnam could choose to locate the family in designated cities in Asia. We chose Bangkok as it was nearest to South Vietnam. Once the family was established there I went on to Saigon. After a short orientation there, I was assigned to a province advisory team in Quang Tin Province in the northern part of South Vietnam.

Saigon had changed. It was no longer the French oriented city of the past, but a bustling and much more Americanized City, with plenty of blockades and barbed wire to remind people of the war. Danang, in the north, when I saw it last, was a sleepy little city called Tourane. It had totally changed to a sprawling military encampment in complete disarray.

It seemed the U. S. Army had lost all military discipline. Soldiers, in their personal behavior and dress, and in whatever they were doing, had lost all semblance of a military force. If for no other reason, withdrawing our military from Vietnam was essential for the sake of our own national security.

On that first day, after signing into my temporary room in a barracks, I stepped out for a short walk and immediately was surrounded by young boys, one of whom ripped my watch from my wrist, and they all ran off laughing. That night I had dinner with other Foreign Service Officers and John Gunther Dean, then the district director of the C O R D S program in the north. When I left, I remember him saying that the best advice he could give is that before boarding the small plane that was to take me to Quang Tin Province, I should take a shot of cognac.

We landed at Tamky, the capital of Quang Tin Province. Tamky was really just a wide place on Route 1 - the main north-south road in Vietnam. It was under government control during the day. At night we had to stay barricaded in various compounds behind bunkers and sandbags. The advisory team was made up of both military and civilians, each group having their own compound.

I often went to outlying villages in the province, but only during the day, and with careful arrangements for return to Tamky before nightfall. The trips were made by helicopter only. In the often foggy weather, we would fly just above the treetops, following the road at some 150 mi. per hour. The choppers were flown by very young pilots They would go on to other places during the day, returning to pick us up later. Though we were often shot at from the ground, we luckily had no hits.

One night in the compound we apparently had a probe by Viet Cong (VC) to see if they could get through the barbed wire and cause havoc. It was the only time since Korea that I handled a weapon. The malaise we made preparing for it probably aborted their effort.

On another occasion I arrived at a village just after an American patrol had passed through. A small boy had just been made an orphan as his parents were killed by the patrol in a firefight. The soldiers had claimed the parents were VC as they had a weapon. The village elders gave the boy to a lady who claimed to be an aunt.

The province was also home to Chu Lai, a U.S. military base. A walk on the roads around the base revealed literally hundreds of roadside stands selling a lot of things, including heroin at U.S. $2 a packet. The American Division there also maintained a battalion size outpost in the triple canopy jungle in the western part of the province. Its purpose was to interdict the VC path used to infiltrate from the north. During my time in the province, on one night, the entire battalion was overrun. Reportedly, the forces sent to retrieve the dead found many with supplies of drugs.

I once was invited to join in a military assault by the provincial soldiers against a reported VC post to the west of Tamky. A lot of lead was fired at a spot near the top of the hill, but whether any of the VC were there is another matter. We received no return fire.

There was also some interesting events in Tamky. The seacoast was nearby, and at times fishermen would sell us a bushel of some of the best lobsters one could find. They could not transport to their normal markets. I would occasionally meet up with Nung people, who are a separate ethnic group that spoke and accented Mandarin. Other times I would visit a nearly Cham ruin (the Chams predated the Vietnamese invasion from the north several hundred years ago), but I couldn't get too close as such places were often mined.

Every month I could take a trip, through Saigon to Bangkok to visit the family. Having flown in the planes of the predecessor to Air America in the 1950's, I found that the same planes were still being used, but with a different name. Many of the crew were from Taiwan. Leaving the north. even for two or three days did give time to reflect on what we were doing. The original purpose was to help restore government structure throughout the country by training local people at the local level. But after a few years, the Vietnamese knew much more than we, but the program continued nonetheless. Then came a request for me to move to the embassy in Saigon.

Saigon 1971-72

My formal assignment was to be the embassy's commercial attache. There was a lot of shipments of goods and people to Vietnam from the U.S., but very little Commerce, so the job was used for special assignments. Aside from routine work, I had three such assignments: scrap metal; helping in the local procurement program; and as embassy liaison with the Chinese community.

Of all the elements of the broad relationship we had with South Viet Nam, scrap metal would hardly seem to be much of a priority. Yet there was a White House connection; as our troops were withdrawing, the amount of scrap was not only multiplying, but it was worth considerable money. Further, there was a need to assure that sensitive equipment was not being classified as scrap and exported to the wrong places.

The military did most on the latter two points, assuring that open bidding took place for the lots of scrap as they built up, and to uncover efforts to hide unauthorized items in the scrap pile (a whole army tank was once discovered). The White House connection was a retired American Brigadier General who had a letter from President Nixon supporting the good general's effort to relieve the U.S. of the onerous task of disposing the shiploads of scrap it was now doing. The general and his associates-all Vietnamese retired generals-wanted to buy all the scrap and ship it out under one grand contract. My job was to be sure he had not get such a contract.

The reason for this skullduggery was brass. Brass scrap - worth at that time $1,000 a ton - came from the bottom half of artillery shells and bullets. The brass scrap that accumulated rather quickly in some of the South Vietnam Army units, including some a safe distance from any fighting. Our intelligence suggested that the good general, and his well-connected ARVN generals had already hidden in the jungle some 22,000 tons of it. The problem was getting it out of the country, which the proposed contract would do much to resolve.

All officials pointed the general to my office, and my job was to develop reasons why a process of drawing up such a contract was having difficulties. That went on for several months before the General, after threatening reprisals from the Oval Office, apparently gave up. I do not know if the brass is still in the jungle, or whether the general found some other way to get the brass out of Vietnam, or, more likely, whether it was inherited by the new owners after 1975.

When the decision was made to phase our military out of Vietnam, the economic section of the embassy began a program of encouraging the ARVN to procure its needs locally to the greatest extent possible. As a part of this effort, I began researching for a report on what the ARVN could reasonably be expected to do. As information accumulated, it became clear that what ARVN was doing wasn't exactly what we had in mind. They had established a bank, already had a hold on port facilities, and were in the process of acquiring a lock on trucking goods. They also were into some agriculture projects and a trend clearly was developing that they would indeed be buying more locally-but from themselves or those who cooperated with them. Though the report I wrote was not what was expected by the economic section, they reacted quickly to get the Vietnam government to point the ARVN back to fighting and away from business.

The main reason I was asked to move to Saigon, however, was to liaison with the important Chinese community. For this purpose the ambassador agreed that I could bring my family down from Bangkok. It was important. To establish relationships, the Chinese entertained lavishly, and with most Americans being temporary bachelors, entertaining was done in the big restaurants that included friendly hostesses found in Cholon, (Saigon's very large Chinatown).

We zeroed in on the top 10 to 15 businessmen in Cholon, and entertained husband and wife. They reciprocated in kind, and we were able to know each other more quickly and more closely than I would have been able to do on my own.

These were the people that own much of the economy of Vietnam. They each had their own networks around the country and with government. They were paternalistic toward those working under them - some would keep their factories running even during crisis periods, as they felt a responsibility toward " their people". They gave generously, some as bribes, some for a humanitarian purpose. And they cooperated with both the Vietnam and the U.S. governments when asked to do so.

But they also made very much money. Most of them had " small wives" in other places-Singapore, Hong Kong, Taiwan, for example. With one exception, they remained loyal to the South Vietnamese government, and with that one exception all left the country with the fall of Saigon. To my knowledge, of those that left, only one remained successful after moving to Hong Kong. The others, like a fish out of water, soon lost most of what they had been stashing away in Hong Kong or Singapore banks.

But in Saigon, in 1972, when my tour in Vietnam was nearing an end, I received a cable from my former boss in Taipei, who had become the Counselor for Commercial Affairs in Tokyo. He asked if I would like to replace the commercial attaché there, and I accepted.

CHAPTER FIVE
*Tokyo, Senior Seminar, India, Hong Kong,
Washington, Botswana*

Tokyo 1972-74

Though yet another assignment as commercial attaché clearly branded me in the Foreign Service, Japan was our largest trading partner and therefore offered a good opportunity to shine. Technically, Foreign Service Officers working in "commercial" positions came under the Economic Bureau of the State Department. The Commerce Department did have a say in assignments to these positions, and did have a seat on State Department promotion panels. Though the State department traditionally gave low priority to the commercial function, Commerce Department promotion panel members more aggressively supported officers who have done well in pursuing Commerce objectives. I believe that was instrumental in my rapid rise, getting promoted every two or three years at each level.

The principal task of the commercial unit was promoting trade and investment, providing information to the Commerce Department, and rendering services to U.S. businesses. It included a trade show unit from the Commerce Department that had a modestly large display room and other facilities, and, for an embassy, a large staff of local and U.S. personnel.

The facilities and services were a form of subsidized support to small and medium-sized companies that needed the help to expand our exports to the large but difficult Japanese market. Large companies had their own resources for this purpose, and when they needed help it was more often to lobby, delicately, for equitable treatment in getting a large scale contract or sale.

Business receptions, by Japanese and American companies, were an almost daily event. And receptions were large, in expensive hotels, with special buffets, and always with some small gift given on departure. Dinner at home was a rarity.

We had transferred directly from Vietnam to Japan, scheduling our home leave some months later. As I got into the work of the commercial attache, I became very impressed with the large Japanese trading houses and the conglomerates of which they were a part. To learn more about them, I not only visited their offices but collected considerable information from their publications and other research. From this came four reports about these groups-how they operated, their networks, and their competitiveness both in trade and in forming special groups within their network to win big projects around the world.

While on home leave, I received news of my promotion to senior status. Shortly thereafter, still on leave, my boss sent word that he was retiring. With his support I asked the State Department to replace him. Commerce in this case held back, because there were two senior Commerce officers both wanting the position. In the and, Commerce agreed, because they couldn't resolve the problem.

At this level there was less to do directly on programs and projects, but more on policy and bureaucratic politics. The latter lasted for the rest of my time in Tokyo but was generated in Washington by a familiar struggle between the State Department and the Commerce Department. Commerce once again complained that State was not giving commercial issues the priority they deserve. State, once again claimed they were. This time, it agreed that commercial and economic units, in our embassies around the world and in Washington, would be combined. The struggle, within the embassy, in carrying out the new policy, lasted for months. Ultimately, years later, Commerce succeeded in establishing its own foreign commercial service.

During this time it was U.S. policy to encourage Japanese investment in the U.S.. Commerce organized a large exhibition in Tokyo of 35 states, each with its own personnel and publications, at one of the city's largest hotel. The purpose was to " sell " one's State on the advantages for a company to locate in the state. The best I heard was from a Japanese businessman, who thought the effort gave Japan much face. The picture of 35 states competing with each other to attract Japanese companies into their state must have been a very satisfying event. The most unique, and perhaps most effective, presentation was from the mayor of New York. He was able to quote statistics of all kinds, from the cost of power, or water, and rents for offices, to the number of Japanese grocery stores and Japanese schools in the city. The Japanese later bought Rockefeller Center, which probably wasn't what the mayor had in mind.

During this tour, President Nixon created a "schockoo" in Japan by embargoing the shipment of soybeans to that country (to stem the rise in price domestically). For us the closest thing to that would be cutting off wheat to the economy. Two days later, there was a partial lifting of the embargo when it was discovered that a certain type of soybeans, used to make the almost indispensable miso soup, was grown only in Ohio, and could only be sold to Japan. Eventually the rest was also lifted, but the damage had been done.

I visited a senior director of one of Japan's largest trading firms during this time. He told me that the company had decided to buy an enormous plot of ground in Brazil, clear it, and raise soybeans for shipment to Japan and Europe. The company did just that, followed by others later. Japan and Europe are our largest customers for soybeans.

Another incident in the same vein occurred a year later, when the Senior Seminar class visited the Winery Association of California. The members complained to us that our government was not helping them sell wine to Japan. I was able to remind them that a year before, Japan's largest retail house had approached me with the proposition of buying some California wines labeled by the producers, but wanted also a tanker ship load of wine which they would bottle with their own label in Japan. We found no sellers for them. The association members explained that the previous year had not produced sufficient grapes so they could only sell to customers in the U.S., but that this year there was a surplus. It was, unfortunately, a common problem in trying to market American goods - foreign markets are secondary markets.

Toward the end of our tour in Japan, I received a call from the embassy's DCM. He had good news, he said, as well as bad news. I had been selected to attend the prestigious one year senior seminar, and that was the good news. The bad news was the embassy was not willing to release me. By sheer chance, it turned out, three senior officers had been chosen from the Tokyo embassy, and clearly the embassy could not accept this. One volunteered not to go because he had a good next assignment he liked. The other wrote a 27 page rationale why he should go. The State Department made the decision that I should go.

Twelve senior Foreign Service Officers are selected each year to attend the Senior Seminar at the Foreign Service Institute. Another 10 senior personnel from other government agencies with some foreign relations responsibility are also selected. All need at least 20 years experience in their work (including military, intelligence, AID, USIA, and sometimes others such as Justice or Treasury). The objective was to hear lectures and meet with leaders in almost every field, from cabinet officers to dock workers; to travel to different regions of the country and meet with similar people there; and to present one paper on a subject the member had never been involved with.

Probably the most useful part of the year was simply getting to know and learn about the experiences of our fellow members, and to understand foreign relations as seen from their perspective. We also, throughout the course were reminded of how we were selected for the Senior Seminar because we were considered to be slated for the top of our profession.

My paper, on India in Asia, allowed me to take a trip that covered discussions with experts in Tehran, Islamabad, New Delhi, Katmandu, Dacca, Rangoon, Bangkok, and Jakarta. I did not know then, of course, that some years later, I would be assigned to New Delhi, but the background I gained from this exercise was useful to me later.

In terms of a Foreign Service career, the seminar could be especially useful for an officer who would then be assigned as a DCM at a large post, or an ambassador to a smaller one. The course had covered America - it's politics, economics, culture, and its problems. A graduate of the seminar would be well prepared to tell host country leaders about America in all its diversity. Unfortunately, it is at this plan - the follow-on assignment - where the system breaks down. It is the exception rather than the rule, that a graduate gets such an assignment. The letdown, felt by most in the class after the school had raised expectations so high, was severe.

Washington-Treasury 1974-75

At the end of the seminar, I and several others were without assignments. My former boss in Saigon had become an assistant secretary (OASIA) in the Treasury Department. He called one day and asked whether I would take the position of deputy executive director for the U.S. in the Asia Development Bank. I accepted, but he later called back to say the Treasury Department was insisting on a Treasury person for that job. Of course I was disappointed, but he offered another one year special assignment, which is where I went. About two months later, the man from Treasury, who had moved to Manila to become the new deputy, was killed in a small plane crashed while inspecting a project. My new assignment was just a temporary job without much help in my career, but clearly it turned out better than the first one offered.

My assignment was to make a study, mandated by Congress, on what the U.S. Government could do to encourage U.S. companies to participate in bidding on projects financed by the multilateral banks. U.S. firms had complained that the U.S. had the largest equity in these banks, but few U.S. firms were competitive in winning bids. It was a yearlong study which was not very taxing, and kept me "out of the loop" in terms of lobbying for my next assignment back in the Foreign Service.

In making the study, I developed three separate actions that could be taken in improving U.S. performance on winning bids for large projects abroad. These were to make changes in: the International Development Banks procurement systems; U.S. government services to business; and U.S. private sector organization.

The first suggested standardization of procedures, possible insurance to lower the high risk involved, and regional procurement centers. For the U.S. government, a better communications system a better communications system between government information sources and U.S. business. The third was my favorite, which I had encouraged in the past - to amend antitrust legislation to permit American companies to form development companies (akin to the Japanese Keiretsu conglomerates) for bidding on projects abroad.

I completed the study about the time I received my next assignment as economic counselor in our embassy in New Delhi. This was not a step up -at best sideways - but as usual I chose an overseas assignment because it would have better opportunities to show good performance, then a domestic assignment in the bureaucracy at the State department.

India 1976-79

Before going to India, on home leave, I reached age 50, and thought long and hard about my future. At age 50 I was eligible for retirement, and it would likely be the last chance to change to the private sector if I wanted to. With the post Senior Seminar record of assignments, continuing on wasn't looking very well. I stayed in the service, but it was not an easy decision. If there had been a definite opportunity, I might have done, but during this assignment I did get my last promotion, which helped my morale.

The economic counselor in New Delhi had broad responsibilities. The commercial counselor's office; the then small AID office; the agricultural attache and agriculture research offices; science attache; and Drug officer; all came under my supervision. When the DCM was out of Delhi, I was acting DCM.or Charge. My office, in fact, was a part of the front office (when the embassy was built it was supposed to be for the AID director of the then very large USAID program in that country).

AID developed into my major preoccupation. It wasn't because it had become large, but it was the U.S. bureaucratic politics of keeping it from getting too large. The time was shortly after our withdrawal from Vietnam. Among many other casualties, the large AID program there, with a considerable number of personnel, was one of them. The only USAID program left in India was the PL 480 program (i.e., wheat). AID was anxious to restart the large programs of the past.

In the embassy, we argued that whatever program was developed, it should primarily be in joining with a multilateral program to avoid the political problems that existed when we ran a large bilateral program their previously. That was not what AID had in mind. At one point, AID sent their equivalent of an assistant secretary for Asia to Delhi to complain to the ambassador that I was obstructing their objectives. Ambassador Godeen, a former Princeton President born and raised in India, supported me. The huge aid program (and bureaucracy they had envisioned) did not materialize. I believe the fact that in the meantime Egypt was to get a large program may have relieved some of the pressure on us.

In the country at large, Indira Gandhi's emergency rule was being challenged, and in an election she was defeated. The scope of an election in India is hard to imagine: 600,000 polling places, each with observers throughout that vast country. The first non-Congress Party government took power-creating problems but strengthening democracy. It was heartening to spend much time informally explaining U.S. policy to senior bureaucrats who had to prepare their ministers for the questions in the Lok Sobha. It was, and remains, unnatural for our two democratic countries not to have a much closer relationship.

In addition to taking in the Taj Mahal with the family, I took many trips around the country, one to the very tip of southern India, and another to a place called Gazaphur, not far from Benares (Veranasi), the holy place on the Ganges. Gazaphur had a factory built in 1826, still in use, to process opium. This was legal opium, controlled by government and exported to foreign pharmaceutical firms including the U.S. Controlled, that is, except for the many monkeys in the area. From the tree tops, they could breathe in the fumes and behaved accordingly.

Gazaphur is also the site of a small monument over the grave of General Cornwallis, the same general who surrendered to the Americans ending the war of independence. He was apparently rewarded by being made the Viceroy to India, but died of cholera on a trip up the Ganges River from the then capital of Calcutta. The opium being made there at that time was shipped to China through Hong Kong, eventually bringing on the opium wars.

On the personal side, we lived in a very nice section of Delhi. The household, in addition to the family, had to have about six servants (as each could do only one task according to their caste). Their families came, and we had 32 people living in the servants' quarters. There were five mango trees, each bearing a different variety of mangoes; and a very large and tall tree that was a favorite for vultures. They made a mess of the lawn underneath and didn't do much for the tree. A special bell ringer was hired who managed to have a bell rung periodically in the tree, which annoyed the vultures and kept them away.

We had a near disaster when our son, Luke, came down with a case of typhoid. He was cured with the help of a Sikh doctor in a British hospital, but it was painful and a near miss. We also had a happy event when our daughter joined us, at about the same age as our son. She was put in the same class at school without having any English, and was fluent within three months.

Nearing the end of our tour in India, I received a call from my former boss in Tokyo, then the DCM there and now the Consul General in Hong Kong, asking if I would come there to be his deputy. It was no great leap up in terms of career, but it did put me back in the jurisdiction the East Asia bureau and I accepted.

Hong Kong 1979-81

On this assignment to Hong Kong, my third, there were again many changes from the past. In the past two experiences, however, the change was based more on changes in Hong Kong. This time it was more based on outside factors that affected my work. .

The Consulate General in Hong Kong, as in the private sector, had become a regional office for many U.S. government agencies - at that time there were 16 such offices. The Deputy Principal Officer (DPO)-the official designation of my position-spent much of his time on management and coordinating the work of those many disparate offices. As is the case for any deputy, he must also stay informed to temporarily replace the Consul General whenever he is out of the country.

Before settling in, we took our second trip to China. The first, during our tour in India, was in 1976 shortly after the death of Mao. We went entirely by train to Beijing, Shanghai, and Guangzhou. It was still Mao's China then, with all the people wearing the single color suits, the communes, and the discipline of a closed society. By 1979, there had been considerable change, with people willing to talk with us, but still a restricted society. We traveled by air to Beijing, by train to Xian, by air to Chungking, by boat down the Yangtze River to Wuhan, and a train to Shanghai and then to Guangzhou.

Back in Hong Kong, the second wave of Vietnamese boat people hit the colony during our tour. In fact, a much larger invasion was happening by Chinese coming across the border from China. The old rules of getting past Boundary Street in Kowloon was still in force but obviously not sustainable with such a large influx. The boat people were arriving in small boats that couldn't possibly have taken the voyage from the northern part of Vietnam. Since most of the refugees were actually " overseas Chinese" and were Vietnamese citizens, it seems the boats would hug the Chinese coastline, where food and water could be bought, or boats repaired, as long as they continued on past to Hong Kong.

While this created problems for the British colony, the U.S. took the lead in urging other countries to except the refugees. Though these refugees were from the north and the exodus was not caused by the war or by the American withdrawal, still many in the U.S. looked on this as an American responsibility.

For Americans to sponsor a refugee, both a place to live and a job had to be assured. Even with this rather difficult condition, there were actually more sponsors then eligible refugees available.

The U.S. switch of formal relations from Taipei to Beijing in 1979 brought quite a change. In the Consulate General, by reading the communications from Washington and Beijing, and press reports from Taipei, we could see the degree our policy toward China was focused on the Soviet Union, and how harsh we had made the break with Taiwan even with our own people. In a short visit by Secretary Haig enroute to Beijing, the discussion, mostly with people accompanying him, was on the problems the Soviets were having with Warsaw, not on the imminent visit to Beijing. From Taipei, we heard of the anger of foreign service people in the former embassy, having had communications cut, and salary stopped. Like the Taiwan issue, they were being treated almost as the enemy. The U.S. also, incidentally, sold off all its considerable properties on the island, reinforcing the notion that we were arranging our leave of Taiwan in a way that would only give them a " decent interval" before being swallowed up by China.

For us in Hong Kong the change in this relationship meant that anything that was PRC-owned was no longer off limits, and people from there could now be met. The Amcham was gearing its organization to take on a whole new orientation - doing business with China. And the American businesses began streaming to that " huge potential market ". We often briefed those asked for it about China, and advised against having too high expectations. They could not be stopped, however, and within a year, there was a reverse flow as the difficulties of doing business in China began to sink in.

In the Consulate General, I took the lead in rearranging the offices within the building to provide for much greater security. This did not sit too well with political and economic officers who liked the convenience of local employees and visitors working in the same area. It was encouraged by Washington, however, and the changes remained though grumbling continued even after we left).

Prices, especially for real estate, continued to escalate in the colony. A mid-level apartment, for example, then went for $10,000 a month - in 1980! Washington sent out experts to negotiate the sale of several properties, which was to be used to generate funds for building an apartment building, and other multifamily housing. As usual when people from Washington come to deal with property matters, we were not a part of the negotiations, which inevitably generated rumors that these negotiations were not exactly clean. However the sales and the building plans were still only on paper when we left Hong Kong for an as yet undetermined assignment in Washington.

Washington 1981-85

Returning to Washington without an assignment is a worrisome situation. One has to lobby fellow officers with about the same rank who are themselves seeking their next assignment. At the senior level it is not a comfortable time. I was given an assignment to write a study on the opportunities for our commerce in the Pacific Rim. It was a required study, but it was also meant to provide time to find an assignment.

Very fortunately, after a few weeks, I was interviewed by the principle Deputy Assistant Secretary of State in the Bureau of Intelligence and Research (INR) and shortly thereafter was offered the position of DAS for long-term analysis. It was a stroke of luck without which my foreign service career could easily have ended. After 26 years in the foreign service, I was to work in the State Department for the first time, and that the DAS level.

INR is both a bureau in the State Department, and a member of the intelligence community. It was established by Secretary George Marshall to provide the Secretary with a second opinion on any substantive issue facing his department. Further, as an intelligence function, it was to provide an analysis but not policy recommendations. At its beginning, INR supplied only long-term analysis. Current issues were done by the CIA. When I began working there it had completely changed. The long-term function had been reduced to one office, while current analysis had eight regional and functional offices.

The long-term analysis office, with about six officers all of whom had been there for many years, was not very exciting. But it did give me the time to learn about the INR system and how the State Department works. After a few months, the DAS for Current Analysis retired, and I replaced him. The breadth and the pace of my work suddenly increased several fold.

In the eight offices, there were 122 analysts. The directors of the offices and I met every morning at 9:00 a.m. (which provided everyone time to read the cables, and the information of that day beforehand). We would decide what should go into " the front of the book", and what three analyses should go in "the back of the book".

"The book" was INR-speak for the Secretary's daily morning summary. It contained current information on matters he should know, from sources ranging from the media to the most compartmentalized intelligence, in six typewritten pages. The first three pages (the front of the book) were short items, each about 2 inches of horizontal space, telling the Secretary something that happened in the last 24 hours, and why he should know about it. The back of the book had three one page analyses of some issue or incident which he should know in more detail.

In the State Department only three copies were distributed, to the top three officers. Bureau chiefs were briefed by INR analysts on any item in it that pertained to their bureau. A copy was also given to the Vice President, Secretary of Defense, Directors of CIA and DSA, and the National Security Adviser. Different secretaries' treated this summary differently. In my time Al Haig scrawled all of over it, expletives and all, but gave the CIA briefing at least equal treatment. Schultz wanted our summary first thing every day and seldom commented, but read it and regarded it highly. There were also frequent memos to the Secretary on current issues that were being debated internally.

The book was put into final form by INR personnel in the Operations Center, sometimes with some input by the Executive Secretariat, who supervised the Ops Center. This led to problems between INR and the Executive Secretary office, when either side objected to some item in the book. The Executive Secretary's office became increasingly intrusive, often in the middle of the night when the book was being put in final form for the Secretary. From the INR viewpoint, these differences often had policy implications which we would not tolerate. The struggle got increasingly bitter, so when the DAS in the Executive Secretariat insisted that its items would run whether we agreed or not, I instructed the INR people in the Ops Center to pull out all INR items from the morning's summary. It went to Schultz, who was in California at the time, with only three items. Obviously that triggered queries from the Secretary's office. I insisted INR had to control the summary and be policy-neutral if it was to serve the Secretary. I won.

Differences we had with the CIA and the regional bureaus in State were not turf oriented. A few were differences within the analysts level, but most were in politically or policy motivated conclusions. With the CIA it was primarily the Director, Mr. Casey. With the regional bureaus in State, differences could often be attributed to policy orientation. In the latter we had differences over the Contras in Nicaragua, actions in Beirut, the Indigenous Defense Fighter in Taiwan, the ANC in South Africa, and many more.

One example was our repeated warnings that the Marines sent into Beirut as a peacekeeping force had completed their task but were now bottled up in a large compound. We pointed out repeatedly the vulnerability of this situation, but State insisted it was symbolically necessary to keep them there. Then the compound was blown up with a large loss of life. We immediately hunkered down. Nothing is worse than being right, but we managed to keep a low profile until the atmosphere improved.

Sometime later the deputy director of our Middle East office was attending a welcome ceremony for the King of Nepal in front of the White House. By chance standing next to him on the lawn was Vice President George Bush.

After introductions, the Vice President said INR was often differing with current policy. The deputy director thought he would be done, but instead, Bush told them to continue " saying it as we saw it - it was healthy to get other opinions".

Another interesting incident that demonstrated a problem likely to grow in the years ahead, was trailing, through intelligence reporting, a Russian ship. It had left a Black Sea port normally used for shipping military equipment to other countries. Crates aboard it were similar to those in which MIG 19ts were shipped. Every morning around 7:00 a.m. I would have a highly classified cable describing where the ship was heading, an increasingly it looked like Nicaragua. Every morning, at about 9:00 a.m., I would get a call from Johns Scali (ABC), telling me precisely what I was reading in the cable, and then asking what I thought of it. The information age had already begun.

Our differences with CIA were centered around the intelligence community estimates put out by that agency. We often found the executive summary and the body of the estimates were not saying the same thing. The word we heard (unconfirmed) was that Casey took the draft estimate home and rewrote the summary to reflect what he thought it should say. As a member of the cabinet, he knew what it was he wanted the estimate to say, and he knew that the busy real decision makers would only read the summary. The intelligence community system provided that when a member of the community could not accept an element of the estimate, a footnote would be permitted. INR was well known in the community, as small as we were, for dominating in the number of footnotes we had in these estimates.

At the end of my assignment, informally I was asked by the DAS for Personnel, my former boss in INR, if I would accept an appointment as ambassador to Botswana. He encouraged me to take it, and given the personnel situation at senior levels of the State Department at that time, I decided to do so. That was very quickly followed up by a call from President Reagan asking me if I would become his ambassador to Botswana. This was a Reagan feature that was very commendable. The family, later, was then offered to have pictures taken with him.

Botswana 1985-88

Though we had been well briefed, having been through the Senate confirmation process and the " baby " ambassador (first time) course, we entered a country, a climate, and a culture that was entirely different than anything we had experienced previously. Perhaps because our expectations werte more akin to West Africa, we quickly realized it was a friendly place, and we came to like and respect the people. A country larger than France, with only a million people, a huge desert but also a large swampland, two of the largest game preserves in Africa, a stable democracy with no ethnic, tribal, or racial problems, and the largest source of gem diamonds in the world, with no corruption attached to it. That wasn't exactly what we had envisioned a typical African country to be like.

It was not all a placid spot in an otherwise contentious continent, however. Botswana's economy was completely dependent on South Africa, where apartheid was the law, and incapable of controlling or even influencing the African National Congress infiltration into Botswana and from there into South Africa (and little will to do so). The result was an occasional raid into Botswana from its neighbor South Africa. Though careful not to overdo it, Botswana was an active member of Front Line States.

The U.S. mission included the embassy, USAID, USIA, and the Peace Corps. The embassy occupied the second and third floor of a small office building, with no marine guards, which closed down completely every evening, USAID (typically) had a larger office with somewhat more people. USIA had another small office in another modest building. The Peace Corps headquarters had a modest office, but it supervised one of the largest Peace Corps programs - around 200 volunteers.

These volunteers were scattered throughout the country, mostly in villages accessible only by either a primitive road, or by small plane. The Director of the Peace Corps came once and we traveled by small plane, meeting all 200 in villages around the country. The local people welcomed the Peace Corps volunteers, and amazingly we had almost no problems with them despite their isolation.

There were about 15 embassies in the diplomatic corps in Botswana. Most other countries accredited their ambassadors resident in neighboring countries. the next door neighbor from our residence was the Soviet Ambassador, a friendly Ukrainian with whoml we got along well. At receptions, however, he often became visibly concerned as there were three of us - myself, the Indian Commissioner whom I had known in Delhi, and the Chinese ambassador who spoke no English - who engaged in conversation in Chinese.

On one other occasion my Chinese language became handy. The Foreign Minister had called me to the ministry late one night to ask if the U.S. could help with a potentially serious problem. The capital, Gabarone, was located close to the border with South Africa. The Botswana we're hearing a movement of military tanks and trucks on the other side and were very concerned that another raid into Botswana was imminent. Since the embassy was shut down and would take at least two hours to warm up the communications equipment, I called Washington on an open line. We new South Africa intelligence had the capability for eavesdropping, so I called another Chinese language officer working in the Africa Bureau front office at State, and explained the situation in Chinese.

He called our Ambassador in Pretoria who contacted the foreign office there, and after an hour or so (the foreign office had not been informed), I was able to pass on to the Botswana Foreign Minister that what they were hearing was a military exercise, not an attack.

The Botswana Foreign Minister, Madame Chiepe, a former schoolmarm in the countryside, was respected in diplomatic circles in Africa, including in South Africa. On a visit to Washington she met with Secretary Schultz. She talked about democracy and its problems with South Africa. Shultz was very impressed, and on his planned visit to Africa, insisted that he should stop briefly in Botswana to make a speech about democracy in Africa (meant largely for the nearby neighbor to the south). At the last minute the trip was canceled when President Reagan suddenly arranged a meeting with Gorbachev in Iceland.

We had a fair number of members of Congress visiting, who usually stayed at the residence. On one occasion Jesse Jackson flew in with a large number of anti-apartheid activists. They arrived in the evening but refused to stay in their hotel as it was partially owned by South Africans. Jackson persuaded Madame Chiepe to talk to them about Botswana's dependence on South Africa -" we can choose our friends, but we can't choose our neighbors". They accepted, but as if to punctuate the point, the next day their departure was delayed by several hours as a part had to be flown up from South Africa to fix some malfunction in their airplane.

Another well-known visitor was a U.S. representative to Botswana on its 20th anniversary of independence - Maureen Reagan. She was quite an attraction for the crowd, and from my standpoint gave me an opportunity to take her to meet with other dignitaries-then Vice Premier Li Peng for one.

My predecessor, a construction company owner in San Francisco and a rabid hunter, had persuaded Washington to build an embassy building, and had spent much time personally working on the blueprints. I never got to see it completed, but it was during a period of special security consciousness. The blueprints were altered for security considerations and what was being built seemed to be more of a fortress than an embassy. Lift-up barriers for autos, narrow windows, all kinds of security devices, and a place for the yet to come Marine guards. This, in Botswana.

When we first arrived, we used to drive or fly to Johannesburg almost every month, to shop mostly. With time, we went there increasingly less frequently-everything could be found with a little effort in Gabarone. In the end, I had hoped my assignment would be extended beyond the election at home. Unfortunately, my time for was just a few days from the set date decided by the State Department, and so we had to depart yet again without a specific assignment.

87

Washington 1988-90

When we returned, election campaigns were taking place, and senior level assignments-overseas and domestic-had been arranged, with the exception of a few that most would avoid at any time. The Director General of the Foreign Service insisted that I take one of them - International Adviser to the Industrial College of the Armed Forces (ICAF) at Fort McNair in Washington. It and the War College were both located there as the nucleus for the National Defense University.

This was the kind of job I had resisted for all my career. Responsibilities were few, work was devoid of any pressure, and no opportunities to make a mark. In addition, following an assignment as an Ambassador, it was a very deflating letdown. The people I worked with were great, and the surroundings pleasant. Had I been planning on retiring, this would have been the perfect assignment. Plenty of time to think and to search for my next career.

It was instructive during this time, to watch military colonels start their course with a very low opinion of Foreign Service Officers. By the time they finished several months later, they had broadened in many fields, including a much better understanding of the role the Foreign Service plays in national security.

During this tour, two trips I remember was one to Mexico City with an ICAF group. With all the traveling I had done as a courier and in the regular service, I had never been south of the border. The purpose was to visit with the military and with some of the private sector industries. There was time to sightsee, however, and for me a pleasant surprise.

The other was a combined ICAF-War College trip to China. It took place as the demonstrations in Tien An Men were growing in early May of 1989. In Beijing the authorities steered us away from Tien An Men, but we inevitably saw much of the activities despite this. We also had meetings at the National Defense University and several think tanks in both Beijing and Shanghai; their airplane factory in a Shenyang; and another military facility in Xian. The changes from a decade before were obvious, but the ferment and openness most attracted my attention. It apparently changed quickly after June 4th, but seems to be moving to even greater openness a decade later.

That tour at ICAF was our last in the regular Foreign Service. Toward the end I was furiously lobbying and searching for my next job. It was a pretty depressing time, but fortunately it did not last too long.

(Meetings with current Indian Prime Minister Manmohan
Singh and former Prime Minister J. Nehru)

(Presenting Ambassadorial credentials to President Masire of Botswana)

(Top: Meeting with former ROC Vice President Lian Chan; Bottom:
meeting with Thabo Mbeki, former President of South Africa)

(Meetings with President Lee Teng-hui of Taiwan and his advisors)

(Meeting with Madam Chang, widow of Generalisimo Chang Kai-Shek)

(Meeting with President Chen Shui-bien of Taiwan)

To Natale Bellocchi
With best wishes,

Ronald Reagan

(Meeting with President Ronald Reagan)

To Lilan Bellochi
With best wishes, *Gg Bush* *Barbara Bush*

(Meeting with President George Bush)

CHAPTER SIX
AIT: The Unique Relationship

In the years following WW II, Taiwan was turned over to the Republic of China (ROC) by the U.S., on behalf of the victorious Allies until such time as the Allies determined how, when, and to whose sovereignty, this was to be given. For the U.S., that has not changed. The issue of Taiwan's status, i.e. its sovereignty, is a fundamental issue for the three major players, the U.S., China, and Taiwan, and divides the politics within Taiwan. China insists Taiwan is a part of China, Taiwan insists it is a separate entity, and the U.S. insists the difference must be determined peacefully.

During this time, until 1979, the Republic of China (ROC) on Taiwan was recognized as "Free China." Most of the rest of the world, however, by 1972 recognized the Peoples Republic of China (PRC). In the U.S. and especially in the Congress, however, the ROC, despite its authoritarian system, was considered "Free" as opposed to the communist PRC on the mainland. The ROC lost its position in the UN in 1971, (Chiang Kai-shek turned down America's offer to support Taiwan remaining in the UN General Assembly).

From the post World war period through the 1980s, Taiwan's economy mushroomed. American aid until 1965 and Taiwan's almost textbook implementing of its development policies made it America's second largest economic partner in East Asia (after Japan). Economics had joined security and ideology as priorities in the relationship.

In the U.S., however, pressures grew for America to recognize the PRC, and in 1979, the U.S. changed its recognition of China to the PRC. President Nixon had signed an initial communiqué with China in 1972, and President Carter signed a second communiqué in 1979. There were some wording on both that was deliberately ambiguous by the U.S. side to overcome differences between the two countries.

The bill written by the State Department on how the U.S. was to deal with Taiwan was sent to the Congress. This was done by the Executive Branch with little concern on security matters and many other important issues. While the American constitution gives the Executive Branch of government preeminence on matters of foreign policy, it does not prevent Congressional authority on policy oversight and allocation of public funds.

The Congress immediately held hearings which resulted in passing the Taiwan Relations Act (TRA). It was then, and still remains, a very unique law, making our Taiwan policy a matter of domestic law. The Congress clearly pointed U.S. policy toward Taiwan in a different direction than the Executive Branch had intended. Its influence on any changes in America's Taiwan policy remain.

Anyone working in AIT should know the Taiwan Relations Act (TRA) in detail; the guidelines for conducting the relationship established under it; the three communiqués that form the basis for the U.S. - PRC relationship, including our commitments and China's position on sovereignty over Taiwan; and the intricacies of the language used in both our relationships with the PRC and Taiwan.

One should know that though we have a "one China" policy, we have never defined "China" (there have been many in China's long history); that we recognize the government in Beijing as the government of China; that we have never said that Taiwan is a part of China; that the U.S. position on the sovereignty of Taiwan is that it is yet to be determined; and that we have no preference for any resolution of the issue between the two sides of the Taiwan Strait other than it be peacefully resolved.

The breaking of our diplomatic relations with the ROC (Taiwan) in 1979 was the first time the U.S. had ever done so with a friendly country. It was done surreptitiously without the knowledge of Congress or the general public. The Congress was further upset by the State Department's weak proposal for continuing the "unofficial" relations with Taiwan. It inevitably further aggravated the constitutional differences between the Executive and Legislative Branches that have always existed on their respective roles in foreign policy.

This bit of history is important to know, as this rivalry between the two branches on the subject of our Taiwan relationship persists to this day, though the rationale for its continuance evolves with the changes that have occurred in both China and Taiwan. The law that was produced by Congress (the TRA) and forced on the Executive Branch is unique: the only foreign relationship we have based on domestic law.

While the Executive Branch (the State Department) had submitted a draft bill to Congress that was mainly the details of establishing an institution to conduct an unofficial relationship. It would have left policies largely open to whatever the Executive Branch wanted to do. Congress completely changed the policy purposes of the law. It installed very important security commitments to Taiwan, and explicitly established that a peaceful resolution of the PRC-Taiwan relationship is a *sine quo non* of U.S. relations with the PRC. It also stated that Taiwan was to be considered a country under U.S. law for legal, counselor, and commercial purposes. If largely left to the State Department to establish the institution (AIT) to conduct the relationship, and to establish the rules on how the U.S. Government should conduct itself with the Taiwan authorities.

The continuous struggle between the two branches of the U.S. government has had some unintended results. The Executive Branch has hamstrung itself in adapting to a far different Taiwan, and a far different China, by becoming overly sensitive and overly ambiguous on matters dealing with China, not just to accommodate an overly sensitive Beijing, but to work around congressional oversight. Congress on the other hand, until just recently with the democratization (and higher profile) of Taiwan, was less than stalwart in its oversight function causing members to mandate, or solicit from the private sector, specific reports on the subject at hand. The TRA, in the meantime, caught in the struggle, remains untouched and less able to help accommodate our policy to the changing realities.

If the security commitments in the TRA had not been legislated, Taiwan would now be a province of the PRC against the wishes of the people on that island. Further, if the provisions in the TRA treating Taiwan as a country for commerce and other reasons had not been legislated, Taiwan could not have reached the level of prosperity it enjoys. The Act deserves enormous praise. The task here, however, is not to praise it, but to suggest where policy assessments might focus to further strengthen it.

At the time the TRA was enacted, some Administration officials of that time expressed the view that the Act would not be needed very long, as unification was inevitable. Though Taiwan remains separate, succeeding Administrations have continued to conduct this relationship under a short-term perspective.

Changes in the guidelines over the years have been very few and not important. Changes could better address the realities of today and what they are likely to be in the near future. The most fundamental need is to generate the political will to interpret what has been written to better serve our interests. We have been overly sensitive in assessing the impact of any action we take with Taiwan on our perceptions of the PRC attitude toward them.

I do not personally have much confidence in this attitude. For example it was conventional wisdom among our China watchers that establishing the direct election of the president on Taiwan would be perceived by the PRC as an unacceptable step toward independence. It was not. It was also conventional wisdom that the elimination of the provincial government level in Taiwan would be perceived by the PRC as an unacceptable step toward independence. It was not. Obviously our perceptions of PRC perceptions have not always been very accurate.

In commenting on some of the problems experienced in implementing the TRA, there are some points to make on some specific sections of that Act. The struggle between the Executive and Legislative Branches over the degree of authority each has over foreign policy has existed since the constitution was written. That document does not address this point though the Executive Branch is generally granted pre-eminence in this field, while Congress asserts its authority mainly by its control of the purse. The TRA, in establishing itself as the basis for a foreign relationship, was an exception, and the third communiqué between the U.S. and the PRC was seen as a challenge to it.

One result of this experience, therefore, was that the Congress over several years made an effort to have the administration publicly acknowledge that a law such as the TRA took precedence over any communiqué. It never fully succeeded in getting this acknowledgment in law, though then Secretary of State Christopher more recently did agree to send a letter to Senator Murkowski to that effect. Not entirely a satisfactory means of assuring future executive agreements do not contradict domestic law.

Another shortcoming in the system is that the Administration has taken advantage of the requirement in the law that it should notify the Congress if a threat to Taiwan's security exists. Only then would the two branches of government consult on what to do about it. That interpretation has resulted in the Administration being very reluctant to even use the word "threat" in describing the situation at any time with regard to activities in the Taiwan Strait.

Another matter that is clearly based on what was perceived to be the PRC's perception, are the guidelines for what is acceptable conduct under an "unofficial" relationship. It should be noted, incidentally, that the word "unofficial" is not to be found in the TRA. These rules were established unilaterally by the Executive Branch, (under Section 13 of the Act, but after the first three years, did not even need to be transmitted to Congress). We now tend to call these rules "policy", and our policy review of 1994 largely involved with some of them. The rules in large part range from the inefficient to the silly. They restrict the liaison and coordination between the two sides in both economic and security matters at a time when coordination should be increasingly important for us.

The guidelines contain matters that include meetings, contacts, travel, correspondence, and terminology, among others. They serve the purpose of keeping the relationship, in appearances at least, as unofficial. On occasion, some new guidelines must be developed to cover unanticipated situations (such as transits through the U.S., or visits by senior level officials from Taiwan). Once established, of course, they set a precedence which whenever one is changed, becomes an issue between the U.S. and the PRC. These rules quickly became a part of "policy"

They are clearly based on what was perceived to be the PRC's perception of what is acceptable conduct under an "unofficial" relationship, however. We now tend to call these rules "policy" and our policy review of 1994 largely dealt with some of them. The rules in large part range from the inefficient to the silly. They restrict the liaison and coordination between the two sides in both economic and security matters at a time when coordination should be increasingly important for us. In fairness, Taiwan's own priorities often seem to be more on the guidelines than on the substance of policy.

Another example was the dispatch of the carriers during the missile crisis of 1996. We can recall that the PRC first fired missiles at the time of the Legislative Yuan elections in late 1995. The Administration complained publicly but did not consider the PRC exercises (that the missile firing were supposedly a part of), as a threat. Then in 1996, again there were exercises but the missiles were now being aimed much closer. The Administration called them 'irresponsible", but again, even at a formal Congressional hearing called by the then even more concerned Congress, the word "threat" was not used.

Later a second carrier was dispatched, with repercussions in both Beijing and Washington that are still being felt, but still without touching the "threat" button that would call for initiating consultations with the Congress under the TRA. Many have thought that the Lee Tung-hui visit to Cornell caused the China's missiles, but I believe Taiwan's establishing of its first Presidential election by the people was more important to China.

Two other important issues that received some attention in the TRA used wording that was relevant at the time of the drafting of the law, but now require an explicit interpretation to make them applicable to today's Taiwan. As a result they have been largely ignored.

Section 2 (C): Nothing contained in this Act shall contravene the interest of the United States in human rights, especially with respect to the human rights of all the approximately eighteen million inhabitants of Taiwan. The preservation and enhancement of the human rights of all the people on Taiwan are hereby reaffirmed as objectives of the United States.

Section 4 (D): Nothing in this Act may be construed as a basis for supporting the exclusion or expulsion of Taiwan from continued membership in any international financial institution or any other international organization.

The first is on human rights. Clearly at the time of the drafting of the Act, there was concern in the Congress that the people of Taiwan might not be given the right to determine their own future. There was at that time, as we can recall, a different political system on Taiwan. The situation, of course, has changed. The principle that people have the right to determine their future remains the same, but especially in the Administration, there now is a concern that the precipitate exercise of this right might bring disaster not only on Taiwan, but for the U.S. as well. Since the missile crisis, there are some both in and out of the Administration, and some in Taiwan, who would prefer to drop this principle entirely. At minimum, there should be a clear, explicit statement by the U.S. Government that the U.S. will oppose any change in the political status of Taiwan that does not have the consent of the people of Taiwan.

The second issue is membership in international organizations. Here again, the situation was different. Today the issue is not staying in the international organizations, but getting in. The wording in the Section, however, does include "exclusion" as well as "expulsion", and could be interpreted in a different way. The present Administration, in the Taiwan Policy Review of 1994, actually took a step backward by formally stating it would not support Taiwan's membership in international organizations that require statehood, a distinction the TRA did not make.

Section 12 of the Act spells out the reporting requirements for the Executive Branch to make to the Congress. Formal agreements are to be reported to the Congress whenever they are completed. Subsection (d), however, is the only reference to any continuing reporting on the conduct of the relationship, and that is limited to two years after the Act is passed, and only on economic relations.

Congress cannot, and probably should not, maintain a separate monitoring office for this purpose. But given the special nature of this relationship, the domestic law on which it is based, the influence of our policy toward the PRC, and the importance of this issue in our presence and interests in the Western Pacific, an independent annual report to Congress on the U.S. Taiwan relationship might be appropriate.

Yet increasingly, our economic relations with Taiwan are handled in a multilateral context. Globalization of economies is the trend, with information, services, capital moving instantly, and internationally. Ignoring an economy the size and importance of Taiwan, as the World Bank does now, for example, makes no sense, nor is it in our interest. Based on the intent implicit in section 4 of the Act, Congress should more vigorously insist that it be implemented.

In terms of policy, the second most important element of the TRA is the commitment to retain all the laws and regulations necessary for continuing the commercial, consular and cultural relations between the U.S. and Taiwan that existed before. That has permitted the relationship to blossom both in mutually beneficial commerce but in people-to-people relations that is such an important part of that relationship.

That the relationship grew so much during the first decade of the TRA is a tribute to the efforts made by both sides on the two important issues of arms sales and commercial/cultural relations. This emphasis continued in the second decade. But Taiwan has changed, and other issues that result from Taiwan's democratization need addressing. The government and its officials, which have normally been referred to as "authorities", are now as legitimate as any found anywhere. The society, broadly speaking, is as open as any found anywhere. And the conduct of its foreign affairs as subject to the will of the people as found in any democracy.

Given this transformation of Taiwan into an entirely different kind of entity, what are the challenges that now face the U.S.-Taiwan relationship in the future, and has the TRA any role to play in efforts to adapt other policies to the new realities? My answer to the latter is yes, but not with the idea of changing the TRA. That carries with it many difficulties and is therefore unlikely. By placing our focus on that possibility, we could be making the TRA a roadblock to change rather than a basis for it.

More likely is the use of the TRA, with its statements on various policies toward Taiwan, as support for separate commitments on specific issues. For example, the TRA contains the two paragraphs which are directly relevant to the changes that have taken place on Taiwan, i.e., Section 2 on human rights, and Section 4 on international organizations. They were written at a time when Taiwan was different than it is today. So was the entire Act. But on some issues, where there was political will, the language was interpreted to accommodate to the circumstances of the day. For these two issues no change in the TRA would be necessary, but polices that better accommodate to democratic Taiwan could be pursued with the support of the Act as written.

In human rights, for example, there was considerable disappointment in Taiwan when President Clinton made his statement on the three no's in Shanghai. In rationalizing the statement, the Administration claims that it represents no change from the past. In at least one sense, it does. From 1979 to 1995 it was standard policy by all who implemented policy toward the PRC and Taiwan, that the U.S. does not respond to questions of support or non-support of independence. U.S. policy has remained that the two sides were to determine Taiwan's status, peacefully.

The rationale behind this approach is that while there was always a concern that the U.S. could be dragged into a confrontation with the PRC if this was mishandled, and therefore a good reason to hope no unilateral change by either side would be tried, the U.S. in this way would also avoid not supporting a fundamentally human right—the right of people to choose their own future.

Now that there has been an explicit statement from the U.S. in this matter, I believe there should also be an explicit statement that any change in Taiwan's status should have the consent of the people on Taiwan. If one reads the hearings and the subsequent comments by drafters of the Act, it shows that such a position was clearly the intent of Section 2 (C). Arguments that this requirement is implicit in the U.S. position that there be a peaceful resolution, does not sufficiently cover this commitment.

In another area, the globalization of economics, even with the problems that have been encountered in recent months, has put Taiwan at a disadvantage in dealing with the increasingly important international organizations. And its democratization has forced domestic political factors to be given a much higher priority in its international relations. The U.S. has said, both in the Taiwan Policy Review of 1994, and in the Shanghai statement made by President Clinton, that it would not support Taiwan's membership in any international organization that requires statehood. That statement in both instances has not been challenged directly by the Congress, even though such a requirement does not appear in the TRA. To change it abruptly now would create a serious strain in the U.S.-PRC relationship. The TRA could still be used, however, as a basis for beginning the process of seeking support for some kind of participation by Taiwan in the international community.

In the U.S., it is understood in government and among experts that Taiwan is fully qualified, and even needed, to participate in the International community. It is also clear, however, that it is PRC objections that prevent this issue from being equitably addressed. There may be other means of accomplishing the same purpose, but first it is even more important to encourage the U.S. to adopt a different public stance toward this issue in its relationship with the PRC.

This would require more political will in Washington than the recent past has shown. Beijing's strong opposition is no small obstacle to overcome. Still a more realistic approach by the U.S., and hopefully by the international community, that recognizes the changed circumstances democracy has brought to Taiwan, but which does not seek to interfere in the ultimate resolution of the differences on the two sides of the Strait, might gradually take hold.

In yet another area, even recent weeks, it is seen that changes in Taiwan's security requirements are likely to continue. The missiles that already exist opposite Taiwan are real, and responsible leaders both in the U.S. and Taiwan must contend with that fact. Sections two and three of the TRA, a domestic law that establishes the relationship with Taiwan (and which takes precedence over the communiqués), sets forth U.S. policy regarding arms sales. Included therein is the statement that "...the United States will make available to Taiwan such defense articles and defense services in such quantity as may be necessary to enable Taiwan to maintain a sufficient self-defense capability." From a legal and policy standpoint therefore, the TRA is sufficiently flexible to accommodate whatever is decided with regard to Taiwan's defense against this kind of threat.

Enabling Act was sent to the Congress in 1979. Substantive issues, especially security, were overwhelmingly put into the act by Congress. State thinking the issue of Taiwan's status would be settled in a short time while establishing guidelines and protocol that would make the PRC least unhappy. The Congress on the other hand treated the issue as one that will treat Taiwan as a country to the greatest extent possible, and committed as closely as reasonably possible American support for Taiwan's security and well-being.

The system was costly and inefficient. Some changes have been made in the system over time, but still far from what is needed, in America's interest, in addressing security and political matters. This is also true in the administrative managing of this unusual system. It was clear from the outset of my assignment to AIT, that the government's need to provide an acceptable means to carry on an unofficial bilateral relationship with Taiwan, and the private sector organization needed by law, were often incompatible. There was little interest in the State Department for the support needed to make the changes necessary in AIT's financial system. It eventually was completed, but it took far too much time unnecessarily.

My Chairmanship

As for my objectives as Chairman, the impression that stayed with me throughout my tenure as Chairman of AIT, was of the very fundamental change from an authoritarian system to a democracy that was taking place in Taiwan, and its fragility. Thus my continuous reminder to the policy makers at State that we show more support for it not only in principle, but realistically, as without such support instability could result with very uncertain consequences to U.S. interests. Though I spoke and wrote often about this internally with my State Department colleagues during my time as Chairman, it seems to have taken Taiwan's own unwelcome assertiveness, the shock of a democratic change in government, and the changing security environment that has after more than a decade brought serious attention to the changed circumstances on Taiwan.

My views were also shaped by my experience with the American-Taiwanese community, many of whom were blacklisted from returning home. Both in talking to individuals seeking visa assistance and in questions and answers session after a speech to their association, there was a strong atmosphere of delight that what for them passed as the U.S. Government was aware of the new reality in Taiwan as they saw it.

Especially in my initial few months, but throughout my tenure, I was sensitive to the State Department preference that our Taiwan relationship remain low profile and trouble-free. But from the beginning, I also recognized that this attitude was not sustainable given the profound changes that were taking place on that island. Low profile and an active democracy are a contradiction in terms. It was always necessary in dealing with the policy makers at State, to avoid losing credibility by challenging a conventional wisdom that complicated policy: A Taiwan that was raising its profile was making trouble. A Taiwan that kept quiet was doing the right thing. Within these parameters I began making changes to the methods of carrying out my duties.

AIT speeches about our relationship with Taiwan had been infrequent and largely devoid of references to the political changes taking place there. It was clear to me that America, even among experts on foreign policy, were unaware not only of the changes taking place, but of the implications of these changes on our relationship. In large measure, it was—and is—the U.S.-PRC relationship that occupies the mind of our China watchers, in and out of government. That relationship is difficult and complicated—and important. Distractions, even the democratization of an island and its people so close to, and so culturally akin to China, (and therefore with such potential for setting a favorable example to that great country), was to be avoided. Few in our government, much less outside it, followed Taiwan affairs. This remained the case until the turn of the century, a decade after the democratic peaceful revolution on Taiwan, when America began understanding the reality and perhaps beginning to understand the potential in the changes that have occurred on that island.

So I began making speeches at first largely to American organizations interested in China, then increasingly to Chinese-American groups. The American groups seemed a little uncomfortable with what I was saying, as it didn't fit with their long-held perception about what Taiwan's objective should be. The first priority for the people there was not longer China, but democracy and self-government. This unease was also apparent with the older Chinese-American associations. But younger ones, and especially Taiwanese groups, were very enthusiastic. They seemed genuinely pleased that the American government was at last meeting with them and talking with them about what was happening on Taiwan. The State Department did not focus on this, and when they did, asked that I clear speeches with them. After testing the clearance process for a speech I was to make in Cleveland I reverted to speaking from notes. it seems those that were doing the clearance thought I should be boosting our China policies. I thought my audience was more interested in our Taiwan policies.

I also often met with members of the large Taiwan media group resident in Washington, both socially and formally. It is one of the largest such groups in

Washington. They too had to go through changes brought on by democratization back home in Taiwan. I learned as much from them as they from me and enjoyed it in the process. With the media and in the speeches and discussions that followed them, I always stayed within our policy parameters, however, even when it didn't seem to make sense.

Even in the too infrequent trips to Taiwan, I insisted on doing much more than an administrative inspection of our organization there. On my trips to Taiwan, I set my own agenda, though always taking with me a colleague from AIT. In many cases it was the first time that colleague had met the person I was calling on.

Aside from meetings in AIT, I usually met with the President, the Vice President, several cabinet officers, mayors and legislators, businessmen, news publishers, human rights activists and military personnel. Most of my time was spent in Taipei, but I spent time in Kaohsiung and Taichung, and sometimes by car, made calls on most of the county magistrates throughout the island.

I was the first AIT Chairman to call on the opposition party Chairman in his office. On that first call to the late Huang, Chin-Chieh, the office was in a walk-up third story, crammed with stacks of handouts, and little space for us to sit and talk. It was a stark contrast to the wealthy ruling party. I was also the first Chairman to be given a reception by the Legislative Yuan. The host was the vice president of the Yuan—a Taiwan elected member. There were many speeches, predictably, mostly about the new Taiwan and the solid relationship with the U.S. The President of the Yuan came in to give a short (for a politician) speech— about the heroes of the Kuomintang Armies in China's northeast. Needless to say, he was a "senior" member elected on the Mainland. That, too, made a stark contrast in the old and the new Taiwan.

Except for the last year, my visits to Taiwan were resisted not by the State Department, which would have preferred more, but by AIT Taipei. I won't speculate on the motivation for this problem, but it was not helpful. My trip reports, which were well received in Washington, emphasized the trends I saw developing, and the mood of the leadership in both political and economic circles. On returning to Washington, I always made a point of briefing not only the State Department, but other departments and agencies, and congressional staff.

Thus, beginning in 1990, I pursued three changes in conducting the relationship—by more realistic speeches to the public and in reports to State; by maintaining a good rapport with the Taiwan media and community in America; and in my trips to Taiwan. Inevitably, changes developed some problems within AIT between Washington and Taipei. In 1990-92, these problems were more in political differences over how best to conduct the relationship. The differences in 1992-95 were administrative in nature with regard to our Taiwan operation.

The latter was serious, causing me, in cooperation with the State Department, to spend much time in those years trying to make the organization's administration more transparent and compatible with the requirements for handling public funds. Eventually this spilled over into public charges by my successor about some of these problems after we, working with the State Department, had already resolved.

My first two plus years in AIT were under the Bush Administration. The early months of trying to understand the system revealed several unexpected matters. The first was that there is very little institutional memory in either AIT or Taiwan Affairs in the State Department. The second is that the lowest policy official—DAS level—in the regional bureau responsible for Taiwan, spent little time focusing on Taiwan. Another was that AIT officers with the best in-depth knowledge of Taiwan, were not sufficiently involved in the policy making process at the State Department. It was the main incentive for me to liaise with other government agencies and Congress.

Books and other commentary paint the Bush White House as very pro-China, apparently based on his quick dispatch of senior officials to Beijing soon after Tien An Men. I did not have that perception, perhaps because I "arrived" into Taiwan affairs somewhat after these visits, when Bush was trying to repair the domestic reaction to them. While the actions were clearly domestic politics inspired - public endorsement for Taiwan's membership in GATT, and later the sale of F-16s - policy level personnel with whom I work seemed disposed to see Taiwan as a friend more than a troublemaker. This attitude changed with the change of administration.

In mid 1990, when I began working at AIT, our relations with the PRC was at one of its low points—the result of the Tien An Men massacre. Despite efforts to restore the U.S.-PRC relationship to at least a higher level (which lead candidate Clinton to accuse of "coddling dictators"), the Bush administration took two actions critically important to Taiwan - membership in a major international organization (GATT) and lifting the ban on the sale of military equipment long denied them (F-16). Conventional wisdom persists that our relationship with Taiwan is better when our relationship with the PRC is good - but these actions hardly support that.

CHAPTER SEVEN
American Institute in Taiwan 1990

American interest in East Asia focused mostly on the aftermath of Tien An Men. For the U.S.-Taiwan relationship was the beginning of lost opportunities throughout the decade that followed, to bolster democratization in Taiwan as well as in East Asia generally.

There were issues that seem to dominate the relationship—trade problems such as the Pell Amendments, the deep sea fishing problem, and the large but improving imbalance of trade. These were important and legitimately concerned that were important to address.

But the important changes that were turning Taiwan from an authoritarian political system to democracy were given rhetorical support but brought no differences managing the rapidly changing government system. It was a decade that saw this development while at the same time U.S. Administration priority was to improve the U.S.-China relationship.

This was also a time when Washington was receiving reports that President Lee, Tung-hui was "a closet independent" supporter and therefore not to be trusted. This attitude remained through out my time in AIT and beyond. In later years people still thought this and I believe eventually he wanted to have a separate country. I believe he even then was moving in that direction, but he moved carefully around his party's conservatives, America's concerns, and China's intentions.

I believe a different attitude in the early years—supporting but also sharing U.S. concerns with him, might have steered him in a strategy that supported democracy but in a way at least less likely to increase tensions in the Taiwan Strait.

Instead, we witnessed in these years alone, the striking difference in quelling a student riot in Beijing's Tien An Men and the then CSK Memorial in Taipei. A more enthusiastic public support by the U.S. would have done much to demonstrate to China and the world the positive direction Taiwan was taking.

In my Foreign Service career, I had been posted to the democratic Philippines (before Marcos), Japan, Botswana, and the largest democracy in the world, India. Watching a new one emerge from a far different system of governance I had seen in earlier years was for me fascinating. In my first trip to Taiwan as AIT Chairman, I found the AIT office kept such a low profile that it was seen as unfriendly.

I broke that impression to some degree by meeting individually, with a wide variety of leaders—cabinet officers, scholars, businesses—traveled by car to the south and met with several county magistrates from Ping Tung to Tao Yuan. Back in Washington, I spoke of my impressions to the Sino-American Society—another AIT habit. They had expected the regular annual report on U.S.-Taiwan trade, and for some of the elderly members, were deeply disturbed that "Free China" was changing.

When I was preparing for my assignment, much of all this was important but distant background. Learning of the immediate past was urgent—preparing for my first trip to Taiwan as AIT Chairman. It is useful to review those first few years before democratization began to take hold among the people of Taiwan. After the new unofficial relationship with the U.S. which had begun in 1979, domestic political developments were mainly a continuation of the authoritarian system of Chiang, Kai-shek. The largely Mainlander KMT establishment kept control of the central level government, politics, and security functions, while allowing native Taiwanese to participate politically at the local level and in the private sector of the economy.

Chiang, Ching-kuo (CCK) had been the *de facto* political leader of Taiwan for almost five years before the change in the relationship with the U.S. He maintained the fundamental structure inherited from his father, with some loosening of the system to accommodate the needs of the growing economy. An election to fill some vacancies in the Legislative Yuan had been postponed when the break in U.S.-Taiwan relations occurred. Political activity of this kind was set aside as the regime felt its way with the new situation. Even when the election did take place in 1980, it made little difference in the profile and power of the Legislative Yuan or in the central government or the ruling party.

Pressures were growing for political reform, however, generated not only by its internationalized economy, but by the loss of its membership in the UN, and the external pressures for political reform from such sources as the important American annual human rights report. The growing number of rallies and lectures by various "tang wai" ("outside the Party", or opposition) groups ultimately led to the high profile "Kaohsiung Incident" on December 10, 1979, which resulted in the imprisonment of several tang wai leaders. This galvanized more support for the loosening of political restrictions and the internal pressures for more participation by the Taiwanese grew. Some opposition represented by moderate but anti-KMT personalities such as Henry Kao and Kang, Ning-hsiang, were allowed to engage in political activity, but during this period no change was considered in government organization as it was believed that such an action would loosen the hold of Mainlander and KMT power.

In 1984, CCK was reelected by the National Assembly for a second term. One decision he took then was to become significant: his choice of Lee, Teng-hui as his vice president. Tang Wai activity continued to increase and apparently, at least in part, stimulated his thinking on the need to reform the political system. Presumably his objective was to develop changes that would maintain stability while permitting continued mainlander and KMT control of that system.

By 1986, CCK had initiated several meetings with political opposition leaders to discourage them from forming a political party. The results were clearly not what he had hoped. In March he informed the KMT that he had decided on political reform, and had a task force established in the Party Central Committee to recommend steps that would be needed to move toward a constitutional democracy. In June the task force recommended elections for the Legislative Yuan, the Control Yuan, the National Assembly, and for the mayors of Taipei and Kaohsiung.

In the fall, Tang Wai leaders held a joint assembly and published a draft charter, even before opposition parties were legalized. CCK did not oppose this and subsequently privately informed the visiting Katherine Graham, publisher of the Washington Post, that he had decided to lift martial law at an appropriate time. (In addition to continued pressures from the U.S., that year saw the fall of Ferdinand Marcos in the Philippines and Chun Doo Hwan in Korea, which could have had some effect on CCK's thinking as well). By December, in the supplemental Legislative Yuan elections for unfilled seats, a competitive party participated even though opposition parties were yet to be legalized. The KMT won 70 percent of the seats being contested, while the still illegal Democratic Progressive Party won 22 percent.

In July of 1987 CCK announced that martial law would be lifted after the passage of a new national security law. When the new law passed it was criticized by some for covering many of the constraints that had been a part of the martial law, but it permitted the legalization of political parties and it clearly did not deter the opposition from gaining public attention through vociferous and loud arguments in the LY, and demonstrations. The ban on travel to the Mainland was partially lifted and new laws regarding freedom of speech, association, public assembly were drafted (and passed in early 1988).

On January 13, 1988, CCK passed away and Lee, Teng-hui was sworn in as president. Two weeks later he was elected as the KMT Acting Party Chairman. As the first Taiwanese president, and an outsider in the inner core of KMT power elite, his hold on power was tenuous. To calm concern, and gain support, he paid calls on many of the politically important people in government and around the island, however, and by mid-year, at the 13th Party Congress, he overcame opposition and was elected Chairman. In the following year he replaced Premier Yu, Kuo-hua with Li Huan (both mainlander Party leaders) as he gradually consolidated his position within the Party and in government. Among other things, he supported a new law that would give generous retirement payments to national representatives in the elected bodies who voluntarily retired.

In Taiwan, in 1990, Lee, Teng-hui emerged from two years of jostling within the KMT/Government to retain his position as President and Chairman of the KMT. While CCK had started a process by lifting martial law and some travel to the mainland, just where he intended to take the country was not clear. The struggle over that in the KMT must have been intense but largely closed to the public. My guess is that CCK eventually would have preferred the Singapore type of democracy—the Asian values. Though Lee was still far from having grasped full control from the KMT establishment, by 1990 events forced him to begin openly working for the kind of democracy he had in mind, which as time made clearer, was a populist type of democracy.

In Taiwan, and as I began reading into U.S.-Taiwan affairs in the late spring and early summer of 1990, Lee, Teng-hui had emerged from two years of jostling within the KMT/Government to retain his position as President and Chairman of the KMT. While CCK had started a process by lifting martial law and some travel to the mainland, just where he intended to take the country was not clear. The struggle over that had been intense but largely closed to the public. Though Lee was still far from having grasped full control from the KMT establishment, by 1990 events forced him to begin openly working for the kind of democracy he had in mind.

In 1990, therefore, political activity heightened, within the ruling party and in competitive two-party domestic politics. From 1988, at the death of CCK, through 1989, Lee, Teng-hui's energies had been absorbed in consolidating his position as President and as Chairman of the KMT. In the party and government, which in practical terms were in distinguishable, the struggle for power was between the older generation elite, especially Mainlanders, and the younger, more liberal elements of the party, including Taiwanese, calling for changes.

This internal struggle for control, which included differences based on ideology, generation, ethnic (Mainlander and Taiwanese), and fundamental control of power within by Mainlander/KMT leaders, narrowed Lee, Teng-hui's option not only in gaining power, but in establishing the direction he wished for Taiwan to take. It slowed the process of change, put constraints on his power, and led him to use forces outside the reaches of the ruling elite to accomplish his objectives.

By 1990 he began openly to use this indirect strategy. This emergence on Taiwan of an active President bent on democratization was largely ignored by the U.S. Among most of the China experts he was considered a "closet independent type", and therefore a troublemaker. From 1988 to 1989 he had spent his energies gathering support within the KMT power structure. By 1990 he was beginning to establish himself outside the elite as well.

On February 11, President Lee announced his preference for a running mate in the upcoming election for president—Li, Yuan-tsu. It was unexpected and clearly meant to co-opt efforts by some senior party officials to name a strong "establishment" vice president candidate to keep Lee in check. The old guard within the Party wanted to maintain the system much as had been done when Vice President Yen, Chia-kang succeeded Chiang, Kai-shek. At that time, the constitution was observed, but it was clear President Yen was to be an interim figure only. Since Lee was not of that mind, and since there was no pre-appointed successor, the old guard within the KMT Party made an attempt to nominate Lin, Yang-kang (a conservative Taiwanese member), and Chiang, Wei-kuo (brother of CCK), as the party ticket. After much debate, the two were eventually persuaded to withdraw (with the help of student riots supporting Lee). The Party, therefore, proposed only Lee arid Li as the presidential candidates to the National Assembly. That body had the constitutional responsibility for electing the president.

The long-standing first National Assembly, elected on the Mainland before the retreat to Taiwan, convened in March of that year. It was the first time opposition members who had been elected in Taiwan were to fill some of the empty seats participated in that body's proceedings. The rejection of these members on the grounds of their refusal to take the oath to the ROC, and their raucous actions intended to attract the media, as well as the effort by the National Assembly majority to assume more power, generated an unusually large protest by university students on March 3 that quickly grew to significant proportions.

As in most cases in these early days of opening the society to the human rights long denied, the demonstrations by the students were unprecedented and caused shock and concern. The Taiwan Garrison Command advised putting down the demonstration forcefully, with weapons, to quash any precedent. The Minister of Interior, a Taiwanese who had studied with the President in Japan, with the approval of the President forbade not only military involvement, but any armed police from intervening as well. Lee, through the media as well as personally, talked to the demonstrators, promised to convene an extraordinary National Affairs Conference made up of all segments of the political spectrum to discuss the nation's problems, and succeeded in defusing the demonstration. It was a stark contrast to the events that had taken place the year before in China's

Tien An Men. It was a message that few in Taiwan, and even fewer in America grasped—peaceful change was the leadership's objective, but other means were just below the surface.

On the 20th of March Lee replaced Premier Li Huan with Hau, Pei-tsun, partially to assuage the "non-mainstream" (conservative, mostly Mainlander) elements in the party, and partially to address the growing law and order problem on the island. Lee was elected president for a full term on March 21 by the National Assembly. On June 21 the Council of Grand Justice announced that senior parliamentarians must retire after December 31, 1991.

The National Affairs Conference (NAC), promised by Lee, formally met on June 28. All segments of society were represented, including some opposition leaders from abroad who were on the "black list" and heretofore had not been permitted to return to Taiwan for years. The party "establishment", and the media they largely controlled, were very critical of this action. They feared the invitation of such elements elevated their status, could open the political system for public debate, and even threaten the foundations of the kind of society they wanted.

In fact the NAC did just that. Many of the agreements, or more accurately understandings, that resulted from the conference were later challenged by one side or the other. Nonetheless, the conference opened up public discussion of issues that previously had been either illegal or impolitic to debate. It was generally agreed that a new National Assembly would be elected entirely from the Taiwan constituency and that it would address constitutional revisions; that the special laws connected with the communist rebellion on the mainland that gave the president extraordinary power, would be lifted; that a new strategy would be developed regarding the Mainland; and that dissidents would be allowed to return home, among many other things.

The Taiwan Garrison Command, feared by many Taiwanese since its establishment after the reversion of Taiwan following World War II, was relocated, signaling a reduction in its status. Another result of the Conference was the tacit acceptance by the opposition party that they would pursue their objectives (i.e. independence) within the law — and not on the streets. It was yet another indication that though peaceful change was everyone's objective, other options were not too far under the surface. The National Affairs Conference was concluded on July 4.

By August "supplemental" legislators (elected in Taiwan) outnumbered "senior" members (elected on the Mainland) for the first time. In September DPP members boycotted Premier Hau's formal dinner, an unprecedented act. The discord continued to mount between the "Breakfast Club" (supporters of Lee, Teng-hui) and the "New KMT Alliance" (or non-mainstream, who opposed him).

During this time, the growing contacts between Taiwan and China also engendered a range of issues that needed careful handling. A set of unofficial institutions began. In September, the National Unification Council (NUC) was established (largely to satisfy the unification elements of the party).

Later in the year, the Grand Justices announced an interpretation of the constitution that required all "first term" representatives (i.e. those elected on the mainland to such elective bodies as the Legislative Yuan, the National Assembly, and the Control Yuan) to retire by December 31, 1991. The president also issued a special amnesty pardoning many dissidents, including Hsu, Hsin-liang and Shih, Ming-teh, both of whom subsequently served as chairman of their party.

American interest in East Asia in 1990 focused mostly on the after effects of Tian An Men. For the U.S.-Taiwan relationship, while it meant to bolster democratization in Taiwan and in East Asia generally, in stead as I saw it, was the beginning of lost opportunities throughout the decade that followed.

My first trip as AIT Chairman came as these many changes were taking place. Though the AIT director in Taipei had seldom been seen there and was not keen on my meeting with a variety of people throughout the island, he nonetheless had his people help me. My first job was to visit within the AIT. I then made a special effort to meet with as many people as possible, from government officials to workers, from the President and much of the cabinet, separately, to Legislators, politicians of both parties (for the first time), academics, business leaders, military, organizations, and old friends through out the island. Most had not met with AIT.

I made a special effort to meet with as many of the new legislators from both parties as possible. They were to be the political future of Taiwan. Most of them were moderate and responsible, and as most of them were American-educated, we would have much good will there. These LY members were already leading Taiwan toward a much different political future than we had known.

There, and in the Executive including the President, members of his cabinet, and other leaders as well, there seemed to be a genuine eagerness to see us and this very definitely included my wife. They are well known for their hospitality. There was also an element of curiosity generated by the media, and by my wife, Lilan, as a native of Taiwan. There was also the ever-present effort to raise the officially of the relationship at every opportunity. This explains the eagerness for many if not most of the people we saw. But there seemed to be desperation brought on by events, both domestic and international.

But the important changes that were turning Taiwan from an authoritarian political system to democracy were given rhetorical support but little change in managing the rapidly changing government system. This was a decade that saw this development while at the same time both U.S. Administration priority was to improve the U.S.-China relationship.

This was also the time when Washington was receiving reports that President Lee was a "closet independence supporter" and therefore not to be trusted. This attitude remained throughout my time in AIT and beyond. In later years, his advocacy for independence is seen as part of this impression. I believe a different attitude in those early years—supporting but also sharing U.S. concerns with him—might have steered him in a strategy that supported democracy but at a pace less likely to increase tensions in the Taiwan Strait.

Instead, we witnessed in this year alone, the striking difference in quelling a student riot between the Tian An Men incident in Beijing, and the CSK Memorial in Taipei, the considerable list of human rights that returned to the people. A more enthusiastic public support by the U.S. would have done much to demonstrate to China and the world the positive direction Taiwan was taking.

In my first trip to Taiwan as AIT Chairman, I found the AIT office that kept such a low profile that it was seen as unfriendly. I broke that impression to some degree by meeting individually with a wide variety of leaders—cabinet officers, local leaders, scholars and businessmen—traveled by car to the south and met with magistrates from Ping Tung to Tao Yuan. Back in Washington, I spoke of my impressions to groups ranging from the old "Free China" believers to ultimate unification and ultimate independence groups among the "overseas Chinese". It shook up the former, and pleased the latter.

Leaders understand quite clearly that the PRC, sensing Taiwan's drift towards its own identity both internationally and domestically, was putting increasing constraints on Taiwan's maneuverability. At the same time the leadership is faced with the domestic political chemistry: that the momentum toward a more Taiwanese dominated democratic system was simply irreversible. This assessment is not based on either ideology or newfound liberalism. It is based on the pragmatic analysis that the momentum would be impossible to stop. Just a short time ago (pre-June 4, 1989), there seemed to be a growing sense of confidence in Taiwan that their economic power would make it possible to deal with the Mainland from a position of strength. Now a more hostile PRC which is undermining Taiwan's international support, and a quickened pace in political change domestically, have eroded that confidence very substantially.

Taiwan's critical relationship with the Mainland, including its considerable trade, investments, and remittances must be seen in its domestic context. The stock market crash was still reverberating; the Asian games were in full swing; the Iraqi crisis was news, but what dominated the media and dinner conversation was politics and the Mainland relationship. The two are not only interrelated, but unlike the past, openly debated. The debate is complicated by the heavy flow of visitors from Taiwan to the Mainland, including many LY members. The visits between these unofficial persons and officials in the PRC give outsiders the impression that a behind the scenes dialogue is going on. This is categorically denied by Taiwan officials at the highest levels. Clearly they would be at a disadvantage doing so now, and further, in domestic terms, it would be political suicide. Gradually, the government started to set up government and private sector institutions to handle Taiwan-China issues as needed.

In my judgment, the PRC has ample reason to be concerned. A Taiwan identity is emerging and already beyond suppression. Even those in both the executive and the legislature whose ultimate objective is unification with Mainland, insist on equal status in any negotiations with Beijing. This means a separate identity, and though for this group that means an "ROC", that is a weakening position. When the old National Assembly and Legislative Yuan members are retired next year, there will be a definite shift in the power structure—and this will be toward a separate Taiwan identity.

At this point, Taiwan identity does not mean Taiwan independence. Except for a small (but growing) constituency, independence is seen as too risky by those, mostly Taiwanese, who would like it: not practical for a long time seems to be the overwhelming view; and undesirable by a shrinking minority, mostly mainlander, conservatives. Beijing's actions undermine the pro- unification conservatives at a time when they are already quickly becoming a threatened species.

In domestic politics, the opposition party is given recognition by the ruling KMT. In the few short years of the DPP's existence it has already accomplished much. It is not a strong party, however, either financially or organizationally. To keep it together, the party leadership finds it necessary to take more pro-independence positions than the more moderate majority would like. At the present time, it is the independence versus unification issue which stands as the major difference between the KMT and the DPP. Public debate, therefore, tends to focus on this difference. Among the leadership, I was repeatedly told that the issue is largely a media event without substance. In my judgment, if they really believe that, it could be a dangerous attitude. History has plenty of examples where the media led rather than followed events. If on the other hand, government is taking it seriously, their stated option was to pursue the dissolution of the opposition party—an act that would have led to immediate instability had it been done. Either way the issue has reached a worrisome level.

The stock market crash was a blow to confidence but it had less relevance substantively. Their perception of a deteriorating economy has to be seen in the context of a people whose only memory is of annual double-digit growth. But Taiwan's policymaking machinery has a thirty-year record of success. The caliber of people at the top of this machinery almost assures the island successfully coping with its economic problems except, of course, if there is a worldwide recession. In addition, though there is much to be done, especially in infrastructure, they have plenty of money to do it with.

Domestic economic problems seem to me to be manageable. International, or multinational ones, however, are another matter. Beijing's efforts to isolate Taiwan politically are not new, and Taiwan's increasing presence in the international economic arena undeniably has political implications in its contest with the Mainland. But Beijing's policy of more aggressively thwarting Taiwan's efforts to expand its international economic ties will only strengthen the move toward a separate Taiwan identity. Already there is growing sense among native businessmen that a separate Taiwan identity is the only alternative.

We all accept that an economy with the resources and the trade impact that Taiwan has, is eligible for GATT. A good case can be made for participation in the World Bank/IMF structure. The discipline membership in these organizations brings is desirable and in our interest as well. For Taiwan, too, there is a need to maneuver in coping with this international presence. Beijing's placing constraints on this could cause Taiwan to seek other, less desirable alternatives, that run counter to our own interests (and Beijing's as well).

In terms of our relationship with Taiwan, we have our own challenges. How do we deal with a Taiwan that is seeking to exercise its economic presence internationally, and at the same time with a Beijing which is hostile to this development? In strictly bilateral terms, how do we continue our low profile policy within an increasingly open society where Taiwan's and our actions are open to public debate? And finally what should our policy be toward the inevitable and now relatively short-term prospect that Taiwan will assert its separate identity in increasingly stronger terms?

These three policy questions are important in determining where the relationship will go, and therefore influence any proposals on how best to structure AIT to cope with it.

Back home, after the trips and meetings in the Executive Branch and Congress, I accepted a request from the Sino-American Cultural Society (SACS) to give a talk on the subject of Taiwan—an annual requisite.

ADDRESS BY NATALE H. BELLOCCHI

SINO-AMERICAN CULTURAL SOCIETY DINNER

DECEMBER 2, 1990

INTRODUCTION

The changes taking place in Taiwan can easily capture the imagination and interest of anyone who takes notice. With pride in their economic achievements, the people of Taiwan are now moving to establish a democratic, open political system. The atmosphere is alive with change, and those of us who work in this area must be alert to the implications these changes. The transformation that continues to take place in these areas very much shapes Taiwan's future and our relationship to it.

First, what we might call the people relationship: The character of this people relationship has changed very considerably. The loyalties and attention of the Chinese community in America and others with an interest in that subject have become more diffuse. More specifically, with those active in following Taiwan affairs, political preferences in broad terms generally follow the same division now arrayed on that island—i.e. support for unification, or independence. The same rule seems to apply here as it has elsewhere, that the farther away from the problem, the stronger the views of the observers.

But the ease of travel and communications, and the almost pervasive American influence there can too easily get America caught up in the ferment of domestic politics. Last year, for example, 218,000 non-immigrant visas were processed by AIT. When one considers that most of these visas are five year multiple entry ones, as many as 1 to 2 percent of the entire population of Taiwan traveled to the U.S. last year. And then there is the travel elsewhere: a million to the Mainland. Thailand is another favorite, and smaller numbers reach almost anywhere in the world.

Taiwan and the PRC vie for first place among the number of students they have here in our institutions of higher learning. Over 90 percent of those students from Taiwan who study abroad choose American schools. There are about 28,000 of them, or about five percent of all their students in higher education. Many of the supplemental members of the Legislative Yuan—those elected most recently on Taiwan and likely to be the nucleus for the new LY, are American educated. So are 17 of 31 cabinet level officials. So is a high percentage of business leaders. Their universities are generously staffed with American-Chinese professors, and some of their scientists made their reputations here.

This liaison continues. Every year under USIA's International Visitor Program, 12 leaders from Taiwan are invited by AIT to spend 30 days in the U.S. in an intensive program of professional observation and consultation to promote greater understanding of American society. There are many former grantees now in a position of leadership in the Legislative Yuan, among senior academics, editors of newspapers, and well-known artists.

While the number of exchanges sponsored by AIT are no greater than would be the case under ordinary circumstances, the interchange that actually takes place, in terms of percentage of the population, must be among the highest in the world. The potential in this kind of relationship, for both cooperation and contention, is clearly very great.

In science, too, there are strong bonds between our two peoples. Since 1979, AIT and CCNAA have developed a broad range of scientific and technological (S&T) agreements which enable both sides to cooperate on such matters as disease prevention and control, atmospheric research, meteorology and forecast systems, agricultural sciences, and motor vehicle emissions. In addition, there are seven S&T annual meetings: Scientific and Scholarly Cooperation; Biomedical Sciences; Physical Sciences; Technical Information Exchange; Dam Design and Construction; Environmental Protection; and Nuclear Research. During the period of October 1979 to October 1990, AIT and CCNAA have signed nearly 40 S&T agreements.

So in travel, in education, and in science, there are very strong bonds between the U.S. and Taiwan. What makes it even stronger is the economic relationship. This bond has grown in parallel with the Taiwan economy as it transformed itself from a less developed Country status to a newly industrialized one, and then to an important presence in the international economic area, all within one and a half generations. Like elsewhere in the region (but unlike Eastern Europe where the opposite is taking place), economic changes tended to lead political reform.

This economic growth and the American association with it, can be divided into three stages. The first is from 1950 to 1965. A U.S. aid program was channeled into building infrastructure, importing industrial equipment, and promoting agriculture development. It was fundamental in transforming the economy from a mainly agriculture one to labor-intensive industrial production. The U.S. was able to end all economic assistance in 1965 and to phase out all military aid in the mid-1970s. Our present strong economic relationship, therefore, is based on our original and effective involvement in the building of Taiwan's foundation for its present economic development.

During this early period, Taiwan's security concerns dominated the political leadership's priorities. Though the extremes employed during the 1940s to maintain firm control of all political activity moderated somewhat, martial law was strictly enforced and political dissent firmly quashed. Security measures, however, clearly were beginning to put constraints on economic growth.

In the second stage, from 1965 to 1984, the so-called technocrats among the political leadership were increasingly effective in bringing about the political changes necessary for continued economic expansion. Travel by Taiwan citizens was liberalized, tourism permitted to expand, and foreign investment encouraged. The press was allowed some liberties, but not many, and political dissent was still proscribed. Martial law, perhaps somewhat less severely enforced, was still in place. Pressures were growing, however, for more liberalization.

Because small and medium sized enterprises dominated the course of industrialization, income distribution actually improved during this period of rapid economic growth. The standard of living on the island rose perceptively and Taiwan became an important player in the economy of the Pacific region. This continued economic progress was made possible very substantially by Taiwan's access to the U.S. Market.

From 1984 to the present, Taiwan has been characterized as an economy moving toward more liberalization and internationalization. Per capita GNP is expected to reach US$8,500 in 1990. Trade has been the engine of growth, exceeding $118 billion in 1989, making Taiwan the worlds' thirteenth largest trader. Emphasizing exports, Taiwan's global trade surplus totaled $14 billion in 1989, generating foreign exchange reserves which peaked at $76 billion in 1987 and now total about $70 billion. In the commercial relationship, K. S. Sheu, Director General of BOFT recently said that "in the last 10 months there have been 13 rounds of trade talks, which may be one of the highest frequency of talks among nations with which the US has trade relations.

The United States remains Taiwan's largest trading partner, its largest export market, and its second largest import supplier after Japan. These figures give some indication of the depth of our trade relationship. One must remember that a population of just over 20 million sells us about $24 billion worth of goods each year, and buys from us about $12 billion. For us, that makes Taiwan our 6th largest trading partner. At the same time, U.S. investment on the island is about $3.2 billion, and Taiwan investments in the U.S. are growing rapidly.

Apart from bilateral ties, other important factors inevitably must be taken into account in any discussion about the U.S.-Taiwan relationship. Most significant among them are: Taiwan's presence in the international economy; its relationship with the PRC; and the fundamental changes taking place in its domestic political scene.

Taiwan's policy of economic internationalization has been given impetus in the recent past, with the authorities encouraging outward investment. The result is that the island's direct investment overseas has risen sharply. Among other investment shifts, manufacturers of conventional, low value-added products have moved their factories offshore to low-wage Southeast Asian countries and mainland China. Taiwan's direct outward investment is now second only to Japan in some Southeast Asian nations and ranks first in the Philippines and Indonesia.

Eastern Europe also has been a major focus of Taiwan's internationalization policy and is likely to remain so for some time. Taiwan—backed by its economic strength and the world's second largest foreign exchange reserves—is actively seeking to participate in international economic and financial organizations. After two years of absence, Taiwan returned to the annual conference of the Asian Development Bank in May 1989. In January 1990, Taiwan applied to accede to the General Agreement on Tariffs and Trade. Looking ahead, Taiwan would like to be included in any Pacific Basin initiative (such as the Asia Pacific Economic cooperation initiative) as well as additional programs of the Organization for Economic Cooperation and Development, Translating Taiwan's undeniable presence in the economic area of international affairs into some kind of internationally accepted legal status, however, is clearly going to require some imaginative diplomacy—and probably some compromises.

But it is important to remember that this is not a bilateral matter between the U.S. and Taiwan. As a member in these international organizations, we play a part, of course. Our influence may be important but by no means dominant. A status, however defined, would have to receive international acceptance, and this, as we all know, often requires long, frustrating, patient groundwork. When we see what it has done worldwide on a bilateral basis, Taiwan clearly has demonstrated the ability and the means to meet this challenge.

No discussion about Taiwan can be complete without including the PRC-Taiwan relationship. Given the overwhelming importance of the state of that relationship to the island, it overhangs all of Taiwan's external actions, and has a very substantial influence on domestic politics as well.

In 1981 the PRC announced a nine-point set of principles or conditions with regard to their relationship to Taiwan, and later Deng Hsiao-ping extended his principle of "one country-two systems" to include Taiwan. There have been various informal interpretations and nuances added to this from time to time, but the original PRC position has remained largely the same. The fundamental point—that it will only negotiate with Taiwan on a party-to-party or central-government-to-provincial-government basis also has not wavered and remains unacceptable to Taiwan.

There has been some movement on the Taiwan side in the last four years, though hope and wishful thinking often exaggerate the extent to which this represents any meaningful progress in resolving the issue. The Taiwan authorities continue to maintain their policy of "3 no's" (no contact, no negotiation, and no compromise). The authorities state there has been no authorized official contacts, much less any negotiations, and that the conditions set by President Lee Teng-hui, i.e. no talks until the PRC drops the communist system, forswears the use of force against Taiwan, and ceases its interference in Taiwan's external affairs, remain valid.

This does not mean there has not been significant change on other than the political front, however, and in time these changes could well have profound effect in the political arena. Indirect trade is now allowed and is estimated to have reached $3.5 billion in 1989. while there is a significant surplus in Taiwan's favor, remittances from the island likely redress that imbalance. In line with Taiwan's outward surge of foreign investment, it has become what is estimated to be the fourth largest "foreign" investor in the Mainland, (some estimate about US$1 billion). This private sector, largely indirect commercial engagement has already made evident the need for some means of coping with problems as they surface.

In 1986 Taiwan began permitting visits by its people for humanitarian reasons. Once this small opening was made, the door has opened ever wider to a point where the number has surged well over a million. One recent American visitor to the PRC commented that the tourist industry there was being maintained largely by Taiwan and Korean visitors.

This new phenomenon has significant implications. The substantial people-to-people contact means people on both sides of the straits will begin to understand each other more. That does not mean that eventual unification of the two sides is either easier or more likely. The realization of the extent of the differences between the two peoples—in quality of life, in ideology, in perspective, in knowledge about the world around them—could encourage a more clear separation of some kind. The difficulties businessmen have in doing business there, given their different perceptions, also could tend to highlight differences rather than similarities. Contacts among academics, scientists, specialists in agriculture, culture and other disciplines, on the other hand, could do much to make some form of association desirable.

Inevitably, so many visitors touring China, and so many commercial transactions taking place call for some kind of channel of communication to conduct routine requirements. Visas, document verification, marriages, claims, deaths, all require some kind of mutually acceptable arrangement. The need is further complicated by the legal status of the citizens on both sides of the straits: i.e. authorities having to cope with the political necessity of recognizing them as Chinese citizens, but the practical need to deal with them differently.

On the Taiwan side a National Unification Commission has been formed to establish policy toward the Mainland. A cabinet-level Mainland Affairs Council under it will implement policy decisions. A non-government agency is now being organized to actually handle these matters and, if agreement can be reached with the PRC, will have offices on the Mainland.

And now we come to the fascinating, and for Taiwan, the profound developments in its domestic political scene. Since 1986, domestic politics in Taiwan has experienced an enormous change. Up to this point, the changes continue to be pronounced and rapid, but gradual and peaceful. After four decades of authoritarian rule under a martial law regime, Taiwan launched a bread program for political reform. Ever since February, 1987, the newly elected KMT and DPP legislators have conducted unprecedented open debates on fundamental policy issues previously considered too sensitive to discuss publicly. These have included the future of Taiwan, the authorities' "Three No's" policy toward the PRC, the procurement of military equipment, self-determination for the people of Taiwan, and private travel to the Mainland. After some delay and a considerable amount of partisan debate in the LY, heralding a newly independent role for that previously docile body in shaping future legislation, the legislature adopted the National Security Law (NSL) and Martial Law was ended in July, 1987.

There is widespread popular support for the reform program. The momentum of change probably is irreversible. Press restrictions have been largely lifted, though electronic media is still controlled, and legislation has been passed to legalize opposition political parties. In addition, there is widespread public discussion of the most sensitive political issues, including reforming Taiwan's legislative bodies, with the ambitious goal of remodeling them into more fully representative institutions. There has been increasingly vocal agitation within the KMT itself for more democratic national and intra-party institutions as the younger members begin to assert themselves in political competition with their elder leaders and press for more pragmatic policies.

This last January, for example, there was opposition in the KMT Central committee to Lee Teng-hui's candidacy for a six-year term as president. The open contest for delegate support that ensued opened a new chapter in the KMT's own movement toward more internal democratization. It also provoked Taiwan's first wide-spread political demonstration in years, bringing a new element into play when thousands of university students camped out in a major downtown square, and encouraged a rising tide of younger politicians of both Mainland and Taiwan origin to urge direct election of the President in 1996.

In response to these student demonstrations, President Lee Teng-hui convened an extraordinary National Affairs Conference. Although differences exist over precisely what was agreed to, broadly speaking there was general consensus for a new Mainland policy and for constitutional reform, including election of the President by the people and the reorganizing of a new Legislative, Control Yuan, and National Assembly. I have already referred to the proposal for determining and implementing Taiwan's Mainland policies. The issue of constitutional reform may be even more controversial than the National Unification Commission has been, and far more complex. There exists now a set of "Temporary Provisions for the Period of Communist Rebellion," under which for over 42 years many laws and even agencies of government were established under special powers given to the president. These must be abrogated, with new laws passed simultaneously to continue those laws and agencies deemed necessary.

Rather than writing a new constitution, indications are that three amendments will be proposed to reorganize the national elected bodies, two of which are the only bodies with the authority to amend the constitution. At the same time, Taiwan's Grand Justices have ruled that old members of the three bodies elected on the Mainland over 40 years ago must retire by the end of next year (a move widely supported by both political parties). The result is that the sequence of elections, the passage of amendments, and the lifting of the Temporary Provisions must all be coordinated.

This complex set of actions must take place in an atmosphere of some disagreement over many of the issues involved. The relationship between the President, the cabinet, and the new Yuans, for example. The make up of each of the elected Yuans, including the possible reservation of "national constituency" seats will be another.

In the public debates that will take place over the next two years or so, the emotional issues of unification versus independence, and the ethnic differences between Taiwanese and Mainlanders will inevitably come up again. Nonetheless, it is well for us as observers to remember, that in all this ferment, and despite the play to the galleries by politicians, and the sometimes outrageous hype of the newly unleashed press, political leaders of both parties, young and old, almost invariably understand the need for gradualism and moderation.

We have then, several trends that influence the U.S.-Taiwan relationship:

A. There is the continuing strong association in our educational systems.
B. There is the very strong economic and commercial relationship between us.
C. There is Taiwan's relatively new and important international economic presence.
D. There is the new economic and people-to-people relationship with the PRC.
E. There is the relatively new and substantial expansion in the number of people who travel abroad from Taiwan.
F. There is the growth in the perception of Taiwan's own identity, both at home and abroad.
G. There are the now irreversible political reforms and the new generation of leaders spurring the changes.
H. There are the fundamental issues of ethnic power and national status now openly debated.

There may be other important issues as well, but these are the impressions I came back with from my recent trip there. If these observations are valid, then what are the implications? In my judgment, they are first, that the bilateral relationship, through education, travel and commerce, remains as strong as ever, and that we will continue to be a vital factor in Taiwan's future. Second, that a large percentage of the people of Taiwan, traveling as extensively as they do, have a heightened sense of their identity, are more aware of what they have accomplished, want recognition for it, and strongly support their leaders in seeking it. Third, that the expanding contacts and economic activity with the Mainland have both negative and positive influence on any movement to resolve the issue between them. Fourth, that democratization, bringing full participation by all the people in the governing of the island, will also heighten debate on sensitive issues that will challenge the leadership and its changing institutions.

As for the U.S. and Taiwan, we have developed a close, effective and strong relationship over the years. The first Taiwan we knew was a bulwark against the expansion of communism. Given the continuing differences in ideology, Taiwan clearly considers it must continue to play that role. The second Taiwan was a model of economic development, and it still is today. The third Taiwan was that one of the large trade surplus—a situation that is improving but still there. And now, the fourth Taiwan, is democratizing at home and seeking a still undetermined presence internationally. Over the last ten years of this changing Taiwan, our relationship has remained solidly based on the Taiwan Relations Act. Under this, we have expanded both the cultural and economic relationship, and maintained our commitment to provide adequate military supplies for defensive purposes.

CHAPTER EIGHT
American Institute in Taiwan 1991

In 1991, a Mainland Affairs Council, with cabinet level authority but with special ties to the President's office, was established. A major political event was the convening of a special meeting of the National Assembly to address elections for a new National Assembly, a new Legislative Yuan, and a new Control Yuan. Each would be elected entirely by the Taiwan constituency. It also voted on terminating the special laws of "The Period of National Mobilization for the Suppression of the Communist Rebellion," abolishing the powers of the president, and recognized the PRC.

By the end of the year, all remaining "senior officials," i.e., those elected before the ROC retreated to Taiwan, retired with a generous pension. The election for the second National Assembly took place with 71 percent of the seats going to the KMT—almost the three-quarters necessary for passing constitutional amendments.

During the year, the criminal code was restored, returning constitutional protection for individuals. Taiwan independence advocates who were incarcerated were freed, and many dissidents living abroad returned as the "blacklist" was abolished. The Legislature ordered the destruction of political dossiers, the feared Taiwan Garrison Command was relocated, signaling its now lower rank in government, and the DPP opposition party placed an independence clause in its platform.

Lee, in co-opting issues from the opposition, such as pressing publicly for entrance into the UN, was further straining the rift between the mainstream and non-mainstream factions within the KMT. Lee's relationship with Premier Hau, Pau-tsun, who had been appointed by Lee to both satisfy the conservative wing of the party as well less strengthen law-and-order, was deteriorating. The differences between the KMT factions included: the UN issue, establishing the three links with China, revising the constitution, and the direct election of the president.

On November 21, the Straits Exchange Foundation (SEF), was established. It was meant to be a semi-government entity as a liaison with what was hoped would be a counterpart on the mainland side. On October 8, the National Unification Council was established and convened by the President. It produced the National Unification Guidelines, which represented for the first time a clear three-step strategy for eventual unification. The opposition party refused to participate as it objected to the word "unification" in the title. The Council, also for the first time, stated the new ROC position that two separate areas of China existed and that each was governed by two separate political entities. In effect, it recognized for the first time that the PRC was in control of the mainland.

However, it also laid out the policy that the government's first priority was to assure the rights, interests, welfare, security and prosperity of the people on Taiwan; and that unification would take place only if the same human rights, democracy, and way of life that exists in Taiwan also existed on the mainland, For the KMT generally, it was hoped that the establishment of the Council and this new strategy would not only demonstrate a commitment to unification, but also, could be the basis for a consensus on this sensitive subject in Taiwan. The Council and its Guidelines, however, were not a part of the government. The Mainland Affairs Council was established in February. It was to be a part of the Executive Branch but especially close to the Presidential office.

On the cross-strait issue, the SEF and its PRC counterpart—ARATS—began low-level beginnings to addressing some of the technical issues that were in urgent need of attention—hijacking (several commercial aircraft had been landed in Taiwan from China), fishery problems, family issues, and others. Visits to the PRC by Taiwan residents continued to increase. The National Unification Guidelines—setting three stages of gradually moving toward negotiations on unification—were adopted by the National Unification Council.

Much to the dismay of potential shipbuilders in the U.S., Taiwan purchased Lafayette frigates from France. While the U.S. continued to press Taiwan on several trade issues—the trade deficit, deep sea fishing methods, International Property Rights (IPR)—a major breakthrough came when President Bush replied to a letter from several senators, saying that the U.S. "will work actively for Taiwan's entry into GATT."

On the other hand, the U.S. pressed Taiwan to accept a compromise formula for its entry into APEC, (the economic minister would be the leading official while other countries would have their foreign ministers perform that function). It may have been a disappointment, but it was the first time a minister would sit on an equal basis with other ministers in a formal multilateral organization.

In the meantime, my speeches were having an impact among the overseas Chinese organizations in the U.S., and in Taipei. At a seminar at Pennsylvania

State, I largely repeated what I had said previously at the Sino-American Society, but this time the seminar was well covered by the Taiwan media corps from Washington. I talked about the greater assertiveness democracy was bringing to leaders of Taiwan, and the openness of a society which would change how we conduct the relationship. I said the larger flow of people visiting the PRC from Taiwan was not necessarily drawing the two people closer, and the notion that the people of Taiwan were rapidly developing their own identity was particularly highlighted in Taiwan. In retrospect, such frankness may not have been helpful. It may have conveyed the idea that America was aware of the peaceful revolution taking place in Taiwan, when in fact the policy makers in Washington were avoiding reality because it was complicating efforts to rebuild a better relationship with the PRC.

Another speech with much the same content had an impact in a different way. The Taiwanese American Chamber of Commerce, (which then had only eight chapters) asked me to speak to some 700 members in Atlantic City where their annual convention was being held. Some of them were prominent businessmen in their community around the country, and many of them expressed their happiness that someone in government was aware of the changes in Taiwan and was talking to them about it. The Chamber now has many more chapters in the U.S., and is a worldwide organization with an annual convention in Taipei. It remains non-partisan in both U.S. and Taiwan politics.

After my trip to Taiwan in March, I reported the broad situation after meeting with most of the top political leadership and almost a hundred others ranging from cabinet officials, to county magistrates, businesspersons and academics, around the island. Stability was paramount on their minds. The political ferment was unnerving for many. Opposition legislators, seen on TV in disruptive behavior, were considered a symptom of instability. In reality, the media was still largely controlled by government and party, and their loud shenanigans got them the attention they could not otherwise get. But it didn't build confidence, especially among the older generation mainlanders.

The old KMT party elite, though gradually becoming weaker, nonetheless still could block or at least stall reform. This resulted in the younger (usually Taiwanese) KMT members cooperating with the opposition in among other things, pressing for the retirement of "senior" officials in elected bodies, and preventing the newly established National Unification Guidelines from being made into law.

In my assessment, I again (as in the previous report of my first trip the previous year) suggested that it was in America's interest that Taiwan participate in the international community, and that our low profile conduct of the bilateral relationship was not possible in the increasingly open Society developing there. Already it was clear that Taiwan was quickly developing a separate and more legitimate political identity, and that its future relationship with the PRC was likely to become a choice between a loose association of some kind, or independence, but not absorption.

The Taiwan leadership was already making it clear that whatever relationship it was to have with the mainland, it was necessary for them to develop a consensus and gain the support of the people. They pressed then, as they still do, for higher-level contact between the officials of the U.S. and Taiwan. The U.S. side saw this as an effort to gain more officiality only, whereas to an important degree, it was also the pressures on the leadership for more international recognition from the increasingly enfranchised voters. I also complained that many European countries were treating a one China policy as increasingly hollow, by higher-level contacts, while we were not participating in this trend. I also suggested that while the PRC annoyed by the moves in Taiwan for greater democracy, there was little they could do about it. They were, however, likely to press us to block Taiwan independence.

The second National Assembly met in the spring and passed eight amendments, mostly specifying procedures for future appointments to the Judicial, Examination, and Control Yuans. The Criminal code was revised stipulating that a finding of treason must be based on action and not intention, in effect making it legal to advocate independence. The National Security law was revised to reduce the "blacklist" from 282 to five, and the Taiwan Garrison Command was disbanded. After the sedition law was repealed, 19 dissidents were released from jail. Peng, Ming-min, a highly respected Taiwan University professor who fled into exile, returned.

The first election for the entire membership of the Legislative Yuan was held in December with the KMT capturing only 53 percent of the votes and the DPP 31 percent. Prior to that, in July, the Statute Governing Relations Between the Peoples of Taiwan and Mainland Areas was passed. China is defined as one country with two regions governed by equal political entities.

During this year, with reform measures continuing to be implemented, the strain between the mainstream and the non-mainstream in the KMT continued to grow. The struggle in the party was more open, but in the latter part of the year, the election campaign for the legislature, with all seats being contested and with many new faces and open debates on previously prohibited subjects, drew all the public's attention.

Taiwan was moving, quickly, toward democracy. The U.S., however, continued to focus on trade problems; reject requests for purchase of military aircraft despite the fact that aircraft in use were literally falling apart; and offered no support for Taiwan's offer to contribute several millions of dollars to countries in need during the Mideast conflict with Iraq. America's support remained subdued—it was seen then, as for many it still continues to be, a problem, not an opportunity.

At the same time, Taiwan is preparing its policies inter-nationally and with the Mainland, for the long term. One can never discount any sudden change such as happened in Eastern Europe. But aside from that unlikely possibility, the leadership in Taiwan says flatly that unification is years away.

Our policies on military sales, on levels of contact, on science cooperation, and others are often short-term oriented. It seems to me we should begin basing our longer term, and on the more likely prospect that the bicoastal issue eventually is more likely to be resolved in some loose association, rather than in absorption. Any change would still have to be pursued gradually, and the safest and most immediate need is to ratchet up the levels of contact. Following our practice with high-level military personnel, we could be responsive to the President's request for higher-level contacts by getting an assurance that they can manage to be responsive to our needs: i.e. low profile, quiet visits. Then proceed in a measured way to increase the frequency of two-way visits.

With the ferment of the new politics in mind, another area where change may be necessary in the short term is public diplomacy. There, too, a ratcheting of cultural programs on Taiwan and perhaps other more visible but non-political programs as well, could help maintain our special (and in important area advantageous) relationship. In any event, we have to find ways of offsetting public criticism of our relationship, an area that is quickly becoming fair game for politicians and media.

Some trends seen at that time.

This section includes some thoughts I wrote down at the time.

With rising labor costs, large financial reserves, and a more representative political system, Taiwan's leaders face the need to upgrade the economy and the quality of life through very substantial domestic investment. At the same time, its already growing economic strength, an undeniable factor on the international scene, provides it with the influence and the confidence to assert itself more aggressively in both foreign policy and mainland relations. Taiwan is slowly developing other options as it seeks to diversify its commercial and other interests, and the reduced threat of military attack by the mainland over the long time will loosen the strong influence we have had on the island's external policies.

The main thrust of its foreign policy is to gain legitimacy through membership in international organizations, and over the medium term to work for the acceptance of what would amount to a one-nation, two-government status for itself and the PRC. In its mainland relationship, the future options are realistically either some loose accommodation with the PRC, or independence. Economic activity between the two will grow, and the appearance of movement towards accommodation will be maintained, but the status quo is the objective of the authorities while domestic political reform is in process. In the longer term, any meaningful movement toward accommodation will require consensus building on Taiwan, and more realistic conditions offered by both sides.

Underlying all of this, and increasingly the dominant factor in the policies and actions of the leadership, are the very fundamental political changes occurring on that island. With the National Assembly election at the end of this year, an important step in the transfer of power from the minority mainlander community to the native Taiwanese will have taken place. The people will have leaders and representatives directly elected by them by next year. The separate Taiwan identity, already evident, will become even more pronounced as the political and economic gap widens with the mainland. And government will have to be far more accountable and responsive to the electorate.

The political reform program continued to move broadly in the direction set out for it over four years ago. We will hear a very noisy, perhaps even rambunctious debate as very fundamental political issues (method of electing the president, distribution of power within the central government and with local governments) are being considered. Despite this, the leadership—government and political parties, young and old—understand the risk of instability and is committed to non-violent gradualism and moderation, as they search for broad consensus. The PRC, sensitive and worried over this clear strengthening of Taiwan's separate legitimacy and international standing, will strongly oppose these developments, but essentially will have few realistic options to contain the trend.

Despite growing diversification of trade and other interests, the breath and depth of the U.S.-Taiwan bilateral, through education, travel, military, science and commerce, will remain very strong. As long as their relationship remains unresolved, we will continue to be Taiwan's foremost foreign relationship, at least for the foreseeable future. The TRA will continue to be the basis for our relationship.

Democratization will: (A) heighten domestic debate on sensitive issues such as national status, making any meaningful movement toward either unification or independence even more difficult; (B) make unlikely any-near term resolution of the bicoastal relationship, given the very different political climate on each side of the Taiwan Strait, the enormous gap in living standards, and the need to have public support on this issue; (C) make increasingly difficult the conduct of our essentially low profile relationship with Taiwan in what is now becoming an open society where the relationship comes under more public scrutiny, and alternatives to U.S. positions are supported by various interest groups; and (D) make authorities more accountable and responsive to the electorate and therefore more assertive and less flexible in the conduct of their bicoastal and external affairs, including that with us.

PRC opposition to developments on Taiwan will include pressure on the U.S. to publicly commit ourselves to a subordinate political status for Taiwan. There will also be pressures from there and from some elements in Taiwan to publicly oppose the independence option will grow. While neither unification or independence is a feasible option at this time, the need for some kind of internationally recognized status during the expected long interim the issue remains unresolved, will be pressed by most political elements in Taiwan. At the same time, the long-term nature of the bicoastal issue will require our own policies to be structured accordingly.

Pluralization of power centers and decision makers makes it necessary to reach out to other groups beyond the Executive Yuan. To cope with this new open society and public debate. I suggested:

heavier dose of cultural and trade shows clearly sponsored by AIT would help, but calls by high level authorities from Taiwan in the economic, education, trade, agriculture and other fields on high level officials here, would be significant and be most justifiable in terms of our PRC relationship.

We could take care that in organizations that are clearly not political, it is in our interest and that of the international community, to include Taiwan's participation. We could at that time make equally clear that this in no way prejudges any eventual resolution of Taiwan's political status. The PRC position that any international organization, even clearly economic ones, is political in nature clearly runs counter to our interests. To reduce our exposure on this issue, we could seek G-7 acceptance and inclusion in a summit communiqué.

- Taiwan's economic strength puts it in a position to be supportive of U.S. objectives in multilateral organization.
- Membership in the GATT would provide support for LOC graduation.
- Accession process would also allow U.S. and others to press Taiwan hard on market opening without some of the heat of our bilateral consultations.
- Membership in international financial institutions could be used to get Taiwan to contribute to LDC's on a basis other than "the ROC".
- Involvement of Taiwan other than as the "ROC" supports that government in maintaining the status quo against unrealistic calls for independence or unification.

Taiwan's technical capabilities would make it a useful participant in international scientific and if some way could be found, a signatory (and financial contributor) to conventions such as the Montreal protocol.

The democratization process on Taiwan will make the management of instability in the western Pacific more complex. It may even add another burden to our PRC relationship. But to respond or put pressure in any way that tends to subvert that process would be politically unacceptable. We should in fact show more support for the process, even if it is largely symbolic. One area that is clearly in our interest and would be difficult for the PRC to oppose, is help in dealing with the PRC, and reduce the prospect for activity that is taking place. Premier Hau recently shelved the plan to create a Coast Guard, turning it over to the Navy. This is not a good development in terms of our interest. Our support for a Coast Guard might turn this around.

Our present policy of non-interference in the question of eventual status of Taiwan would be essential to maintain. Statements indicating any preference for the options facing the two sides in the Strait, and the factions/parties domestically in Taiwan, (other than peaceful resolutions) would in fact disrupt the domestic democratization process and risk causing instability across the Strait. The gradual, tacit, movement to develop the kind of one-nation, two government situation (which already exists) toward one that can more easily be dealt with by the international community is in our interest (and the PRC's) because it would preserve the unification option and defuse the potentially destabilizing efforts at independence.

CHAPTER NINE
American Institute in Taiwan 1992

Domestic change continued apace. The LY passed the "Statute Governing Relations Between the People of Taiwan and the Mainland Area". The Taiwan Garrison Command, a super military police unit that was much feared by the local people, was finally disbanded. Toward the end of the year, the Legislative Yuan's second election, now completely local members, saw the KMT win 53% of the seats (its smallest number), and the DPP win 31% (its largest number).

Before mid-year, the front office in EAP/State Department changed. A think-tank China specialist assistant secretary was replaced by a career Japan expert, and the deputy for China and Taiwan also changed career officers. From my perspective the previous deputy was overworked and had little time for Taiwan, but was relatively objective when he did. The new assistant secretary was much more open on the subject of Taiwan, but the deputy was very much a pro-China oriented specialist.

From this changeover in personnel in EAP until the end of the year 1992, when a new Administration began moving in, I submitted several memoranda to the new Assistant Secretary. Some were briefing him on AIT operations, others on trends I saw developing in Taiwan, and some on recommendations on policy. It was a rare opportunity, though short-lived, to get around the normal bureaucratic wall put up by lower level officials who resisted direct contact between the Chairman of AIT and the Assistant Secretary. It was possible because he and I had worked together in the embassy in Tokyo.

Events in the U.S. brought even more favorable agreements with Taiwan. Last year, the pressure for supporting Taiwan in the GATT was headed by Senator Baucus, whose state sells considerable wheat to Taiwan. Now the GATT has (check) agreed to give Taiwan observer status white awaiting full membership. In addition, agreement was reached on the U.S. leasing three Knox frigates to Taiwan, and toward the end of the year, and for the first time since 1979, a cabinet level office from America, USTR, visited Taiwan officially. (Taiwan was the second largest importer of American goods in Asia). Election necessities, it seems, overrides unhappy PRC leaders.

The aircraft manufacturers and some subcontractors in the U.S. saw this quite differently. Jobs were at stake, and a candidate Bush could do something about it. The State Department suddenly thought we should oppose the French sale of Mirages. I took the word to the then Secretary General of the KMT James Soong who was visiting Houston. It was too late, he said, the terms of sale had been agreed to and only the signatures of the two sides were needed. Candidate Bush, at the Fort Worth factory that made F-16s, announced that the U.S. was approving the sale of one hundred and 50 F-16s to Taiwan, From almost no credible air force, Taiwan suddenly had 60 mirages, one hundred and 50 F-16s, and their own DF planes (an indigenous clone of America's F-16) were rolling off the production line.

In March 1992, I had to shift my speech routine. The State Department put out a routine circular to remind officers that public speeches must be cleared by the Department beforehand, only this time the Chairman of AIT was specifically included. I sent my next speech over to test the waters. They came back the day before I was to deliver it, badly mutilated. The principle, that public pronouncements by officials should accurately reflect administration positions is normal and necessary, but this in my view was excessive.

There were two broad objections to what had written: it did not include our policy regarding MFN for China, and it did not like my describing the changes on Taiwan that were not to China's liking. I argue that my audience wanted to hear about events in Taiwan, not China. Furthermore not to tell Americans how democratization was changing Taiwan, even if this development was annoying China, would be irresponsible. I simply reverted to speaking from notes to avoid controversy, but the "clearances" demonstrated how we would rather avoid reality (i.e. the changes democracy was making on Taiwan), if it was inconvenient to our China relationship.

I have included at greater length my briefing of the new assistance secretary and my experience with the speech process, to demonstrate the deliberate efforts to avoid addressing the fundamental changes on Taiwan and the implications of this to both Taiwan and China policies. Even in the relatively more savvy (on foreign policy) Bush Administration, important changes pertinent to Taiwan's support for Taiwan's membership in the GATT (later called WTO); the important sale of F-16s; and the visit by a cabinet officer to Taiwan: were not based on foreign policy considerations but on our own domestic politics. Even with the visits of new legislators, more assertive and nationalistic than we were accustomed to, did not influence thinking in Washington. Especially among China experts, these developments continued to be seen as a problem, never as a potential opportunity.

The December 21 vote for the new National Assembly passed calmly and ended with a substantial victory for the KMT. The issues that this assembly must address and presumably on which the members ran, are profound and immensely important for the future of democracy in Taiwan. Yet, they are abstract for most voters, and the personalities running were relatively unknown. Though their educational levels in general are very high, few have backgrounds in law and even fewer on the nuances of constitutional matters.

In retrospect, the KMT strategy to run on a platform of stability, and ignore the independence versus unification challenge of the opposition, was right on. The resounding victory has left, at least for the time being, a relaxed atmosphere. Some say the election settled the I-U issue, but most believe the vote simply set it aside for the sake of stability. The prohibition against discussing the issue, in any event, now seems permanently ended. The election of the new National Assembly was the first time an elected institution of the "ROC" was entirely chosen by the people on Taiwan.

Shortly after the election another event took place, almost equally as significant, but almost unnoticed—the retirement of the elder, mainland-elected members in the elected bodies of that government. This is how I remember it. That government is now Taiwanese. Even the KMT party is numerically Taiwanese though power has not yet shifted to them. And another result, less permanent, is the ferment within all these institutions, that the resulting necessary realignment of factions has caused.

The political parties are now beginning the process of developing constitutional amendment proposals for the National Assembly to consider. Given their huge majority, the KMT reform committee led by the Vice President was obviously the main point of action. Through negotiating and consensus, the difficult process of arriving at acceptable proposals has begun. It was expected that process would culminate with KMT Standing Committee (and perhaps a Central Committee) approval. The approved guidance will then be given to KMT Assembly members when they meet in March to start their deliberations.

The issues were: the method of electing the President; the relationship between the President and the Premier, cabinet; the powers of the Control, Examination, and Legislative Yuans: the role of the Provincial Assembly; and the distribution of power between the Central and local governments. Though the issues are clearly very fundamental, the only really "popular" one was the method of electing the President.

On this issue, the President was neutral publicly, but privately apparently favors direct elections. The conservatives, including Hau, oppose it. The Party leaders also want to oppose it but are worried about the enormous popularity of direct elections among the general public as well as among many in the KMT itself. On all other issues, the guidance of the Party will probably be effective with Assembly members. One other area where the Party may have difficulties is the inclination of the newly elected Assembly members to expand their authority and perks. Clearly, the main battle over constitutional reform will be within the Party. The Party will hold a plenum in March but will hold off calling a Party Congress, already overdue, until later in the year. The main objective of the liberal pro-Lee forces, is to gain control of the Party; and for the conservatives, a last to ditch stand to retain it. The retirement of the elders and the recent elections have left substantial uncertainties on the relative strength of the two sides within the Party. Personnel changes or policy actions by government are all taken with this basic struggle in mind.

Just over the horizon, after the more "gentlemanly" conclusion of the constitutional reform process in June (and coinciding with our own presidential campaign), comes the campaign for electing a new Legislative Yuan. Unlike the National Assembly elections, this will be a very intense struggle for political power by political factions. Money and almost any issue will be used indiscriminately, and given the stakes, will likely become personal as well.

In assessing the possible results, there seems to be two possible scenarios developing. One is made up of at least three strong factions within the KMT, and a somewhat stronger opposition party. (Most likely faction leaders are Kao Yu-ren, Kuan Chung, and Chiu Chuang-huan.) In essence, an "LDP" scenario. Another is a possibility of weak factions, with individual members coalescing in different groups for different issues (with much money passing hands and much stronger influence by interest groups). In neither case will the Party be as influential as now.

The stark differences in style as well as objectives continue to be apparent between President Lee and Premier Hau. The Premier said the election proved the people did not want independence, that no decisions had been made regarding constitutional reform, and that the EY should have the authority to dissolve the LY. The President emphasizes the importance of stability, moves to strengthen the Presidency, and suggests that the people would have to decide on the method of electing the president. Still, as long as the relative strength between Lee and Hau supporters is so uncertain, they may still have need for each other.

Some short-term trends are coming into focus. 1992 in politics will be a time of uncertain alignments as well as uncertainties about the relative power in the various political institutions. Mainland policies may continue to move forward, but it seems at a slower pace. On this point, liberals are wary of the conservatives moving too fast on the political side, and conservatives are wary about liberals' support for the growth in economic relations.

There will be growing public support for enhancing Taiwan's international position. We can expect continued pressure for membership in IOs, name changes, and higher-level contacts. Though both sides should have learned that trying to use US policy toward Taiwan for partisan purposes was not very productive. The emotions the LY elections are likely to generate may make that a continuing problem. Pressures for advanced aircraft will also continue. The "new" strategy may, in fact, narrow our flexibility with regard to the TRA requirements by reducing the number of their requirements.

The Taiwan leadership was already making it clear that whatever relationship it was to have with the mainland, it was necessary for them to develop a consensus and gain the support of the people. They pressed then, as they still do. for higher-level contact between the officials of the U.S. and Taiwan. The U.S. side saw this as an effort to gain more officiality only, whereas to an important degree, it was also the pressures on the leadership for more international recognition from the increasingly enfranchised voters. I also complained that many European countries were treating a one China policy as increasingly hollow, by higher-level contacts, while we were not participating in this trend. I also suggested that while the PRC annoyed by the moves in Taiwan for greater democracy, there was little they could do about it. They were, however, likely to press us to block Taiwan independence (which they succeeded in doing eight years later). Taiwan was moving, quickly, toward democracy. America's support remained subdued, it was seen then, as for many it continued to be, a problem, not an opportunity.

The fast pace of democratization continued into 1992. Before the opening of the third plenum of the 13th Party Congress of the KMT, President Lee let it be known that the plenum should consider approving the direct election of the president. During the March 14-15 Central Committee meeting, now open to media coverage, the people of Taiwan witnessed a heated debate on this issue, however.

The non-mainstream faction, bitterly opposed to direct elections (because for one thing they thought this would favor Taiwanese nationalist sentiment), cleverly lined up to get on the speakers docket during the lunch period of the first day, and were thus able to monopolize the floor during the debate. Though he may have had sufficient votes, Lee agreed to postpone consideration of this issue until sometime before May of 1995, fearing the deep division in the party on this issue might cause a split.

The second National Assembly met in the spring and passed eight amendments, mostly specifying procedures for future appointments to the Judicial, Examination, and Control Yuans. The Criminal code was revised specifying that a finding of treason must be based on action and not intention, in effect making it legal to advocate independence, The National Security law was revised to reduce the "blacklist" from 282 to 5, and the Taiwan Garrison Command was disbanded. After the sedition law was repealed, 19 dissidents were released from jail. Peng, Ming-min, a highly respected Taiwan University professor who fled into exile, returned.

The first election for the entire membership of the Legislative Yuan was held in December with the KMT capturing only 53 percent of the votes and the DPP 31%. Prior to that, in July, the Statute Governing Relations Between the Peoples of Taiwan and Mainland Areas was passed. China is defined as one country with two regions governed by equal political entities.

During this year, with reform measures continuing to be implemented, the strain between the mainstream and the non-mainstream in the KMT continued to grow. The struggle in the party was more open, but in the latter part of the year, the election campaign for the legislature, with all seats being contested and with many new faces and open debates on previously prohibited subjects, drew all the public's attention.

The conduct of the relationship over the last two or three years has been affected most notably by the domestic political changes on Taiwan, the 6-year economic plan. the appreciation of the NT$, Taiwan's international economic strength, the state of U.S. relations with the PRC, and the growing political activism of the Taiwanese-American community.

There has been a sea change in the politics of Taiwan over the Last 4-5 years. Though old conservative mainlanders still hold control of the critical Central Committee of the KMT, it is their last redoubt and will inevitably fall. Government has effectively passed to the control of a new generation of largely Taiwanese leaders. The Legislative Yuan (LY) has begun exercising its full array of legislative power. The society is open (the print media almost completely so, the electronic media still are restricted), and some 10% of the people travel abroad each year.

In conducting the relationship, AIT now must not only work with the President and the Executive Yuan but also with the LY to advance our interests. On the Taiwan side it means our policies and actions come under intense scrutiny. It means political leaders and bureaucrats must observe the constraints put on the leadership by legislative and media accountability. It means increased pressure from the Taiwan electorate for international recognition. The move toward even greater openness and greater people power is clearly irreversible, and will increasingly complicate how we conduct the relationship.

The six-year development plan will create enormous domestic demand (reducing Taiwan's dependence on exports). It also will involve up to $50 billion in foreign procurement. It will upgrade not only infrastructure but industry generally, to more service oriented and high tech facilities. This in turn means the content of our trade will follow that trend. The effect on us is the much stiffer competition we face from not only Japan but the Europeans. They are greatly attracted by the money and willing to pay a price (ministerial visits, for example) to get at some of it.

Pressures from our business community have likewise increased in their efforts to stay competitive with the Europeans by urging that we also raise the level of "official" contacts. Our own recession has added to this pressure in terms of both commercial and military sales...

The result of NT dollar appreciation on Taiwan's economy is the growth in outward investment. Taiwan is now the largest foreign investor in Malaysia and Indonesia, and one of the largest in Thailand, Philippines and south China. It also is growing here (one estimate is $1 billion in the Bay Area alone, excluding real estate).

Taiwan's growing clout in the international economic arena is a result of the above two factors. It is also based on Taiwan's position as the world's 12th largest trader, our 6th largest trading partner and holder of the world's largest foreign exchange reserves. There is more need for Taiwan to share the same constraints and responsibilities other major trading nations have, ranging from respect of GATT norms to reduction of CFC emissions. USTR, Treasury and Commerce have active negotiating agendas with Taiwan. Given the market opportunities there, more countries are willing to support Taiwan's entrance in international economic organizations. Taiwan is in APEC and the ADB and the US supports Taiwan's entry into GATT on suitable terms. AIT has traditionally played an active role in bilateral economic negotiations and will be called on increasingly to make demarches on multilateral issues as Taiwan's international involvement increases...

A change here in the U.S. which impacts very substantially on AIT is the growing political activism of Taiwanese-American organizations. The most active and vocal are the independence types, although the broad-based associations, such as the Taiwanese-American Chambers of Commerce, are at least superficially apolitical. They are Taiwanese, however, and their perceptions and preferences are not those the old guard mainlanders on Taiwan like to see or hear. In our public relations, AIT and anyone dealing with the public, must straddle Taiwan's "official" position and the views of the Taiwanese community here.

There are some policy issues awaiting a crisis in the military sales area, but our conduct of the military sales process has continued smoothly. The more open atmosphere n Taiwan means more public information about military sales, and the weakened economic condition of military suppliers in the U.S. creates pressures for a loosening of the reins on sales...

Taiwan, with the world's 14th largest economy, has become an important element in the international economic community. While Taiwan is a member of APEC and the GATT accession process has begun, it is still barred from most international economic and scientific organizations and agreements.

Democratization has made that government more politically legitimate, while complicating issues of national identity and status. Democratization and economic power have strengthened Taiwan's position in the U.S. and helped differentiate it from the PRC.

Conventional wisdom is that there are three scenarios possible for the future of Taiwan: unification, status quo, or independence. The changing realities indicate that there are really only two: accommodation with or without a long-term objective of unification, or independence. The critical element was and remains, developments in the PRC. The very best outcome—continued economic growth with reasonably controllable political development in the PRC—would likely mean some kind of longer-term accommodation between the two sides. Independence pressures would remain, but the unification objective would probably be retained, in a clearly long-term framework, but probably with a decreasing degree of enthusiasm, Taiwan will continue to reach for a separate, equal political status within this framework.

Serious economic competition, or political convulsions on the mainland, on the other hand, would probably create enormous pressure for independence. Whichever of the two scenarios develop, democratization assures that whatever is done will not be a decision made by a small band of leaders on geopolitical grounds only, but a (directed or spontaneous) result of pressure from a free electorate.

In re-evaluating policy, I thought we would want to have certain fundamental objectives:

A. Retain the most successful elements of present policy, i.e. insistence on a peaceful solution to the bicoastal issue by the two sides themselves.
B. In some form have Taiwan included in the international community so that it could be subject to the same constraints and rules we all observe.
C. Expand our flexibility in supplying military equipment and strengthening the processes in our military relationship to retain our influence in the security area.
D. Loosen the self-imposed constraints on a more normal liaison with Taiwan.

There are many things we could suggest, of course. But balancing it with our other important interests, and sticking with what is both responsible and feasible, I suggest:

Permit senior (political) level officials with a clear economic purpose to visit Taiwan. Other countries are doing so with little reaction from Beijing, and clearly using these visits to their competitive commercial advantage. U.S. exports to Taiwan are over $13 billion—our sixth largest market. We have had clear advantage in the past, but that is eroding and will continue to do so if we cannot demonstrate our continued interest.

The U.S. should support Taiwan's full membership, in some form, in multilateral "Global Issues" organizations (i.e.,az science, environment, narcotics, etc.), and in appropriate economic organizations. It is clearly to our advantage, and the world's to have such an important player taking part in both the regulating and planning of these issues. (We are already supporting Taiwan's accession to GATT.)

Perhaps this all could be under a broad umbrella, that the U.S. continues to support the peaceful resolution of the political issue between the PRC and Taiwan by the Chinese peoples on both sides of the Straits. In economic and other areas, however, the U.S. will deal with Taiwan on its merits in ways that further our interests, and clearly are useful to addressing multilateral issues in this increasingly interdependent world.

Much later, after the U.S elections, and with what had become lame duck policy decision makers, I commented on a draft policy paper:

1. "Our One-China Policy." An easy phrase which is starting to creep into speeches by senior USG officials. Outside the China-watching community, few focus on the nuances in that term. We do not accept (only acknowledge) the PRC's one-China policy; we do not accept the ROC; and we do not "strictly adhere" to a one-China policy ourselves. Use of the term gives the impression that in fact we do all of the above.

2. During 1990 China had established its Association for Relations Across the Taiwan Straits (ARATS), counterpart to the SEF. There was continuous exchanges of faxes at a low level toward the end of the year, with the SEF pressing for its National Unification Guidelines issues, and China not accepting them.

   A more recent aspect of this problem was the stalled talks between the PRC's ARATS, and Taiwan's SEF, caused by their lack of agreement over what "one-China" meant. If the protagonists can't agree on what "one-China" means, what would we be doing there? My suggestion is that we reiterate our present policy, calling it the framework within which we will be responsive to the changing realities.

3. There is unquestionably a "mainland fever" gripping Taiwan. It already represents probably 20 percent of Taiwan's external investment and over 10 percent of its trade. It has the potential to grow even larger. I question, however, whether the independence issue would become secondary to

the economic relationship (it is an emotional issue too easily exploitable for political ends).

I also question whether there is "considerable enthusiasm for social and economic integration." What is happening now is profit-driven by the private sector. When put in political terms the commonality of interests drops precipitously. That gap is uncharted and potentially troublesome. As I suggest in the attached memo, that relationship may blossom into something positive; or competition from the PRC and political unrest may raise tensions there dangerously.

CHAPTER TEN
American Institute in Taiwan 1993

This section is written from the perspective of the time. Our policy toward the PRC and Taiwan has been based on the TRA and the three communiqués. Since 1979 there has been bipartisan support for this approach, along with our stated wish that the Taiwan issue would be resolved peacefully, and an unstated expectation that it would be resolved quickly as well. Bicoastal tensions have diminished, and to the degree our policy has contributed to this positive development, it has been successful. But significant changes have occurred in the last few years which affect our interests and which are pushing us (and other countries) toward a re-evaluation of current policy. This section focuses on Taiwan and the changing realities that are affecting our policy, our conduct of that relationship, and three of the broad areas in that relationship that need addressing.

The Changing Realities:

A. Our altered relationship with the PRC, together with the positive changes that have taken place in Taiwan, has changed the atmosphere in which this relationship is conducted.

B. The growing economic interchange between Taiwan and the PRC has the potential for improving cross-straits relations if all goes well. The potential for raising tensions, in economic disputes or convulsive political change in the PRC, is also there, however. And in the meantime, by comparison, improvement in the political relationship has lagged far behind.

C. As the world's 14th largest trader, Taiwan has become an important element in the international economic community. While it is a member of APEC and the GATT accession process has begun, Taiwan is still barred from most international economic and scientific organizations and agreements.

D. Democratization has made that government much more politically legitimate. The issues of national identity and status, once the prerogative of an authoritarian leadership, is now a part of the domestic political debate. The new political scene has significant effect on Taiwan's policies toward the mainland as well as on our relationship with Taiwan.

E. Its growing wealth has given it increased influence and flexibility in its foreign policy and in diversifying sources of supply, including military equipment.

F. The U.S. relationship remains critical for Taiwan but has decreased in importance to them while Taiwan's ability to influence us has increased. (It is our 6th largest trading partner, the largest buyer of Treasury Securities (Certificates), and a growing source of investment in the U.S.).

G. The increased activism of Americans whose origin is Taiwan in our domestic politics has also grown.

Two most Likely Scenarios for the Future of Taiwan:

These changing realities indicate that there are really only two options for Taiwan's future: accommodation with or without a long-term objective of unification, or independence. The critical element was and remains, developments in the PRC. The very best outcome there—continued economic growth with reasonably controllable political development in the PRC—might bring some kind of longer-term accommodation between the two sides. Taiwan will continue to reach for a separate, equal political status within this framework.

Serious economic competition, or political convulsions on the mainland, on the other hand, would probably create enormous pressure for independence. Whichever of the two scenarios develop, democratization assures that whatever is done will not be a decision made by fiat on geopolitical grounds only, but through consensus developed by elected leaders.

Three area of the relationship that need addressing:

International Organizations: Taiwan has become the 14th largest trading economy in the world. It is a major producer of both high tech and pollution-creating goods; and an important source of capital. There is a clear need for Taiwan not only to participate in establishing standards, but in regulating them. International organizations that do this in finance, in trade, in environment, in transnational issues such as narcotics, police, terrorism, etc., in humanitarian efforts, and in regulatory bodies, all could benefit from Taiwan's financial contributions and substantive participation. So could the U.S. The only obstacle to Taiwan's participation is the PRC. One policy issue, therefore, is how best to pursue what is clearly in our interest to do: support Taiwan's participation in international organizations.

Arms Sales to Taiwan:

Taiwan now has the wealth to overcome international reluctance to sell it weapons. The U.S. no longer has a monopoly in this trade. Only the U.S., among major weapons producers, has the serf-interest to pursue stability in that region, however. At the same time, as the newly powerful legislature exercises its over-sight rights, sales of weapons to Taiwan will become more competitive. The PRC also is better able to procure weaponry and has begun doing so. All of the above puts increasing pressure on the inherent dichotomy between the TRA and the '82.

If the U.S. wishes to retain strong influence in maintaining stability in that region, some changes in our arms sales policy will be needed. Some, such as the bucket, and constraints on training, work against our maintaining a strong influence with Taiwan's military.

Contacts Between the U.S. and Taiwan:

As the relationship, especially in the economic and technical areas, contin-ues to expand, contacts across a much wider spectrum, and in much greater depth, are necessary. Many, perhaps most, of the rules of engagement are not specifically, only implicitly suggested in the TRA or the Communiqués. They are based on our perceptions, or on our perceptions of the PRC views, on what con-stitutes an element of officiality. Over the years there have been changes, usually brought about by sheer necessity, but sometimes by the frustrations of dealing with the inherent inefficiencies of the engagement. Some changes can be made by fiat, some require legislation.

Friction within the KMT, in the meantime, heightened and eventually, in August, a small group of conservative non-mainstream, mostly mainlander mem-bers, split from the Party and formed the New Party. Most non-mainstream fac-tion members stayed in the Party however, and continued to wield considerable influence. The 14th KMT Party Congress which occurred almost immediately thereafter, elected Lee to another four-year term as Chairman. Significantly, no military personnel were elected to the standing Committee—evidence that the military had been taken out of politics.

The elections for county magistrates and city mayors took place toward the end of the year. The DPP received 41 percent of the vote, by the KMT still won a majority of the magistrates and mayors, not only through better organization and greater resources, but with the help of Lee's grassroots campaigning. Lee now had a premier more compatible with his thinking. By appointing James Soong, the powerful Secretary General of the KMT to be Governor of the prov-ince, he was able to install a close crony Hsu, Shui-deh the Party Secretary Gen-eral. The military was ousted from Party positions.

Reacting to wide public support for the DPP's efforts to gain Taiwan entry into the UN, Lee co-opted the issue though it was predictably rejected by the UN. It was the beginning of Lee's efforts to gain international recognition for Taiwan, for both security reasons and in response to the pressures from the more assertive electorate's wish for it. By this time, Lee was no longer constrained by conservative members (i.e. mainlanders) that had restricted his efforts to confront the PRC's Taiwan policy.

In cross Strait relations, after a series of meetings over many months, the Chairman of Taiwan's Strait Exchange Foundation (SEF) and the Chairman of the PRC's ARATS met in Singapore. Though semi-official, it was the first formal meeting between two sides of the Strait. It was limited to only administrative issues, but even that had taken considerable negotiations, though the singing ceremony was seen by the media as an historic event that would grow into much greater issues. There was a careful attempt to continue these meetings, with the Taiwan SEF Chairman visiting Shanghai some months later.

The new American Administration moved in very slowly. It was clear from the outset that Winston Lord would be the point man for the Administration on Asia policy. He had been critical of China as had the new President—Clinton—and for most of the year the relationship was adversarial. MFN was tied to human rights behavior; the U.S. opposed Beijing for the Olympics; sanctions were levied based on China's sales to Pakistan; and the U.S. pursued the Chinese ship Yen Ho on suspicion that it was carrying sanctioned material to the Mideast. At the same time there were efforts to reopen military contacts, and increasingly as the year developed, more emphasis was given to the developing a "constructive engagement" with China.

Assistant Secretary Lord asked for comment on a proposal for the coming APEC summit to assure that whatever decision is made on that meeting, takes into account the potential consequences. This memo only addresses what I believe will be the likely reaction of Taiwan should it be asked to limit its attendance at a summit meeting to a ministerial-level official while all others would be represented by their head of state or government.

One of Taiwan's fundamental objectives is to attain international recognition as a separate political entity. The purpose behind this objective not only is to assuage the pressures and dignity of one of the world's most heavily traveled electorates, but to place itself in a status of equality when the time comes for negotiating with the PRC over its permanent political status.

A public downgrading of its status *vice a vie* the PRC, and by the country with which it has the closest and most critical relationship, would at a minimum seriously undercut the present leadership and could even make it difficult for them to survive. Even if President Lee rejected the proposal and publicly condemned it, the opposition party and especially those in it that call for independence, would be enormously strengthened.

Our interest in stability in the Taiwan Straits remains as important as it has always been. Circumstances on both sides of the Straits have changed drastically, however. The PRC may have a greater stake in stability and international acceptance now than previously, but its reaction to an unstable Taiwan is still unclear. On the Taiwan side, it has become for all practical purposes, a democracy. Political power is shared and limited. Popular sentiment is not only a major consideration, it is difficult to manage.

The volatile political climate in this formative stage of Taiwan's democracy, it seems to me, requires considerable sensitivity on our part. The proposal on representation for a summit meeting of APEC members would give an enormous boost to the opposition party's assertion that international recognition is possible only through independence. It would seriously affect if not fatally damage Lee's leadership, and under those conditions, would be destabilizing. The consequences of all this are unpredictable, but clearly run counter to our interest in lowering tensions in that area.

The Legislative Yuan, now a powerful political institution, would most likely move to retaliate even if the result would be counterproductive to Taiwan's interests. Their control of the budget means that procurements and contracts that require government funds would be affected. The involvement of U.S. companies in the largest infrastructure market in the world today, would be at risk. At a minimum, the traditional pro-American atmosphere in which we have conducted this relationship, exerting our influence in economic, political, and security affairs, would be substantially diminished.

One of the important strengths of APEC is its inclusion of China, Taiwan and Hong Kong. It was accomplished by at least superficially de-politicizing the organization (members are "economies"). Having a summit meeting will politicize APEC and create a controversial element in it that heretofore has been avoided.

As a suggestion, we might demonstrate our strong commitment to APEC, and provide a basis for our President's appearance at the meeting in Seattle, by dispatching a high-profile presidential emissary to each APEC capital before the meeting. This should include both Beijing and Taipei. We have already established that APEC matters are not linked to political or "official" status (Taiwan officials have joined APEC functions in the State Department; officials of both PRC and Taiwan have attended APEC functions in each other's territory).

At the APEC meeting in Seattle, the U.S. insisted on an APEC leaders meeting be included annually. The purpose in this case was that a platform was needed for the American president to make a speech which for the first time would explain the importance East Asia (and therefore APEC) was to the Clinton

Administration. The price was pressing Taiwan's acquiescence that though Taiwan was a full member of APEC, Taiwan's president would not be invited, as requested by China. The Taiwan president was permitted to send an envoy to represent him.

In his case, the Taiwan Minister of Economics was to take part in the APEC meetings, and the Chairman of the Council for Economic and Planning Development was, like the Hong Kong member, to attend the leaders meeting. The Chinese president following the meeting at a press conference, strongly charged that Taiwan should not be allowed to participate in APEC. The Taiwan Minister of Economic Affairs immediately opened a press conference of his own and just as strongly criticized the one China policy. I was sent to Taipei soon after to as the President if Taiwan was repudiating the one china policy. The President said he was not.

In our relations with Taiwan, trade issues, and APEC membership was pursued, but the attitude toward an increasingly noisy and therefore annoying Taiwan was seen as a problem, not an opportunity to encourage the democratic revolution that was taking place there. I spent much effort trying to explain to the new team the implications for our relationship of this transformation, and to argue (mostly unsuccessfully) for recognizing this in the ongoing policy review that was resurrected from the previous team.

I sent briefing reports to Winston Lord soon after he was named the new Assistant Secretary of State for East Asia. I explained AIT, its functions and what the Washington office did. Then outlined the changes that had taken place in Taiwan and how they were affecting the conduct of the relationship: how a growing economic interchange with the PRC had the potential for both improving and complicating cross-strait relations; and how the political relationship was lagging far behind. I pointed to the fact that Taiwan had become an international class economy but barred from international participation, how democratization was making the leadership more legitimate, and the impact of the public debate on national identity was having on both our relationships as well as cross straits relations.

I then also explained three areas that needed addressing: international participation; arms sales; and contacts between U.S. and Taiwan. I also briefed him on the four objectives Lee, Teng-bui had for his tenure as President: democratize political institutions that will survive the long term; upgrade and strengthen the economy; win international recognition; and establish a system of peaceful coexistence with the Mainland until the issue between them can be resolved.

In the first trip to Taiwan this year:

I found a Taiwan struggling with many problems. But in most cases, they are the problems that come from progress, not failure.

In domestic politics, Taiwan today is occupied with resolving problems in defining the powers of political institutions that have already been reformed, not in resisting the lifting of constraints on fundamental human rights of the people.

It is coping with problems of meeting the international standards expected of it, and upgrading the economy and the quality of life of its people, not in a struggle to provide only their basic human needs as in a developing economy.

It is searching for initiatives in further improving its relationship with the PRC, not in confronting it with enmity. It is looking for ways of how best to contribute to the international community, not in receiving aid from it.

The relationship, too, has its share of problems. As Taiwan's priorities reflect its changed circumstances, so do ours. The changes around us mean we now live in a more competitive and interdependent world. But, we have a long and successful record of coping with problems. The relationship is too important for both of us, and therefore I see no reason why we will not continue to do so. Perhaps we need only to guard against the natural inclination to take each other for granted, and we will have to work all the harder.

In this most recent trip to Taiwan, I met with President Lee Teng-hui, the head of the five Yuans (including Premier Lien Chan and the "Speaker" of the Legislature), the leaders of both major political parties, businessmen, academics, and about one-third of the legislators, including most of the chairmen of ten LY committees. The legislative elections in December brought on a new cabinet, and an assertive, more nationalistic but still unorganized legislature. The pace of change is breathtaking, so rapid that ground rules, regulations, and implementing laws are lagging far behind the needs of what is actually happening on the ground.

The new premier exudes confidence and pragmatism, but the new members of his cabinet seem more loyal than competent. He is already demonstrating that this new, Taiwanese-led government will not carry some of the old, anticommunist, Chinese-styled baggage of the past, (for example, Lien openly espouses dual recognition, and does not shun the use of the title "Taiwan"). With changes in the President's office, the cabinet, and the ruling party organization, what personalities will now stand out as the movers and shakers of this new administration is still not clear.

The Legislative Yuan, very assertive, is still very unorganized, and who the leading personalities will be there, too, is still to be determined. The institution is reaching, with considerable success, for co-equal status with the Executive Yuan (the cabinet). In this struggle, the rules of engagement are not established, bringing governance almost to a stalemate—at least for the time being. Stalemate does not mean inactivity, however. Debating bills in committee, responding to the demands of their constituencies, questioning the cabinet in biweekly interpellations, the atmosphere is frenetic and fiercely competitive—and often irresponsible.

The KMT, also, seems in disarray. The small, mainly mainlander and vocal New KMT Alliance (NKA) faction continues to seriously undermine the party, not only by acerbating the mainlander-Taiwanese problem, but by the continuous accusations of party corruption and weakness. The electorate seems to be looking for change, and unless the KMT improves its image rather quickly, there is a real possibility the opposition Democratic Progressive Party (DPP) will be able to claim it is the majority party after the year-end local elections.

The Presidential Office, now very much on top of the political heap, seems to be at the same time, a shell. Lee loyalists are in command almost everywhere, in the KMT, in the security apparatus, in the Executive Yuan, and even in the Legislative Yuan. But the Presidential Office staff structure is even weaker than previously.

The U.S. relationship, still critical to them, and still taking up much time and effort to keep healthy, is nonetheless not on the top of Taiwan's agenda. The PRC and Japan are more important issues: the PRC because it still prevents Taiwan from breaking out of its isolation; and Japan because of its serious trade surplus.

There seems to be a better appreciation of Taiwan's problems in entering international organizations. GATT is demonstrating that membership gets Taiwan more than just "face," it brings difficult political problems as well. Taiwan also better realizes that PRC opposition has some international bite that somehow must be overcome. Domestic political pressures, however, demand that the government be seen pushing for membership in international organizations. They will continue to press us, knowing our response will be generally negative, because for one thing we can then be blamed for their inability to win acceptance.

In the economy, aside from the crisis of the moment—our IPR issue with them—the main areas of focus are reinstituting the coordinating role of the Council for Economic Planning and Development (CEPD) among the economic ministries, encouraging domestic investment, putting the six-year development plan in a more realistic time frame, making an immediate impact on the people (with year-end elections in mind) by increasing social welfare programs and environmental projects. The nuclear power project, despite the desperate need for it, faces very difficult political problems which may again delay progress. Finally, how to manage the growing trade and investment relationship with the mainland continues to frustrate the leadership.

The biggest problem facing all elements of the executive branch, is the uncertainty of how to deal with the highly politically charged and increasingly powerful Legislative Yuan. This is especially true of the Ministry of Defense. Not only is the LY (with only a few exceptions) unsophisticated in dealing with matters of international affairs, it has an unhealthy disregard for the sensitivity of national security matters. MND on the other hand, seems incapable of dealing with the LY. The result is the low profile, very restricted U.S.-Taiwan military procurement program has become a political football.

In addition to the year-end local elections, where present indications are that the DPP may make a strong showing, the 14th KMT Party Congress takes place in late summer. It will see the final battle of the mainlander conservatives. Lee Teng-hui may finally get control of the Party, but the cost in terms of party unity may be substantial. The President's own "affirmative action program," originally Taiwanization, is now meant to reassure mainlanders they are welcome to participate in the political process even though it will be under new management. (A majority of the cabinet, for instance, is mainlander.) A major political battleground is the struggle between the newly reformed political institutions over power sharing. The Legislative Yuan, now a rabble of 161 individuals, will likely soon begin to jell into factions and become more coherent in conducting its affairs.

The President, with political reform objectives advancing irreversibly, and with mainland policy now firmly in his bands, will focus increasing attention on this after fundamental problem. Circumstances are pressing Taiwan to do so in any event. The changeover of Hong Kong in 1997 will be important, especially if it goes badly and inspires more support for the independence advocates. The unregulated and growing economic relationship with the PRC threatens to adversely affect both Taiwan's economy and its political options with the PRC. But probably more important to the President and certainly more immediate than either of these two in taking initiatives with mainland policy is the state of the KMT.

The political system on the island is essentially now democratic. The majority Taiwanese direct its destiny. Present trends do not favor the KMT, however, but almost by default do favor the opposition DPP. The DPP is identified in the public mind as a Taiwanese party, its ultimate objective of independence now clothed in what is clearly a more attractive one-China, one-Taiwan slogan. The KMT by contrast, is having difficulty scrubbing its "foreign" (i.e. mainlander) image despite its Taiwanese majority, and remains burdened with the unpopular "one-China" slogan.

To save the power of the KMT (with its unmatched resources and organization), the government is looking to establish an acceptable (to the majority) alternative expression to describe its objective for the relationship with the PRC. The leading option seems to be to maintain a vague obeisance to the concept of an ultimately unified China that will satisfy the PRC but not draw undue attention internally, while seeking a two separate political entities result. This would give Taiwan equality in dealing with the PRC, and international recognition, both politically indispensable, while putting off what is clearly not feasible for some time—a final settlement of the sovereignty issue. Such schemes as a regional security system to which both would join, overcoming the need for the PRC to publicly eschew use of force will be suggested. Pointing out to the PRC that KMT failure will bring on a DPP government is another. Economic benefits to the PRC will doubtlessly also be offered.

Like the past, Taiwan may continue to press publicly for this option despite PRC opposition. Over time, it might gain some acceptance among some elements on the mainland, and some in the international community. But of more immediate importance is the benefit this will give to the image of the KMT. Pursuing a separate (Taiwanese) political entity can do much for that purpose while the party's money and organization are brought to bear to maintain its hold on power.

The question is whether movement of any kind, for any kind of political accommodation with the PRC, can be possible but glacial, and therefore too late to save the KMT. Taiwan can move in that direction only in a very open, deliberate but very circumspect way. The now absolutely essential consensus on this matter will be extremely difficult to attain. All sides of the political spectrum will be mutually suspicious, wary of any unannounced contact, and unable to prevent irresponsible actions or statements by individuals seeking notoriety. The guiding principles for dealing with the PRC as set forth by the new Secretary General of the Straits Exchange Foundation (SEE), (i.e. (a) the security of Taiwan; (b) the welfare of the people on Taiwan; (c) the protection of Taiwan's economic interests on the mainland; (d) the views of the opposition; and (e) the concerns of the "older generation") only partially reveal the delicate and difficult considerations that must be taken into account.

The even more pertinent question is whether the PRC sees any advantage in accommodating Taiwan. And in the intense and sensitive struggle that will be taking place on Taiwan on this issue, as usual, all sides of the debate will be trying to pull the U.S. into it—on their side, of course.

A major obstacle to an IPR settlement with Taiwan at this time is the Legislative Yuan (LY). Frustration with Taiwan over the IPR issue over so long a time, and the behavior of the LY in the past, lower our tolerance level in addressing the present predicament. Nonetheless, we should, as objectively as possible under the circumstances, view the present political state-of-play on Taiwan before making any decision on IPR.

The LY elected this last December is not the same LY of 1989, or even of last year. It is still, internally, unorganized, but it has established itself as a powerful institution on par with the Executive Yuan (EY), or cabinet. Its members are fiercely competitive with each other as well as with the cabinet. The cabinet and its bureaucracy are frittend—almost terrified in some cases—of how to cope with this new and for them dangerous phenomenon. There are still few ground rules, and alliances between individual members of the LY as well as among the still-forming factions that continuously change.

At this formative stage, there seems no visible movers and shakers in the LY that stand out, though factions will likely begin to jell rater in this first session. When that happens, it will be a blessing and provide the beginning of a means to deal with this very obstreperous body. There are two areas of concern during this teething period of the LY: their unfamiliarity with international practice on trade matters (impacting on the PR issue); and their disregard for the islands delicate security situation. Both concerns will presumably need some addressing when and as they establish their rules of...

Over the last two years, I have developed contacts with a broad number of LY members, the leadership of the LY, and faction leaders along a broad political spectrum, including both ruling party members and the opposition. On my recent trip I arranged to meet with about a third of the members, including almost all the chairmen of the various committees, the Speaker hosted a dinner, and a whole pro-Lee Teng-hui faction showed up for a breakfast meeting. Though we discussed many issues, the focus was on the IPR crisis.

My pitch was that we had no wish to interfere in the current differences over power sharing between the EY and the LY. As a foreign trading partner, however, we could only deal with one entity on the other side of the negotiating table, but we were being asked to deal with two. The reservations put on the copyright agreement in effect destroyed the agreement. That we still had many problems with enforcement—or the lack of it—but the legal problems offered no room for compromise. In general, their comments centered around the unfairness of what, we were demanding, and the need for more time. (Their comments on the floor of the LY were much more severe, more nationalistic, more critical of us and of the weakness of the Taiwan negotiators.)

I got little reaction from my personal suggestion that they accept what had been negotiated in good faith in the past, and establish new rules within their government for future negotiations with trade partners. It was also clear that this new, more assertive LY was looking at the IPR problem as a new one that needed time to resolve. Most did acknowledge that for us it was hardly new (after fifteen years of effort, I said, I would be embarrassed to ask for more time).

The most difficult problem for the EY is the public posture taken by the LY members. The EY is apparently prepared to give much on the enforcement problems, but is unable to move the LY on the legal ones, it is a new world for cabinet officers (who are subject to twice-weekly day-long interpellations on the floor of the LY), and they are clearly on the defensive. Vincent Siew. in his private conversation with us, said he was at a loss as to how to deal with the situation. His idea to whittle down the eight reservations to one or two and offer the latter as a face-saver to the LY was admittedly not very original but what else was there to do.

Judging from the first elements of the EY and LY on this issue following our conversation. even Vincent Siew's idea made no headway. Clearly, we ourselves cannot enter this internal and very fundamental fray. We can also not be seen dampening the democratization process which we strongly support. Anything we do might be seen as interference by this much more nationalistic LY, and the result could seriously damage our influence on other important elements of the relationship.

We have set the clock ticking with our April deadline. It is exerting the desired pressure on the Taiwanese, and we should keep the pressure on. But come the April deadline and they have not resolved their very fundamental internal problems, then what? Lowering sanctions on this very emotional atmosphere should be given very careful thought. It would badly hurt Taiwan's new administration, and greatly help its opposition. It could even cause our special relationship with Taiwan to sour badly. Given its delicate position in the western Pacific, are we prepared for that? During the campaign, President Clinton described three overriding objectives for our foreign policy: use our foreign policy (A) to strengthen our economy; (B) to strengthen our national security; and (C) to promote the spread of democracy which enhances both our security and our economy. U.S.-Taiwan relations can play an important role in furthering these objectives.

A major constraint in the past has been a prevalent perception that our relationship with Taiwan is more a burden to our larger interest with the PRC than an opportunity to further our own interests. Maintaining a good relationship with the PRC and Taiwan simultaneously is not a zero sum game, as the past decade has shown. In my judgment it is possible to pursue our broad objectives in our relationship with Taiwan more vigorously without detriment to the process of strengthening our relations with the PRC.

Taiwan's presence and influence in the Pacific Rim is growing. Already it is one of the top foreign investors in the ASEAN countries, number one in Vietnam, and a growing investor in the PRC. It is the world's 14th largest trader, has one of the worlds largest foreign exchange reserves, and one of the highest per capita incomes in Asia. It has, very importantly, a broad network of overseas Chinese in Asia whose relationship with Taiwan offers more opportunity than threat to the countries there compared to their relationship with the PRC.

With us, too, Taiwan has taken on more economic importance. It is our 6th largest trading partner. There is increasing Taiwan investment in the U.S., and it is one of the largest buyers of our Treasury Certificates. One third of the increase in our exports to the Pacific Rim last year went to Taiwan. It has the world's largest infrastructure program in its six-year economic development plan; offering our companies significant export opportunities.

The rapid pace of political reform has transformed Taiwan into very nearly a full democracy. A society based on a Chinese culture has, for the first time in 5,000 years of history, developed a system that permits orderly succession; free, open, periodic elections; open media; respect for human rights; political institutions that provide checks and balances on political power; puts laws above individuals; and holds public figures accountable for their actions. This impressive political progress, like its economic progress, already had significant impact on both Southeast Asian countries and China.

In the security area, for years our military sales program to Taiwan has successfully contributed to our interest in stability in the area. Until last year, no significant military sales were made to Taiwan from countries who do not share this interest in stability. With our initial tacit acceptance, however, French military sales took place last year. It is still possible to limit this diversification of military procurement by Taiwan, and regain our ability to significantly influence any threat to stability in the Strait.

If we see Taiwan as an entity we can work with in furthering our objectives in China and other countries in Asia, there are current issues of interest to us both that we could address. Taiwan's participation in multilateral agencies in...

At the same time we will have to come to grips with the increasingly difficult problem of our self-imposed constraints on dealing with Taiwan. They are based on our perception of what the PRC's perception is with regard to what constitutes "official" conduct. It seems to me we can establish the standards we believe necessary in our own interests, and publicly state they do not constitute a change in the unofficial status of our relationship with Taiwan. The original constraints were intended to be necessary for on the short term. Taiwan has been de facto independent for over forty years. Its de jure status has yet to be settled, and that settlement is likely to take years if not generations. Our interests need not be similarly constrained waiting for that long-term event.

The newly empowered Legislative Yuan is beginning to exert considerable influence on Taiwan's national agenda. This includes the military budget. It will come under increasing pressure as domestic priorities become more subject to legislative action. It is already taking place. Pressures to significantly expand our military sales program, therefore, are likely to diminish. Nonetheless, as in our guidelines on conduct, we should make our military guidelines ("the bucket") flexible enough to provide us with a full range of options in handling our security interests in that area.

We can strengthen the influence of Taiwan's democratization by encouraging a parliamentary association in the Pacific area. Taiwan's Legislative Yuan, with the power of the purse and oversight, and a new generation of political leaders in its membership, sets an important example. Their activism will assure Taiwan's democracy gets ample notice.

Perhaps more meaningful than any other change would be the realization on our part that the political leadership on Taiwan no longer works in the atmosphere of the past. The implications of democratization on the island in terms of our relationship, and the Taiwan-PRC relationship, are profound. An understanding of it can do much to strengthen the relationship and democracy there; the lack of understanding by us, given our enormous influence or the island, could cause unintended instability.

In the following Taiwan Trip Report of December 1993, Lee Teng-hui's grass roots campaigning swung the recent elections to the KMT from an anticipated poor showing. The ruling KMT now, finally, belongs to him. It will remain a fractious party, but the party needs Lee more than he needs the party. The result brought with it a much stronger perception by the electorate that the KMT is now a Taiwanese party, a claim previously made only by the opposition DPP. It also must have sent a signal to the leaders in Beijing that any hope of any significant mainlander role in Taiwan's political system is now dead. The only viable political leader on Taiwan today, who can publicly espouse unification, and remain a viable political leader, is Lee Teng-hui.

And he will have constraints. The ferment within the KMT will continue, but now largely caused by the jockeying for power between political institutions including the presidency. Factions will be open to deals, including with the opposition party, which may remain weak in leadership and lacking in policy direction, but growing in numbers (41 percent in the last election). Lee Teng-hui's actions with regard to the PRC and foreign policy generally, will continue to be largely reactive to domestic political considerations under these circumstances.

The National Assembly meets in late April, and it is widely expected that they will amend the constitution to permit the direct popular election of the president. The KMT understandably wants to speed up the election to take advantage of their present momentum, but realistically, it will be early in 1995 at least before that is possible. The consensus, even within the ruling party, stops there, however, The 458 members of the NA, all elected and many still paying off their campaign expenses, are likely to exact some price for this—probably in a way that strengthens their objective of sharing legislative authority with the LY. The timing of the provincial governor's election is also contentious. On this latter point, perhaps not this time, but certainly soon, the provincial and special municipality level of government will be eliminated. That combined constituency, for all practical purposes, is the same as the Presidents.

Cables from AIT/T have reported conversations of significance with leaders in Taiwan during my two-week trip there. Individuals or groups with whom held discussions are listed in the attachment. The purpose of this report is to give my impressions of events and the trends that seem to be developing as I see them.

The pace of change remains very rapid. As a measure of this pace, two and a half years ago Washington resident (and Taiwan dissident) Mark Chen was being denied a visa to return to Taiwan. Since then he became a member of the Legislative Yuan, resigned and became the elected magistrate of Tainan County. Even in the nine months since my last trip, there has been a degree of change in the domestic political scene that has implications for our relations, the Taiwan-PRC relationship, and our commercial opportunities.

Lee Teng-hui's grass roots campaigning swung the recent elections to the KMT's favor from an anticipated poor showing. The ruling KMT now, finally, belongs to him. It will remain a fractious party, but the party needs Lee more than Lee needs the party. The result brought with it a much stronger perception by the electorate that the KMT is now a Taiwanese party, a claim previously made only by the opposition DPP. It also must have sent a signal to the leaders in Beijing that any hope of any significant mainlander role in Taiwan's political system is now dead. The only viable political reader on Taiwan today, who can publicly espouse unification, and remain a viable political leader, is Lee Teng-hui.

Even under these conditions he will have constraints. The ferment within the KMT will continue, but now largely caused by the jockeying for power between political institutions including the presidency rather than the conservative-mainstream struggle. Factions will be open to deals, including with the opposition party, which may remain weak in leadership and lacking in policy direction, but growing in numbers (41 percent in the last election). Lee Teng-hui's actions with regard to the PRC and foreign policy generally will continue to be largely reactive to domestic political considerations under these circumstances.

The National Assembly meets in late April, and it is widely expected that they will amend the constitution to permit the direct popular electron of the president. The KMT understandably wants to speed up the election to take advantage of their present momentum, but realistically, it will be early in 1995 at least before that is possible. The consensus, even within the ruling party, stops there, however. The 458 members of the NA, all elected and many still paying off their campaign expenses, are likely to exact some price for this—probably in a way that strengthens their objective of sharing legislative authority with the LY. The timing of the provincial governor's election is also contentious. On this latter point, perhaps not this time, but certainly soon, the provincial and special municipality revel of government will be eliminated. That combined constituency, for all practical purposes, is the same as the President's.

The economy is forecast to do well in 1994 (six percent growth rate according to CEPD Chairman Siew). Two broad problem areas were especially notable in my conversations: the political struggles necessary to upgrade the rules and regulations of Taiwan's trade regime, and the even more politically difficult but vitally essential task of transforming Taiwan into a regionally competitive operations center.

Almost all the current trade problems we have with Taiwan are a part of its need to meet international trade norms: IPR, tariffs, subsidies, environmentally sound trade rules, offsets and the lack of government procurement transparency, are examples. As Taiwan meets these standards, we will need to hone our own competitiveness, and Taiwan's political dependence on us will diminish as other countries' economic interests in Taiwan grow.

As the PRC's economy grows, and Hong Kong's role diminishes, competition for establishing regional centers—transportation, finance, high tech information—will intensify. Shanghai, Taiwan, Singapore, Bangkok will lay claim to some role. Vincent Siew wants to use this fact to force reforms on Taiwan's economy. He has a long way to go. I am skeptical that this can be done in time to win even a piece of the regional center pie, but this effort will be his top priority.

They are well aware that the biggest obstacle to becoming a regional center is their policy toward dealing with the PRC. That element of this policy is already under debate. At the same time, I sensed somewhat less enthusiasm among businessmen for doing business with the mainland. Vietnam and (after NAFTA) Mexico is claiming much attention at this time. Big business, especially bankers, seem to be even more skeptical after the recent change in economic policy in the PRC. A small group of big bank chairmen (Bank of Taiwan, CIBC, Chang Hwa and China Trust) agreed that the PRC takeover of Hong Kong would result in a plunge in the value of Hong Kong's currency.

Some ten months later, I was asked to comment on a draft of the Taiwan policy paper. There were many comments, but I will here paraphrase some items of political significance only.
Observations on Draft Policy Paper:

1. The broad thrust of this paper indicates little change in our policies toward Taiwan will be possible relative to the fundamental changes that

have occurred there. At the same time, we have openly and often deterred requests from the Taiwan authorities on the basis that a policy review was under way. This has led to expectations which we will have to deal with as the policy is implemented.

2. The paper lays out the complexities of the Taiwan relationship very well. The setting written in the initial pages places a framework of constraints that is based on PRC policies and potential reactions. Given the importance of the PRC relationship, these constraints must be taken into account. To not do so could lead to the unstable situations we are trying to avoid. My observation is that the paper does not balance this important factor with the potential for instability on the Taiwan side—also a situation we are trying to avoid.

   For example, if the thrust of the paper (given the dearth of any good options) is toward status quo, is this possible under conditions where fundamental changes are taking place on both sides, and on the Taiwan side through democratic processes? It seems to me our focus should be to continue encouraging contacts between the two sides to keep the PRC from resorting to the use of force; and to relieve some of the pressure for independence on the Taiwan side by working to reduce their isolation. Enforced status quo may only bottle up pressures on Taiwan which could ultimately result in instability.

3. The important effects on the Taiwan body politic of their high revel of trips abroad does much to drive Taiwan's mainland and international organization policies. There are a million visits a year to the mainland (with negligible numbers not returning) and as much as three times that number traveling elsewhere. One can argue that this is an important factor in the tendency of the Taiwanese toward separation of some kind and efforts for breaking out of their international isolation. If so, then is this an area where we might be able to help reduce pressures for separation, at the least risk of destabilizing the area? While the PRC will doubtless object strenuously to symbolic changes (i.e. name, or membership in some international bodies) it would do much to relieve pressures from the broad Taiwan electorate. Whether Taiwan officials get to visit in offices are equally important symbolisms, but impact on leadership only, not on the broad electorate, and do little to relieve domestic pressures.

   In the economic relationship. the paper seems to indicate that "NET," a "natural economic territory" exists and will grow stronger. There are considerable differences over that assumption, among both academics and businessmen. It seems to me that this can be seen as causing more problems than profit, whether the "NET" concept succeeds or fails. It will be nearly impossible for this amorphous entity to be disciplined into accepting international standards and rules if it succeeds, or it will create enormous political instability if it fails. Our rationale for encouraging the NET concept is that it could, at long last, bring China into the modern era. But we have no clear idea what we do if it either succeeds or fails.

4. Some options suggest broadening direct access for senior Taiwan authorities to senior economic officers throughout our government. This is desirable for many reasons. On the other hand, it should be understood that direct contacts on official matters will inevitably mean direct correspondence, which inevitably will become public and raise PRC concerns. With regard to senior State economic officers, we should consider the objective. In AIT-hosted meetings the U.S. side is chaired by the most senior USG officer. Permitting direct contact with State economic officials does not automatically put them in charge of an issue chairing bilateral meetings is more likely to do so. Our experience is that senior State economic officers of sufficiently high level to chair meetings seldom have time to perform this function. Permitting direct contact in this case risks repercussions but does not necessarily put State in charge of economic issues.

In Re-evaluating Policy, Presumably We Would Want to Have <u>Certain Fundamental Objectives:</u>

A. Retain the most successful elements of present policy, i.e. insistence on a peaceful solution to the bicoastal issue by the two sides themselves.
B. Put the relationship on a longer-term footing by loosening the self-imposed constraints on a more normal liaison with Taiwan.
C. In some form have Taiwan included in the international community so that it could be subject to the same constraints and rules we all observe.
D. Expand our flexibility in supplying military equipment and strengthening the processes in our military relationship to retain our influence in the security area.

Some More Ideas Regarding Taiwan Policy:

A. Pursue—perhaps in an OECD-type forum—some form of an acceptable separate entity for Taiwan in international organizations by focusing on areas such as finance, environment, and science, where it is clearly in the international community's interest and where political status can more easily be finessed.

B. In the military relationship, do away with self-imposed constraints. Many are counterproductive. The bucket system, for example, has become so complex—and meaningless in terms of its purpose—that it should be abolished: The use of hybrids in supplying equipment (presumably to reduce PRC reaction) invites price gouging and public criticism in Taiwan, results in our more technology than would normally be the case, and not reduce the impact on our PRC relations.

C. While maintaining an 'unofficial" overall relationship, move in phases to "normalize" the conduct of the relationship in a way that does not unnecessarily arouse PRC reaction or violate the requirements of the TRA. Two possible actions that come to mind for the immediate future:

1. Permit calls by CCNAA and Taiwan visitors on USG officials, at all levels, in their offices with the exception of State and White House.

2. Permit visits to Taiwan, under an orderly clearance process, by all levels of USG officials except for national security agencies.

International Organizations:

Taiwan has become the 13th largest trading economy in the world. It is a major producer of both high tech and pollution-creating goods and an important source of capital. There is a clear need for Taiwan not only to participate it establishing standards, but in regulating them. International organizations that do this in finance, in trade, in environment, in transnational issues such as narcotics, police, terrorism, etc., in humanitarian efforts, and in regulatory bodies, all could benefit from Taiwan's participation. So could the U.S. The only obstacle to Taiwan's participation is the PRC.

One policy issue, therefore, is how best to pursue what is clearly in our interest to do: support Taiwan's participation in international organizations. Loosening of the rules of engagement carries with it risks on the Washington side, given our own political system and the impressive capabilities of the Taiwan representatives. At the same time, with the new open environment in Taiwan, we have a need to expand contacts and conduct much strengthened public affairs activities. t.

Over the last two years, I have developed contacts with a broad number of LY members, the leadership of the LY, and faction leaders along a broad political spectrum, including both ruling party members and the opposition. On my recent trip I arranged to meet with about a third of the members, incidents almost all the chairmen of the various committees, the Speaker hosted a dinner, and a whole pro-Lee Teng-hui faction showed up for a breakfast meeting. Though we discussed many issues, the focus was on the IPR crisis.

The changing realities indicate that there are still really only two options for Taiwan's future: accommodation with or without a long-term objective of unification, or independence. The critical element was and remains, developments in the PRC. The very best outcome—continued economic growth with reasonably controllable political development in the PRC—might bring some kind of longer-term accommodation between the two sides. Independence pressures would remain, but the unification objective would probably be retained, in a clearly long-term framework, but probably with a decreasing degree of enthusiasm. Taiwan will continue to reach for a separate, equal political status within this framework.

Serious economic competition, or political convulsions on the mainland, on the other hand, would probably create enormous pressure for independence. Whichever of the two scenarios develop, democratization assures that whatever is done will not be a decision made by fiat on geopolitical grounds only, but through consensus developed by elected leaders.

In Re-evaluating Policy, Presumably We Would Want to Have <u>Certain Fundamental Objectives</u>:

- Retain the mast successful elements of present policy, i.e. insistence on a peaceful solution to the bicoastal issue by the two sides themselves.
- Put the relationship on a longer-term footing by loosening the self-imposed constraints on a more normal liaison with Taiwan.
- In some form have Taiwan included in the international community so that it could be subject to the same constraints and rules we all observe.
- And in international organizations, expand our flexibility in supplying military equipment and strengthening the processes in our military relationship to retain our influence in the security area.

Some More Ideas Regarding Taiwan Policy:

A. Pursue—perhaps in an OECD-type forum—some form of an acceptable separate entity for Taiwan in international organizations by focusing on areas such as finance, environment, and science, where it is clearly in the international community's interest and where political status can more easily be finessed.

B. In the military relationship, do away with self-imposed constraints. Many are counterproductive. The bucket system, for example, has become so complex—and meaningless in terms of its purpose—that it should be abolished: The use of hybrids in supplying equipment (presumably to reduce PRC reaction) invites price gouging and public criticism in Taiwan, results in our more technology than would normally be the case, and not reduce the impact on our PRC relations.

C. While maintaining an 'unofficial" overall relationship, move in phases to "normalize" the conduct of the relationship in a way that does not unnecessarily arouse PRC reaction or violate the requirements of the TRA. Two possible actions that come to mind for the immediate future:

  1. Permit calls by CCNAA and Taiwan visitors on USG officials, at all levels, in their offices with the exception of State and White House.
  2. Permit visits to Taiwan, under an orderly clearance process, by all levels of USG officials except for national security agencies.

Taiwan has become the 13th largest trading economy in the world. It is a major producer of both high tech and pollution-creating goods and an important source of capital There is a clear need for Taiwan not only to participate in establishing standards, but in regulating them. International organizations that do this in financial trade, in environment, in trade, in environment, in transnational issues such as narcotics, police, terrorism, etc., in humanitarian efforts, and in regulatory bodies, all could benefit from Taiwan's participation. So could the U.S. The only obstacle to Taiwan's participation is the PRC.

One policy issue, therefore, is how best to pursue what is clearly in our interest to do: support Taiwan's participation in international organizations.

Contacts Between the U.S. and Taiwan:

As the relationship, especially in the economic and technical areas, continues to expand, contacts across a much wider spectrum, and in much greater depth, are necessary. Many, perhaps most, of the rules of engagement are not specifically, only implicitly suggested in the TRA or the communiqués. They are based on our perceptions, or on our perceptions of the PRC views, on what constitutes an element of officiality. Over the years there have been changes, usually brought about by sheer necessity, but sometimes by the frustrations of dealing with the inherent inefficiencies of the rules of engagement. Some changes can be made by fiat, some require legislation.

Loosening of the rules of engagement carries with it risks on the Washington side, given our own political system and the impressive capabilities of the Taiwan representatives. At the same time, with the new open environment in Taiwan, we have a need to expand contacts and conduct much strengthened public affairs activists. A review of present guidelines is needed to properly measure the extent of the problems involved in any potential adjustments to present policy.

CHAPTER ELEVEN
American Institute in Taiwan 1994

This section is written from the perspective of the time.

The pace of change continues very rapidly, As a measure of this pace, two and a half years before Washington resident (and Taiwan dissident) Mark Chen was being denied a visa to return to Taiwan. Since then he became a member of the Legislative Yuan, resigned and became the elected magistrate of Tainan County. Even in the nine months since my last December trip, there has been a degree of change in the domestic political scene that has implications for our relations, the Taiwan-PRC relationship, and our commercial opportunities.

Lee Teng-hui's grass roots campaigning swung the recent elections to the KMT's favor from an anticipated poor showing. The ruling KMT now, finally, belongs to him. It will remain a fractious party, but the party needs Lee more than Lee needs the party. The result brought with it a much stronger perception by the electorate that the KMT is now a Taiwanese party, a claim previously made only by the opposition DPP. It also must have sent a signal to the leaders in Beijing that any hope of any significant mainlander role in Taiwan's political system is now dead. The only viable political reader on Taiwan today, who can publicly espouse unification, and remain a viable political leader, is Lee Teng-hui.

Even under these conditions he will have constraints. The ferment within the KMT will continue, but now largely caused by the jockeying for power between political institutions including the presidency rather than the conservative-mainstream struggle. Factions will be open to deals, including with the opposition party, which may remain weak in leadership and lacking in policy direction, but growing in numbers (41 percent in the last election). Lee Teng-hui's actions with regard to the PRC and foreign policy generally will continue to be largely reactive to domestic political considerations under these circumstances.

The National Assembly meets in late April, and it is widely expected that they will amend the constitution to permit the direct popular electron of the president. The KMT understandably wants to speed up the election to take advantage of their present momentum, but realistically, it will be early in 1995 at least before that is possible. The consensus, even within the ruling party, stops there, however. The 458 members of the NA, all elected and many still paying off their campaign expenses, are likely to exact some price for this—probably in a way that strengthens their objective of sharing legislative authority with the LY. The timing of the provincial governor's election is also contentious. On this latter point, perhaps not this time, but certainly soon, the provincial and special municipality revel of government will be eliminated. That combined constituency, for all practical purposes, is the same as the President's.

The economy is forecast to do well in 1994 (six percent growth rate according to CEPD Chairman Siew). Two broad problem areas were especially notable in my conversations: the political struggles necessary to upgrade the rules and regulations of Taiwan's trade regime, and the even more politically difficult but vitally essential task of transforming Taiwan into a regionally competitive operations center.

Almost all the current trade problems we have with Taiwan are a part of its need to meet international trade norms: IPR, tariffs, subsidies, environmentally sound trade rules, offsets and the lack of government procurement transparency, are examples. As Taiwan meets these standards, we will need to hone our own competitiveness, and Taiwan's political dependence on us will diminish as other countries' economic interests in Taiwan grow.

As the PRC's economy grows, and Hong Kong's role diminishes, competition for establishing regional centers—transportation, finance, high tech information—will intensify. Shanghai, Taiwan, Singapore, Bangkok will lay claim to some role. Vincent Siew wants to use this fact to force reforms on Taiwan's economy. He has a long way to go. I am skeptical that this can be done in time to win even a piece of the regional center pie, but this effort will be his top priority.

They are well aware that the biggest obstacle to becoming a regional center is their policy toward dealing with the PRC. That element of this policy is already under debate. At the same time, I sensed somewhat less enthusiasm among businessmen for doing business with the mainland. Vietnam and (after NAFTA) Mexico is claiming much attention at this time. Big business, especially bankers, seem to be even more skeptical after the recent change in economic policy in the PRC. A small group of big bank chairmen (Bank of Taiwan, CIBC, Chang Hwa and China Trust) agreed that the PRC takeover of Hong Kong would result in a plunge in the value of Hong Kong's currency.

Another round of SEF-ARATS talks began while I was in Taipei. It, like others since the Koo-Wang talks in Singapore, ended with little result, despite the pressures resulting from the frequent hijackings. It appears both sides want to keep the door open but are not willing to compromise on the fundamental issue of sovereignty, or jurisdiction. The Mainland Affairs Council, like its PRC counter-part, presents an image of conciliation, but keeps expectations low publicly, and is unbending on that important issue. Even if the talks are expanded to include the three links, it seems to me, the jurisdiction issue will be the sticking point. Domestic politics will restrict any give on that point.

Beginning with its UN initiative, in fact, a concerted effort to establish Tai-wan as a separate political entity is being made across the whole spectrum of its foreign relations. At home, the UN initiative was politically popular; the "two sovereign states" statement even more so. Whatever policy exists for mainland af-fairs seems to be driven by the need to balance a gradual reduction of economic constraints on dealing with the PRC, while gradually strengthening Taiwan's po-litical separateness.

I continue to believe that while the U.S. relationship remains critical for Tai-wan, their priority is to generate greater support from the international com-munity, especially in Europe and Japan. We have no fundamental differences over trade (the leadership accepts that they must eventually meet international standards); it will take them some time to digest the military hardware they have already acquired from us.

Taiwan's Key Foreign Policy Concerns

Taiwan's two key foreign policy goals are winning at least de facto recogni-tion from China of Taiwan's status as a "political entity" and persuading the in-ternational community to treat Taiwan as a sovereign nation:

- Last November, its Economic Minister announced that Taiwan would adopt a "two Chinas" policy while maintaining its commitment to even-tual unification.

- Taiwan argues its status as a major trader and market economy qualify it to participate in international organizations such as the UN and GATT. Beijing claims that, as the sole government of China, it represents Taiwan in the UN and has said Taiwan can have GATT status only after China joins.

- Taiwan has courted foreign investment to increase the international stake in stability in the Taiwan Strait. Through investments and aid, Taipei has attempted to build a web of influence overseas to substitute for its rack of formal diplomatic ties.

There is a strong domestic component to this recent foreign policy shift. Taiwan President Li Teng-hui has embarked on ambitious political reforms aimed at transforming the ruling Kuomintang (KTP) from a party dominated by mainlanders to a majority party supported by the Taiwanese. The new strategy is aimed at striking a balance between independence advocates in the opposition Democratic Progressive Party (DPP) as well as in his own KMT and hardline proponents of unification.

Taiwan's abandonment of its "one China" framework and its aggressive campaign to improve its international standing could complicate Washington-Beijing-Taipei relations. Beijing opposes any "two China" policy and warns that a declaration of Taiwan de jure independence could provoke a military conflict, according to the Chinese press.

Transit of Taiwan President Lee, Teng-hui
Honolulu, May 4, 1994

The Setting

The delegation did not disembark, but the President almost immediately invited me to come aboard. In the specially configured SP747, we sat at a table with President Lee, Foreign Minister Fred Chien (as interpreter), Presidential spokesman Raymond Tai (as note taker), Representative Ding Mou-shih, and myself. We talked for about one hour, ending when the refueling of the aircraft was completed.

The Meeting

The President retained his usual politeness, interjecting several times during the hour his apologies that we had travelled so far only to hear his complaints. But he clearly had things he wanted to say, and was anxious to get them said in the minimum amount of time he had set for them to stay on the ground.

He recalled our last meeting (which followed Economic Minister P. K. Chiang's statement in Seattle that Taiwan was a separate sovereign state) in which I had asked him if that statement represented a change in Taiwan's one-China policy. He had replied that it did not, but now, it seems he said, it was the U.S. that had changed its policy toward Taiwan.

Over the past year, the relationship had deteriorated. In the democratic political environment of Taiwan, he said, it has been very difficult managing the reaction of the people. The traditional relationship between us had always been good, and he hoped it would be maintained to our mutual (he emphasized mutual) benefit.

I began to talk about this particularly sensitive period in our relations with the PRC. He politely interrupted and began a monologue that lasted the rest of the hour. (A routine under normal circumstances, but this time he felt under time constraints.) He said that the U.S. was trying to placate "that large country" at the expense of its smaller friends, not only by "slapping us in the face" with the Pelly sanctions, but to the extreme position (tai guofen) we had taken over this transit stop. As a result he had decided not to set foot on American soil under such conditions. He brought up a problem they had had with AIT/Taipei over passports and visas. It was not clear exactly what the problem was, but whatever delays occurred in this process, and the fact that visas in any event are not required for transit, the Taiwan side considered it to be a form of harassment meant to discourage them from using the U.S. for transit..(

The President then said he was deeply worried about the long-term trend in the relationship. He cited the problems over Premier Lien Chan's transit some months ago, the singling out of Taiwan under the Pelly amendment, and this present transit. He again reiterated how difficult this trend was to manage with the people. They had not used Canada for this transit because of the difficulty there would be in trying to explain this choice to the people. (Fred translated this as "We did not choose to use Canada...," but that is not what the President said.)

He then expressed his wish that I pass on to Washington his thoughts on Taiwan's relationship with the mainland. He referred to a recent speech where he had said that sovereignty rested in the hands of the people not the government. He hoped this would have some influence in Beijing. He spoke of his efforts to move Taiwan toward democracy and a peaceful dialogue with the mainland. I told President Lee that I had first heard about his use of the expression about sovereignty from Rev. Kao (a well-known advocate of Taiwan independence) on his recent trip to Washington. The President said Rev. Kao's purpose was a narrow one focused on Taiwan only, while his was meant for all of China.

Since the Koo-Wang talks a year ago, he went on, there had been numerous meetings, and each had been stymied by the problem of sovereignty no matter what the issue. So he has begun to play up the theme that sovereignty rests with the people, and that this is true on the mainland as well. After the constitutional amendments were resolved in the weeks ahead (he estimated that 80 percent of the people supported the direct election of the president), he would begin in earnest to play up the issue of sovereignty.

The President also wanted me to pass on to Washington an example of why he advises that one should not be nice in dealing with the leaders in Beijing. He recalled the "Qiandao" incident of March 31 (24 Taiwan tourists were killed in a gruesome incident on a lake boat in eastern China). Beijing had immediately labeled it an accident, but Taiwan's intelligence sources had informed him almost immediately that both the PLA and local security personnel were involved. On April 6 he had passed a message to "top levels" in Beijing (he specifically mentioned Jiang Ze-min, though Fred did not in his translation), that they should understand the seriousness of the incident. On April 9 he had made a speech to 300 village chiefs in Ilan in which he said that sovereignty rested in the hands of the people, not governments, that the mainland leaders should not cover up the Qiandao incident, and that in doing so they were acting like bandits. He said the speech had been well received, and that it was supported in the international media specifically referring to an editorial in the *Wall Street Journal.*

On April 19 Beijing admitted the tragedy was not an accident. According to the President, Taiwan was aware that there were differences within the Beijing leadership on how to respond to the incident. He mentioned that among other things, a study of official statements as well as an article in the literary section of the *People's Daily* indicated differences existed. Furthermore, Chang, Yung-fa (Chairman of the Evergreen conglomerate) had been told in Beijing that Lee's statement calling Beijing leaders bandits had been too strong. Chang's interlocutor admitted, however, that the incident had been badly handled by Beijing and that they did not want communications disrupted over the incident. The President said he was relating this information to demonstrate his point that firmness was the best way to deal with Beijing.

When he was told the refueling operation was completed, the President insisted on meeting with the wives (who were with Mrs. Lee) for a few minutes. Then he saw me to the entrance, joking that he did not want to get too close as he might enter America.

Comment

Having met with him several times, both privately in his home and formally, his long dialogue was not unusual. He was, also as usual, disingenuous; used strong language; unkind to those who disagree with him; and anxious to be considered a national leader. Yet, on this occasion, he appeared more emotional, with more sorrow than anger in my view, and frustrated, but never to the point where he lost his innate politeness. Fred behaved, since the Presidents English is passable, and Raymond Tai, taking copious notes had plenty of grist for the Taiwan media mill in Nicaragua.

Taiwan—Changes Ahead

According to an interview he gave, President Lee Teng-hui will continue to lead Taiwan on a full-court press offensive for international recognition. His Foreign Minister is now scouting opportunities in Europe. The President is expected to soon rearrange some cabinet members to prepare for the next election, but several sources indicate he will move to "Taiwanize" the Foreign Office as well. Representative to the U.S. Ding, Mou-shih, is likely to be replaced in the process. The more immediate impact on us can well be an acceptance by President Lee of a "private" invitation to the U.S., and a new style, more aggressive representative of today's Taiwan in Washington.

A number of factors—Beijing's growing strength; the concern over the growing private sector economic involvement there by Taiwan businesses; the Taiwan leadership's perception that U.S. support is weakening; and probably most important, the need to keep control of this enormously popular issue from the opposition party—has led President Lee Teng-hui to spearhead an aggressive drive for international recognition. His "Vacation Diplomacy" meetings in Southeast

Asia, and his official visits to Central America and South Africa, are apparently only the beginning. Foreign Minister Fred Chien is in Europe scouting out future forays for his President.

The first direct election of the leaders of three major political subdivisions on Taiwan, probably early next year, are important for the ruling party. President Lee is expected to reshuffle the cabinet to prepare for them, and to provide positions for those not chosen as candidates for the party. It is expected that Lee will, at the same time, restructure the National Security Council in the President's Office, giving it far more influence on international and mainland policies, and placing the present Foreign Minister at its head. He will also make substantial changes in the Foreign Office, as he did previously with the military, making it more 'Taiwanese" and more reflective of his policies.

Taiwan's representative in Washington, Ding, Mou-shih, under some criticism at home for Taiwan being singled out by us for Pelly Amendment sanctions and the Lee transit episode in Honolulu, apparently recently offered his resignation to both the President and the Premier. It was rejected but several sources indicate he will be replaced, probably in conjunction with anticipated changes in the Foreign Office. One intriguing rumor has Eugene Chien replacing him. Chien is a young Taiwanese, former legislator and former head of Taiwan's Environmental Protection Agency. He is now Taiwan's representative to London. Even if it is not him, it is likely to be someone like him—confident, aggressive, and much more representative of today's Taiwan than anything we have seen in Washington in the past.

In Taiwan, it seems to me we are in a quandary about the public debate in Taiwan on the issue of national identity. In the coming national level elections, this issue will inevitably be on the top of the political agenda. We seem concerned on the one hand that the debate could excite passions in Taiwan and in the PRC leading to military or other threatening actions. On the other hand, any effort to constrain the liberties of free speech and open debate by the Taiwan electorate runs against our own deeply felt principles and could in fact also trigger passions that destabilized rather than stabilized the atmosphere of the upcoming elections.

I believe it may be possible to have the debate continue without constraining liberties but to move it away from the risk of igniting external reaction. If we, the PRC, and the Taiwan electorate were satisfied that the debate was over a distant objective, it would not raise the passions and concerns that a more immediate and possibly destabilizing action would do.

In Taiwan today, the very vigorous democratic political system that has been rather quickly put in place, includes three viable political parties. The KMT, the ruling party that emigrated to Taiwan from China ruled authoritatively for over

40 years, has itself been transformed into a largely indigenous, more democratic party that maintains as an ultimate objective unification with China but a recognized separate political status in the meantime.

The DPP is an indigenous party that has grown rapidly, outpacing its ability to organize itself, and which has as an ultimate objective the independence of Taiwan. The third party is appropriately called the New Party, represents a constituency that is mainly a conservative minority mainlander community that places unification with mainland China at a higher priority. It has remained barely viable but can play the role of a spoiler or a coalition partner.

Election contests on Taiwan are highly competitive and very intense. Naturally, oversimplified but pointed slogans are often employed to either hurt an opponent or help the speaker or his/her party. One slogan that has gained currency is that a victory by the main opposition would be tantamount to a declaration of independence. The slogan was quickly picked up by the PRC, who threatens military action if such a victory takes place. Many in the U.S. accept the slogan at its face value.

If the slogan gains broad acceptance, it could have serious consequences. The PRC would have a marker which could gain international acceptance, and intervention, therefore, could be seen as justified. Many in the U.S., accepting the marker, could then also accept the notion that a victory of the DPP could be considered a provocation against which our commitments under the TRA would not apply. In the meantime, to avoid a PRC reaction, it would be argued that the fundamental right to determine ones future should not apply to the people of Taiwan.

The scenario above would not only be unfortunate, it would be based on an erroneous analysis. The first strawman is the "declaration of independence." It is unlikely that the DPP or any other group of consequence would "declare independence." Taiwan for all practical purposes has been independent de facto for many years. What it has lacked is international acceptance, or de jure recognition of this fact. "Declaring" independence would be meaningless unless it leads to recognition. The only question would be, does that statement in fact bring this about, and that seems unlikely at this time.

The second strawman is that the DPP would in fact declare independence on taking power. It is clear that the DPP has increasingly been positioning its independence stance, like the unification stance of the KMT, as a longer-term objective.

In the 1993 election for village, town and city mayor and councils, and country magistrates and councils, the DPP did not do well, both because of lack of organization and because of their image in advocating a potentially destabilizing objective. In 1994, in the elections for Taipei and Kaohsiung mayors and the provincial governor, the independence objective even more clearly affected the DPP's support, with DPP candidates trying to reduce their exposure on this issue. A recent post-election meeting of the DPP, according to press reports, indicated that there was considerable sentiment in the party that the independence plank in their platform should be modified.

In a democracy, people often vote simply for change. In Taiwan it is reasonable to expect that one day, an opposition party will come to power. It may or may not be the DPP, but it will in any event, in Taiwan's largely middle class society, mean that that party would have to capture the broad middle ground of the political spectrum. In some ways, this is already the case, with KMT and the DPP both sharing important elements of their policies. For example,
Both parties openly:

    a. support the same economic system
    b. place the same importance on a strong military
    c. understand the need for U.S. Support
    d. desire economic relations with the PRC
    e. understand the political need for stability
    f. agree that the Taiwan-PRC issue should be internationalized
    g. share the policy of entering international organizations
    h. share the efforts to upgrade foreign relationships

Both parties also at least tacitly understand that:

    a. their respective ultimate objectives are distant
    b. that each one's objectives domestically are political liabilities (status quo being the wish of the large majority)
    c. that some understanding, some day with the PRC will be necessary

The democratic process in Taiwan seems to be self-adjusting in a way that retains the legitimate rights of the electorate to decide their own future, but steers away from actions that threaten stability. External pressure to constrain freedom of choice on Taiwan would be undemocratic unsuccessful, and unnecessary. The actions of the DPP mayor immediately following his election indicates that whichever party gains power, the need for broad support and the demands of governance will temper the pursuit of long-term objectives.

That said, it does not mean that the present state of play is satisfactory. In addition to the enormous organizational work needed to strengthen its viability, the DPP should make much more clear, for the electorate on Taiwan as well as for the international community, its blueprint for the future. If it accepts that independence is a long-term objective, what does it see in the meantime? Will the same "separate political entity" envisaged by the KMT as an interim status also be acceptable to the DPP?

There are several advantages to having this more clearly defined, for the DPP as well as for Taiwan, and for stability in the region generally. Both major parties would maintain their respective ultimate objective, i.e. unification for one, and independence for the other. But an election would much more surely under these circumstances not threaten a drastic change and/or a potential conflagration. Stability could more easily be maintained and any political contest could put greater focus on the ability to govern better, under the present system, with gradualist policies to move toward whatever objective.

It seems to me the alternative is to continue present trends, with one side of the political spectrum advocating gradualism toward an objective that relatively few really want, at least at the present time, but is far into the future. The other side advocating an ultimate solution in a much less clear timeframe, and a very hazy path that will lead the people there. In a period of relative calm, that scenario could likely be maintained in an atmosphere of stability. But if trends are to be heeded, for other reasons, the latter side might one day gain power. Taiwan, and those in the international community that support its democracy, would have only the analysis of trends to defend its actions against any precipitate move from outside Taiwan, not the open commitment by both parties that assures everyone there would be no precipitate action from within.

The November 3 Trip to Taiwan

I began my trip in the south, spending time in Kaohsiung, Tainan city and county, and Wufeng, a provincial capital. The remainder of my stay was in Taipei, meeting with a variety of leaders, and ending on my last day with the Premier and a two-hour dinner next to President. On this trip, I felt the distinction between attitudes in the north and south much more clearly, mainly due to the campaign for the first direct election of the provincial governor. Campaign activities for this year's elections were intense despite the early date (elections are on Dec. 3). Foreign issues, including those with us, were not much in evidence in the media. "National" issues such as identity, security, the PRC, did come to play—surprising in a local election—though the personality, character, record and outrageous promises of the candidates, which are more normal, dominated the news.

As is usually the case in this early stage of Taiwan's democracy, the election will set very important precedents. The election of Taipei's mayor may lead to the highest office held by the opposition. Though there is some concern he has concern he has peaked too soon, and they keep a wary eye for a possible deal between the KMT and the breakaway New Party, the candidate's lead seems to be holding. The New Party candidate is deliberately provoking the introduction of the identity issue to weaken his DPP opponent. The KMT incumbent is not popular and given little chance. In Kaohsiung, on the other hand, the KMT incumbent is almost unassailable. His record has much to do with that, but his DPP opponent (no creditable New Party candidate there) has been hurt by party infighting and changed social values (he has admitted to at least one mistress).

The governor's race is the most profoundly important. The opposition does not have a strong candidate. The KMT incumbent is strongly supported by the President and the Party leadership has been whipped into intense activity to support him throughout the island. But James Soong, the KMT candidate, is a mainlander, and one whose previous positions required him to implement discriminatory laws resented by Taiwanese. In addition, the Party's traditional structure at the grass roots, i.e. relying on faction leaders to bring in the local votes, was crippled after last year's local elections by the vigorous prosecution of widespread fraud and vote buying.

Soong, well ahead in the polls, may also have peaked too soon. The question is can he hold on. He may, despite the strong impression I have that Taiwanese south of Taipei strongly favor a Taiwanese to be the first directly elected governor of Taiwan. The stakes for Taiwan's future are high. If Soong succeeds young mainlanders will have a future in the new Taiwan. If he fails, Taiwan may have a serious problem.

The President, and his party's Secretary General, are already planning the next election. At present, the LY elections are due in December 1995, the first direct election of the President, and electing the next National Assembly is due in early 1996. The KMT Leadership wants to combine them, to save money, curtail the endless political campaigning, and to take advantage of Lee's coattails. If "national" issues such as identity and PRC relations are apparent in this year's campaign, they will be overwhelming in the next one.

In talking with businessmen north and south, big and small, it seems to me Taiwan's "Mainland Fever" has subsided. Government has encouraged that trend, and its leadership's changing of private sector focus from the PRC to Southeast Asia seems to be working. Businessmen generally were complaining that taxes—legal and illicit—and the difficulties of repatriating funds to repay loans in Taiwan—were suffocating any incentive to do business there. The Economic Ministries continue to press for liberalization of economic relations with the PRC, such as direct shipping, but they are getting little support politically. The President himself, citing figures on the extent of Taiwan's economic relationship with the PRC commented that they "should show us more respect." The Chien

Dao boat burning incident early this year has had a lasting effect. Business still wants to do business, but popular sentiment remains deeply affected. The next talks in November in Nanjing, according to the MAC Chairman, are expected to bring an initialing of the agreements verbally agreed to in the last meeting (in Taipei), but not much more. At this pace, we are unlikely to see any significant advances in this relationship unless one side or the other makes a concession—and neither, given their respective political situation, is likely to do so.

Throughout the island, there seemed to be a skittishness about security. The talk about PRC plans for a military attack on Taiwan in 1995 is a topic of conversation throughout the island, and at all levels, with much speculation on the author's purpose in writing it. Questions were asked about Perry's visit to the PRC in the LY, and substantial media play about my visit, probably encouraged by the authorities, was meant in part, it seems to me, as a form of reassurance of America's continuing interest. The interest in the hook, by everyone from taxi drivers to scholars, was largely due to the prediction being based on geomancy and fortune tellers, but to some degree also influenced by Taiwan's greater international assertiveness and PRC objections. The President told me he was aware who was generating this skittishness, and his widely publicized inspection of Taiwan's military exercises and visits to military schools seemed to be ac effort to address this problem. The political leadership's problems are not in believing or disbelieving the book, but in avoiding domestic political problems in disputing it publicly.

All of these matters, as well as a much publicized stock market scandal, have not dampened economic activity. Growth is projected at 6.2 percent. Even better news for us is that our trade deficit with Taiwan is continuing to drop—one projection had it at a new low of $6 billion. The promotion of Taiwan as a regional center has not moved very far, however. A lot of talking, planning, and critiques of the planning, but not much action. Much depends on the Taiwan-PRC relationship, in any event, and that is not moving very much either.

During the year, I put in many of my thoughts on issues that might be of use in completing the Policy Review taking Place.

A positive factor in a DPP victory in the Taipei elections is that it will give the opposition a chance to rule in a constituency that is large, important and difficult, but without significance in terms of national status. They need the experience badly as I detected little progress in their capability to govern. A Soong (KMT) victory as Governor would also be a positive development in reducing ethnic (or provincial) tensions. That, too, is badly needed, as the temptations and likelihood that these tensions will be deliberately generated in the heat of the coming national political contests will be a serious problem.

Lee Teng-hui, it seems to me, is increasingly making decisions on his own, using personal advisors, not the bureaucracy, to provide advice. But his advisors are not an established "kitchen cabinet," or a clique. Individuals among them change from time to time. He continues to have a remarkable "feel" for Taiwan and its people, however, and I suspect this comes from the web of contacts he maintains.

It is even more clear now that Ministry of Foreign Affairs (MOFA) is out of the decision-making circuit. Announcement on Taiwan's APEC ministerial delegation was made without MOFA's participation. Louis Tzen's new assignment in the National Security Council (NSC) was announced before MOFA knew. And despite Fred Chien's colorful (and self-serving) description of how Ben Lu was selected as Taiwan's representative to the U.S., that decision was apparently made not only without MOFA but with the purpose of establishing direct Presidential control over that relationship. The Cassidy contract, in fact, could be further evidence of this.

Taiwan's NSC, which Ding Mou-shih now heads, is still not a vehicle for staffing Presidential decisions. Many think it would be too politically difficult for it ever to be such an agency. Ding now has two deputies—Louis Tzen who joins him in December, and Lin Bih-jaw the head of Taiwan's premier think-tank. An impressive group seems to be taking shape, but ultimately, the NSC will become whatever the President wants it to be. One has to hope that eventually a structured decision-making process for the Presidents office will begin to take shape.

In the meantime, Lee Teng-hui remains a very popular president (a mainlander and one of Taiwan's top businessmen said he is more popular than later-day CCK). He also is a one-man decision maker for government and party, and probably the only one that can keep the very divergent leaders of government, political parties, and interest groups working well enough to avoid destabilizing actions. It is ironic that an authoritarian system that inevitably has an "indispensable" leader has transformed itself into a democracy, but continues to have another "indispensable" leader, which democracy by definition is not supposed to have. One has to wonder, if something happens to him, or he chooses not to run, whether Taiwan could continue its peaceful, stable progress in both economic and political terms.

And there will need to be a strong leader at the top for at least the short term. Other leaders in the ruling party would have to have time to gather support, and the opposition is far from ready to govern. With the next election after this one, the question of Taiwan's identity will doubtless not only have to be addressed, but politics may well force a resolution. At this point, there is clearly no consensus in Taiwan on this issue, even with a strong president trying to develop one.

Some Ideas on the Taiwan Strait

We have always hoped that in time, the two sides of the Taiwan Straits could resolve the issue of the relationship between them peacefully. Though initially both sides considered this a highly emotional, deeply felt matter, the unfinished business of a bitter civil war on the mainland of China, time has begun to change that attitude. On the PRC side there has been some change, hut nothing fundamental, and it is unlikely any major changes take place as long as the old civil war warriors remain in power. On the Taiwan side, however, with democratization, and the Taiwanization of the political leadership, the issue is now seen as a practical problem, not an emotional issue. Presumably, with time, the PRC will similarly change its views. It will remain much more complex for the PRC, however, but practical solutions are more likely to be at least considered.

As the PRC economy grew, the authorities must have surmised that time would resolve the Strait's issue, and in their favor. There appears to be less confidence now that that strategy will prevail. It was based on an assumption that Taiwan could do little to avoid the inevitable. The Taiwan authorities, on the other hand, coming to the same conclusions, and driven by the pressures of an open political system, have decided to use their strengths more aggressively to establish a status of political equality pending a future resolution of the issue.

It has been conventional wisdom that unification now is unacceptable to Taiwan, that independence now is unacceptable to the PRC, and that the status quo, therefore, was preferred by all concerned. In my judgment, Taiwan no longer considers this latter option feasible, for two reasons: they need to establish their political equality while their economy remains relatively strong; and they must be responsive to domestic political pressures or risk losing power. Thus President Lee's message in Honolulu—"Taiwan has always been expected to behave and not make trouble, but we can no longer do that."

President Lee's objective is a Taiwan run by the people on Taiwan, determining their own future. The issue in the Straits, for him, is a practical problem and therefore he opposes independence as impractical. To the old guard in Beijing, that attitude amounts to heresy. But realistically, if one surveys the options of political leadership on Taiwan, Lee and his attitude is the best the PRC can expect. Any other option, from the PRC standpoint, would be worse, except, of course, if instability on Taiwan and a "justified" intervention were more desirable for them.

So where does the U.S. fit in? It goes without saying that we should not get directly involved— more precisely, the U.S. <u>could</u> not do so given the PRC attitude. Yet both sides of the Straits are edging toward a new equilibrium in their relationship with each other. I do not believe that either side has any clearer idea than we, just where this movement will lead. At best, it seems to me, the most we can do is influence events by our own actions, in pursuit of our own interests.

One of our objectives with regard to Taiwan is to work to avoid confrontation between the PRC and Taiwan without ourselves becoming directly involved in doing so. We want to avoid the PRC becoming sufficiently agitated over an issue to damage our relationship with them; we don't want domestic instability on Taiwan as this may trigger confrontation; and we don't want our own domestic politics upsetting this delicate balance.

On Taiwan the leadership's moves to stay ahead at domestic change in Taiwan have had to accelerate or risk losing power. They seek a new equilibrium internally as a democratic entity sufficiently nationalist to satisfy a very international oriented people, and yet avoid crossing an indistinct line that forces the PRC to react.

In my judgment, the outcome best suited to meet our objectives is for a Taiwan that is an active international player but remaining committed to future negotiations to establish their relationship with the PRC. Taiwan's participation in international organizations would come over the objections of the PRC, of course, but we would gain something in terms of our own interests.

Participation by Taiwan in international organizations benefits us. Taiwan should be subject to the same rules and standards as we, should be involved in enforcing the discipline these International Organizations (IOs) require, and should contribute financially to them. There are other benefits to this latter course: frustrations are building in Taiwan with regard to its international position. The ever-cautious political leadership has been steering a course to reduce pressures for independence by posturing and pressuring for international recognition to satisfy these pressures domestically, while declaring its commitment to a future one-China policy with respect to the concerns of the PRC. PRC policies are anything but helpful in this regard (the PRC's efforts opposing Taiwan in IO's gives one of the biggest boosts to those advocating independence). Having Taiwan in IO's would help relieve this pressure, which, ultimately is in our interest as well.

Furthermore, we will enhance our position much more strongly in the commercial area. When Taiwan accedes to the General Agreement on Tariffs and Trade (GATT), the Japanese competition for winning large projects will increase several fold. We are going to need every advantage we can get. Supporting some kind of participation in IO's for Taiwan will help, and we can do so gradually, over several years, thereby supporting the need to keep domestic pressures on Taiwan manageable, while trying to obtain a quid pro quo for each effort.

In my judgment, gestures such as name change, or office calls do not gain us much. MOFA is pleased because it gives their personnel face, but it will have little impact where it is needed—among the electorate on Taiwan. Under normal circumstances, this would be Taiwan's problem, not ours. But the alternative to supporting the present leadership on Taiwan is a bit dicey given the alternative. It seems to me that it is in our interest, at least for the time being, to support this leadership as best we can.

We have done this before—arms sales. The PRC strongly opposed this strategy (it still does), but it has helped to reduce tensions while the two sides work this out. A gradual move to support Taiwan in international organizations could provide Taiwan eventually with sufficient confidence, and buy sufficient time, to enhance eventual negotiations between them.

Our abiding interest has always been in stability in the region and this strategy strikes me as most likely to accommodate the change taking place while promoting the eventual resolution of this issue by the two sides themselves.

Some more thoughts on Taiwan

Last Friday's meeting generated some thoughts on how we might address the problems caused by Taiwan's more assertive and nationalist posture.

One expert had an idea that we informally let the PRC understand from time to time the difficult predicament in which the Administration finds itself with regard to Taiwan policy sounds good. The policy will be energetically defended but we can't wish away the reality.

On the other side of the Straits, even informally talking to the establishment can get us into difficulties. The issue of national identity is going to intensity in the next three weeks, and after a pause for breadth, next year in the run-up to the next elections.

The polls are showing that the KMT is holding a comfortable lead in Kaohsiung, holding the lead in the province, and gaining in Taipei (the DPP continues to hold the lead, but it appears to be slipping as the KMT mobilizes its resources there). If the KMT sweeps all three, tensions may let up for a bit, but I do not believe for very long, as the popular vote count could easily show a DPP plurality.

It seems to me that we cannot be against the democratic process, and that at some time in the future, an opposition party will win. Our own interests are not in who wins or even what they stand for, but in any results that create instability between the PRC and Taiwan. The pace and the pressures being generated in Taiwan for greater separatism are largely (but not entirely) created by the opposition. Some elements in Taiwan, and certainly the PRC, see a win by the opposition as tantamount to a declaration of independence, and therefore, instability.

I am personally still confident that the electorate in Taiwan knows where its interests lie (i.e. stability) and will vote accordingly. On that basis, I'd vote for non-interference. Admittedly, the dynamics of politics on Taiwan make continuing stability there dicey. If we feel compelled "to do something," it might be in talking informally with the opposition. The KMT would use any discussion of this kind for political gain; the opposition, in this case, would not want to.

We could avoid taking sides in a domestic struggle over a very fundamental issue, if we focus not on where the opposition wants to take Taiwan, but on public assurances that the pace and direction of change will be based on maintaining stability.

The opposition is unlikely to "Declare Independence" (the last two Chairmen have said as much). They don't have to, but they do have to get international recognition. The PRC says they will use military force if Taiwan declares independence, but are unlikely to do so. They have too many other options — less costly but effective enough to give Taiwan a serious problem.

As things stand now, however, it is not a formal declaration that will trigger all kinds of reaction, but just the coming to power of the opposition party. That's had because we should not be against a fundamental democratic right to vote the people's choice, what might be helpful, and more acceptable in our own political environment, is encouraging the opposition to forge a manifesto of its own, that would be published and stand as their party's commitment to the people of Taiwan.

We could even suggest some ideas that would, at least in our view, assure us, the PRC and the people of Taiwan, that a government led by the opposition would not result in chaos. The best result from our standpoint it seems to me is for the opposition to establish a principle that no matter what party governs, and whatever ultimate objective they would hope to see, no final status for Taiwan will be established without some kind of understanding between the two sides on their permanent relationship.

The PRC wouldn't like it, but they would then have no basis for intervention solely on the change of governing party, and the ultimate decision would still be well into the future. The task for the DPP leadership would be enormously difficult given their disunity, but it would in the long run enhance their prospects for power, and they know it.

There are times it's convenient to have a "private" entity do things that are a step away from being "official." I've written an article that could be either spoken at an appropriate occasion, a letter to an editor, or whatever, which while getting little play in the U.S., would be read in Taiwan.

It's a subject that would get some resonance in the KMT, but especially in DPP circles. It could, of course, be prefaced by saying this was my own view as an observer, etc. What do you think?

Frustrations are building in Taiwan with regard to its international position. The ever-cautious political leadership has been steering a course to reduce pressures for independence by posturing and pressuring for international recognition to satisfy these pressures domestically, while maintaining its One-China policy with respect to the concerns of the PRC. PRC policies are anything but helpful in this regard (the PRC's efforts opposing Taiwan in IO's gives one of the biggest boosts to those advocating independence). Having Taiwan in some IO's would help relieve this pressure, which, ultimately is in our interest as well.

Furthermore, we will enhance our position much more strongly in the commercial area. When Taiwan accedes to the GATT, the Japanese competition for winning large projects will increase several fold. We are going to need every advantage we can get. Supporting some kind of participation in some IO's for Taiwan will help, and we can do so gradually, over several years, thereby supporting the need to keep domestic pressures on Taiwan manageable, while trying to obtain a quid pro quo for each effort.

In my judgment, gestures such as name change, or office calls will not gain us much. MOFA will be pleased because it gives their personnel face, but it will have little impact where it is needed—among the electorate on Taiwan. Under normal circumstances, this would be Taiwan's problem, not ours. But the alternative to supporting the present leadership on Taiwan is a bit dicey given the alternative. It seems to me that it is in our interest, at least for the time being, to support this leadership as best we can.

In Re-evaluating Policy, Presumably We Would Want to Have Certain Fundamental Objectives:

A. Retain the most successful elements of present policy, i.e. insistence on a peaceful solution to the bicoastal issue by the two sides themselves.
B. Put the relationship on a longer-term footing by loosening the self-imposed constraints on a more normal liaison with Taiwan.
C. In some form have Taiwan included in the international community so that it could be subject to the same constraints and rules we all observe.
D. Expand our flexibility in supplying military equipment and strengthening the processes in our military relationship to retain our influence in the security area.

Some More Ideas Regarding Taiwan Policy:

A. Pursue—perhaps in an OECD-type forum—some form of an acceptable separate entity for Taiwan in international organizations by focusing on areas such as finance, environment, and science, where it is clearly in the international community's interest and where political status can more easily be finessed.

B. In the military relationship, do away with self-imposed constraints. Many are counterproductive. The bucket system, for example, has become so complex—and

C. meaningless in terms of its purpose—that it should be abolished. The use of hybrids in supplying equipment (presumably to reduce PRC reaction) invites price gouging and public criticism in Taiwan, results in our transferring more technology than would normally be the case, and does not reduce the impact on our PRC relations. Avoiding the use of ranks and titles seems inconsequential and in fact accomplishes nothing. It is an unnecessary irritant, however, and is largely ignored outside of government.

D. While maintaining an "unofficial" overall relationship, move in phases to "normalize" the conduct of the relationship in a way that does not unnecessarily arouse RPC reaction or violate the requirements of the TRA. Some possible actions:

1. Permit calls by CCNAA and Taiwan visitors on USG officials, at all levels, in their offices, with the exception of State and White House.

2. Permit visits to Taiwan, under an orderly clearance process, by all levels of USG officials except for national security agencies.

3. Gradually remove restrictions on the display of Taiwan's flag in non-official settings; permit expanded use of Twin Oaks; review other operational impediments consistent with our commitments.

Some Implementation of Policy Adjustments

Below are comments on the implementation draft and some potential trouble spots in those being contemplated.

1. The unofficial system in existence today has some problems and does require some adjustments. One of the problems even now is enforcement, but by and large it is manageable. The draft paper does not mention the very critical need for enforcement once the present system is opened to change. Absent a clear directive from the President to his cabinet officers and heads of agencies, that assigns State the clear authority to implement the adjusted policy, the unofficial system of the Taiwan relationship could and probably would become chaotic and risk collapse. I believe this requirement should be addressed immediately so the directive is issued concurrently with the signing of the review.

2. Another general comment on the draft is that the wording should be thoroughly scrubbed for controversial wording. This town is full of China experts, TRA experts, communiqué experts, etc. Several references to "we acknowledge that there is one China and Taiwan is part of it," for example, may warm the hearts of the PRC readers, which probably could use some warming when they hear the briefings, but could ignite unwanted public controversy in Washington, and would hit Taiwan pretty hard. (We acknowledge <u>China's position</u> that there is one China....) Similarly on page 11, the end of full paragraph 3, I suggest dropping the last two sentences. That wording would be incendiary in Taiwan and goes beyond our stated China policy.

3. Comments on potential trouble spots below assume that whatever we say in individual briefings, the adjustment across the board will become public.

4. Initiation of a sub-cabinet economic dialogue and of TIFA talks with Taiwan.

   I see no trouble with the initial announcement as long as we add that we will get in touch with them in the weeks ahead. Some turf problems and venue questions will have to be faced when actual planning begins, but immediate questions from the media should be easy to put off. Eventually an IWG task force may have to be formed to screen the many implementing decisions that will have to be made.

5. On a selected basis where it is clearly in U.S. interests to do so, we will support Taiwan's membership in organizations accepting non-states as members, and look for opportunities for Taiwan's voice to be heard in organizations of states, <u>in a way that is acceptable to the membership</u>. (underlined words mine)

   This will open up a host of questions, no matter how gently—or how confrontational—it is put. Initially, aside from handling PRC objections, we'd have to make clear to Taiwan an orderly, manageable process would have to be discussed, perhaps sometime after the first of the new year.

   In the meantime, we could develop our own internal policies on what organizations are desirable candidates, how to deal with Taiwan personnel, communications, etc., in this context, and how to keep Taiwan personnel from engaging in direct bilateral discussions under an IO cover.

6. Increase the level of USG visitors to Taiwan in economic and technical fields as the need arises; and where it is clearly in our interest to do so, also permit a visit by a cabinet member in the same fields.

   It should be possible to ward off initial questions on who, when, the definition of "economic and technical," etc. from Taiwan, the PRC, the media and the Congress. More difficult will be the pressures this will generate within the executive branch. Requests will be quick in coming, and an IWG Taiwan task force may have to be organized almost immediately to handle them.

7. Permit USG officials authorized to travel to Taiwan to meet Taiwan officials at any level in government offices.

   Since for all practical purposes this is already happening, the only question is whether this is worth stating, at least to the media. In any event, it should be easily manageable.

8. Permit somewhat longer transits for Taiwan's top leadership.

   This one is a hot potato. In my judgment the best solution is not to mention it to anyone. If asked (such as by the Congress), we say we will be as sympathetic as possible consistent with the nature of a transit. Anything more, it seems to me, will bring more questions from Congress, where this is an emotional subject; will let the media have a circus; and will give Taiwan a golden opportunity to push the envelope.

9. Office calls:

   Below has been extracted from previous comments on this subject. The underlying problem is how to enforce unofficiality if at least AIT is not present at meetings and not handling communications between USG and the Taiwan side.

Meetings with Taiwan in Washington

Meetings below office director level between CCNAA (AIT's Taiwan counterpart) personnel and USC offices are permitted. Below office director level meetings with visiting Taiwan authorities must now be arranged by AIT, but this might be worth reconsidering. In both cases this does not apply to State, NSC, White House. Any meetings above that level become policy decisions and AIT must provide cover in a neutral, i.e., non-government location.

Meetings outside of a U.S. government location between RSP/TC (State) and RSA/East Asia office director equivalent (DOD) have been taking place for several years. This is a policy decision, but AIT/N comment is only on the need to be kept informed (see below on the same problem regarding communicating with Taiwan). Aside from the obvious danger of CCNAA knowing more than AIT/W, and CCNAA efforts to deal directly with State through that channel, the example set for their agencies is delicate, and almost immediately undermines the discipline we are trying to keep. (Our experience is that other USG agencies, including in State, in varying degrees, resent the need for AIT cover.)

If a policy decision determines that office calls can he made by the Taiwan side at the senior levels (always excepting State, NSC and WH), EAP should be aware of the almost certain consequences. In addition to EAP not being briefed on these conversations by AIT/W, follow on communications between USG agencies and CCNAA will very quickly take on an official appearance (see below). While this would make the conduct of the relationship more "normal" and efficient, it would also present opportunities for the Taiwan side to undermine the fundamental difference in this relationship (i.e. its unofficial nature).

Communicating with Taiwan in Washington

As in (3) above, Bureau of East Asian Affairs (EAP) at the State Department is kept informed if AIT/W is the channel for communicating with the Taiwan side. With the special case of EAP itself, keeping AIT/W informed of AIT/T or EAP contacts with the Taiwan authorities, or instructions to do so, takes a special effort. It should be understood that CCNAA/W is informed immediately by MOFA, however. The system for notifying AIT/W of captioned cables is effective, for O-I and other communications less so.

For other elements of State, and other USG agencies, communicating outside of front channel cable with AIT/T, or with CCNAA directly would leave AIT/N and those responsible for Taiwan policy unaware of it, and the Taiwan side could quickly transform such activity into the appearance of officiality.

AIT/W experience is that EAP, as the "gatekeeper" of Taiwan policy, is watched by other USG agencies and they are quick to challenge us on the meetings/communications guidelines.

10. AIT Employees Access to MOFA
    I suggest we add: " ...if the Taiwan authorities so desire. However, it should be understood, the USG does not intend to reciprocate."

11. Name Change:
    Although I personally favor using the word Taiwan in the new name, if our position is that we do not want it, we should avoid being tagged with having rejected the word "Taiwan" in the new name. We use it in our titles, in our statements, in our laws, etc., so there is the problem of appearances. Secondly, there will be vocal objections in Taiwan over the absence of the word, but that is Taiwan's problem. Thirdly, however, we have our own politics to contend with, and though the number of potential critics on the Hill may not carry the day, it will add to the burden of the Taiwan relationship.

Of the different adjustments being considered for the conduct of our relations with Taiwan, only two activities of AIT/W are affected: U.S.-Taiwan contacts, and U.S.-Taiwan communications.

The overriding objective of the Taiwan authorities, since the establishment of the present unofficial relationship, has been to work toward an official one. A previous Vice Foreign Minister told a visiting Codel about two years ago, when asked, that Taiwan's ultimate objective was an official relationship with the U.S. It may happen one day, but as long as our purpose is to maintain at least a veneer of unofficiality, guidelines are necessary to assure this objective. If the suggestion for adjustments in our Taiwan policy now being considered materialize, the veneer of unofficiality will be getting very, very thin, indeed. To maintain that appearance and have a system that is easily understood and reasonably enforceable, we could require that AIT personnel accompany any CCNAA personnel or Taiwan visitor above the rank of division chief on their calls to Executive Branch officials. The communications directive should be the same as present guidelines.

The subject being discussed here is Taiwan and the prospects and strategies for its membership in the UN. For policy makers, this issue is addressed not only as an element of U.S. policy toward Taiwan, but in the context of a much larger mosaic of relationships in East Asia as well. Many of the papers I have seen, discuss this issue in that same broad context.

My brief is more narrowly focused on Taiwan; however, even in that more narrow view, Taiwan's recent efforts to seek membership in the UN is itself also only a part of a larger development—the peaceful revolution that has taken place in the political system of that island. Taiwan has grown in economic strength over a period of years. It became a significant player in international trade and in other areas of international interest some time ago. Why then is the question of membership in the foremost international organization only now being given this attention?

It is Taiwan's democratization. That is a more recent development, and it impacts on almost every activity, not just domestic politics, and definitely including its international status. The implications of Taiwan's democratization are only slowly being recognized. There needs to be much more public discussion, such as this one on the UN issue, on how all area of activity important to us are being affected. Regardless of the activity we focus on, domestic economics, domestic politics, security, international involvement, culture, PRC relations—all have been affected.

In the domestic economy, for example, there has been a clear shifting of economic priorities. The military budget has been reduced, large infrastructure projects stretched out, but pensions have been expanded and a national health care program passed into law. The priorities of the voters are clearly apparent.

It is in domestic politics, however, where a revolution has taken place. The political process has become open, competitive and far more complex. The number of issues under public debate has broadened to include not only its international status but its own government structure as well. Political leadership must now manage governance rather than simply rule.

Perhaps more pertinent to the subject you are discussing, this December the governor and the mayors of the two largest municipalities—Taipei and Kaohsiung—will be directly elected. In a little over a year the first directly elected President will be voted in. The legitimacy of the leadership thereafter—that it represents the will of the 21 million people on that island, can hardly be called into question.

Democracy has permitted the PRC to become another option for the people of Taiwan, but for profit or pleasure. This development has led to the opening of a line of communication between the two sides. But democracy also has brought the PRC into better focus by the people. The "it's a great place to visit (or do business in), but I wouldn't want to live there" mentality probably has strengthened the wish for a more clear, separate political identity.

These economic and political areas of interest are intertwined. They affect each other and no more so than in the wish for—and in their eyes—the need for international recognition. So we get to the point that it is not just domestic political jockeying that generates Taiwan's efforts to enter the UN and other international organizations.

Twenty percent of the people on Taiwan travel abroad each year. This very impressive fact, and the needs of Taiwan's international trade-led economy, have resulted in Taiwan's people being unusually internationally oriented. Its diplomatic isolation is very broadly and very deeply felt. Of course, the political parties jockey to harness this sentiment in their favor. But the issue is there, it was not generated by politics, and it is clearly non-partisan. Furthermore, the very questionable chances for success are hardly an incentive for any political party that tries to manage the issue.

In our relationships in that part of the world, economics has grown in relative importance. The rapid growth of the PRC economy, therefore, becomes an increasingly important factor for us as for Taiwan. We face a far different world now, and a far different East Asia, than that which existed when this special unofficial relationship began some 15 years ago.

As Taiwan's democracy matures, which we have always encouraged arid supported, it takes on a different character—more assertive and more nationalist. As the PRC modernizes, which we also have encouraged and supported, its rapidly expanding economy takes on more importance for us. To the degree that American policy can influence events there, and that remains substantial, U.S. policy has been successful. The commitments made to the PRC, and the TRA, which are the basis for the unofficial relationship with Taiwan, have served us well. We now have lower tensions, and stability has been maintained.

But with the increasing economic strength of the PRC, and the increasing political strength of Taiwan, our own influence diminishes relatively in trying to guide the course of events en both sides of the Straits.

Under this broad background, the administration recently decided that the fundamentals of our policy toward Taiwan would remain in place. With regard to international organizations, the U.S. government will continue not to support Taiwan's membership in the UN. It did state, however, that Taiwan does have a role to play in a number of transnational issues and Taiwan's voice should be heard by some international organizations confronting these issues. On a selective basis, therefore, the USG will look for opportunities for Taiwan's voice to be heard in such organizations.

To anticipate a question, there have been no discussions on which organizations or how the process of deciding will work. I believe it is logical to conclude that the decision will be or a case-by-case basis, and that there will be a process within government to arrive at a decision.

An Extra Paper

The Assistant Secretary invited comments on his paper to the Secretary regarding challenges in Asia. I'm assuming a comment from the sidelines would not be unwelcome even if it is necessarily focused on a narrow subject—our relations with Taiwan, and suggests a course not now being considered. I'm in no position to advise on how this should fit in with your broader concerns, but you may find it useful as the debate on challenges in Asia progresses.

One of our objectives with regard to Taiwan is to work to avoid confrontation between the PRC and Taiwan without ourselves becoming directly involved in doing so. We want to avoid the PRC becoming sufficiently agitated over an issue to damage our relationship; we don't want domestic instability on Taiwan as this may trigger confrontation; and we don't want our own domestic politics upsetting this delicate balance. The rapid pace of change out in that area, however, does not permit us the luxury of working only to maintain the status quo.

From the narrow perspective of Taiwan, we may not be keeping pace with change. In our commercial interests, for example, a visit to Taiwan by the Secretary of Commerce a year ago could have generated some concrete commercial advantage. I do not believe that would be the case today—at least not to the same degree. Another example is a suggestion, offered up by one participant at a meeting of Taiwanese leaders here in America, that Taiwan might accept being a "region" of China, was in fact offered up by Taiwan two years ago. The PRC rejected it, but today, if offered by the PRC, would probably be rejected Taiwan. Other examples are the replacement of a mainlander premier, or the direct election of the president, both of which, just two or three years ago, would have been unthinkable.

In my view, it is not that Taiwan's expectations for our relationship have risen faster than reality permits; it is that the leadership's moves to stay ahead of domestic chance in Taiwan have had to accelerate or risk losing power. They need to find a new equilibrium as a democratic entity that is sufficiently nationalist to satisfy a very international oriented people, and yet avoid crossing an indistinct line that forces the PRC to react.

Taipei and Beijing both put more or at least the same degree of importance on symbolic actions as they do on substantive ones. Taipei, for example, is seeking (A) a name change for CCNAA and (B) office calls. Should we grant either of these, it will be over the objections of the RPC—and we will not have gained much from it ourselves (in fact, the latter especially will complicate our lives).

Taiwan's participation in some—repeat some—international organizations would also come over the objections of the PRC, but we would gain something in terms of our own interests. Participation by Taiwan in environmental, economic, scientific, and transnational issue organizations benefits us. Taiwan should be subject to the same rules and standards as we, should be involved in enforcing the discipline these IO's require, and should contribute financially to them.

CHAPTER TWELVE
American Institute in Taiwan 1995

This section is written from the perspective of the time.

As Chairman of AIT, my time and effort in 1995 was heavily focused on three events: the visit by President Lee, Teng-hui to Cornell; the effort to complete an electronic financial management system for AIT, and the decision to replace me as Chairman.

In 1995, Lee, Teng-hui's political position was unchallenged. He had bested the conservatives in his party: those who had broken with the KMT (the New Party) had become a demonstration to those conservatives who had stayed in the KMT, on how fruitless it could be to challenge what was now Lee's Party. Those who had humiliated him two years before by thwarting his efforts to amend the constitution to permit the direct election of the president, had been crushed by his triumph in last year's National Assembly, amending the Constitution as he had wanted. Party members who wanted to be elected for office needed Lee's support, (though the loss in the Taipei race had been caused by a renegade KMT splitting the Party vote).

On the Taiwan domestic scene, in early 1995, the President made a formal and public apology to the families of the victims of the February 28, 1947 incident (a massacre of native Taiwanese by the recently installed mainlander regime). After returning from his visit, at the 14th Party Congress, Lee was nominated as the KMT candidate for the following year's presidential election, with Premier Lian Chan as his running mate. At year's end, the election for the third Legislative Yuan took place. The KMT won a majority of seats (45), but it was a slim victory. In the balloting within the legislature for the president of the Yuan, the KMT incumbent won over the DPP challenger by one vote. Obviously, during the life of legislature, continuous bargaining and bickering was going to be necessary to make even minimum progress.

On cross-Strait relations, in January, Jiang, Zemin made a relatively moderate proposal for negotiations. It received considerable international attention, but contained the usual unacceptable conditions, Lee's six-point response likewise was moderate but contained equally unacceptable conditions, so little progress was made.

Lee's position externally was different. Our tepid support for democratization on Taiwan caused by our concern about improving our PRC relationship, led to Lee, Teng-hui's conclusion that it was necessary to find ways to raise Taiwan's international profile. This further alienated the U.S. (and even more the PRC). Increasingly, Beijing's leaders and the Washington Administration both saw Lee as a troublemaker. Both saw him as a strong and popular leader—firmly establishing an irreversible democracy on Taiwan, which Beijing opposed and Washington found very inconvenient.

Early in the year, there was yet another effort to assign a political appointee to the AIT Chairman's position. There had been two other attempts since the beginning of the Clinton Administration. Each time I had been asked to write a brief on why this was not a good idea, which presumably was used by the State Department to fend off these attempts. This third one was apparently considered more serious, but the possibility of a visit to Cornell by Lee, Teng-hui occupied much of the attention of those with responsibilities for Taiwan relations. The strong public objection by the State Department to this visit gained so much attention that whatever the results, it would be seen as a major battle, and would generate a strong reaction from Beijing.

At the same time, Ding, Mou-shr was replaced as Taiwan's representative to the U.S. by Benjamin Lu. Lu was not a Foreign Ministry official, but had had several assignments abroad as an economic official in Taiwan representative offices. The year and a half or so that he held his position in Washington was a tumultuous time for anyone representing Taiwan in the U.S.

Assessing his short tenure, from my perspective, is not as simple as reports in both Washington and Taipei would have it. Within his own government, he came as an "outsider". He had little support from his own home office or his staff in Washington. Benjamin was not establishment, much less a foreign ministry official. He was a mainlander but one who was comfortable with, and had contacts with, not only the Taiwanese, but opposition Taiwanese. He had enormous energy, and used it to pursue the objectives of his President's objectives even though they did not have the support of the Foreign Ministry and most of its officials.

On the American side, he came at a time when the State Department, having dumped the Administration's be-tough-with-China policy of the first year, was very anxious to turn that around and saw Taiwan's more assertive efforts as inimical to U.S. interests. The objectives Benjamin was pursuing, therefore, clashed with those of the State Department.

At the same time, it would not be fair to say that all of his troubles emanated from MOFA in Taipei, or from the State Department in Washington. As jovial and as kind as he was, his major problem was his unfamiliarity with the culture and language of diplomacy. Bilateral communications, therefore, suffered badly. It could have been overcome, however, had he developed at least some of the staff to work with him. There were some who had sufficient professional discipline and would have provided the loyal support he needed. He would still have faced a rocky time, given the pressures that the Lee visit generated, but communications would have been better.

Many months later, when I had already left AIT, and on a visit to Taiwan, I was asked by some officials to talk to President Lee about Benjamin—he was, of course, being blamed by many as being the sole cause of the poor state of the bilateral relationship. I did talk to the President, but contrary to what many seem to believe, I did not mention Benjamin. I did talk about the very bad state of communications between the U.S. and Taiwan. They translated that into the message the others wanted.

What even those in attendance at the meeting did not know, was that President Lee, in a private conversation with me in Anchorage on his return from visiting Cornell, had asked me to help Benjamin better understand the relationship. Being on the other side, of course, I could not do very much. The President, who had appointed Benjamin, knew of the difficulties, but was skeptical that MOFA would be willing to carry out his wishes. I have always regretted the fact that Benjamin got caught up in such a difficult position. As a colleague in the U.S.-Taiwan relationship, he was personally a good friend.

Lee seems to be focusing on two objectives in the American relationship: separating the Taiwan relationship from our PRC relations, and looking to us to help strengthen their international status. With regard to Taiwan's PRC relations, he wants engagement with them on a broad front to demonstrate the advantages of dealing with Taiwan, while taking initiatives internationally that strengthen Taiwan's hand in future negotiations.

In early 1995, gaining and preparing for the visit of Lee, Teng-hui to Cornell occupied much of Benjamin's time, and ultimately generated what was a frustrating relationship with the State Department. The hiring by Taiwan of Cassidy Associates, a large PR/lobbying firm in Washington, received considerable media attention as the price was considered quite high—U.S.$1.5 million a year. I was visited by an associate of Lee, Teng-hui who wanted to know my impression of the Cassidy company. At that time I merely commented that lobbying was, in theory a least, a low-profile effort, whereas a public relations oriented firm was just the opposite—Cassidy seemed to be both. I wondered aloud if that was what Taiwan needed.

In fact, from casual discussions with government colleagues, the Cassidy reputation was not all that good with congressional staffers and White House/State Department people as well. The Cassidy people were considered too "pushy", and predictably managed to get credit in the media for almost anything that was supportive of Lee's visit to the U.S. The result was that among those who opposed the visit, it was easier to claim that the Cassidy people were "buying" the visit.

In fact the media attention and the Congressional action in support of the visit was indeed extraordinary. Strong support for the visit in editorials and articles in the major newspapers was persistent and doubtless put pressure on the government to issue a visa to President Lee. Even more telling was the 396 to 0 vote in the House, and a 97 to 1 vote in the Senate, in favor of granting the visa. The Administration, spearheaded by the State Department, despite these pressures, continued to be unwilling to compromise.

Some time later, at a meeting between some of the same policy officials, and visiting Taiwan officials who are among Taiwan's top American experts, there was some probing by the visitors on some form of compromise regarding the Lee visit, but nothing came of that as well. At that time our official position was to refuse granting a visa to President Lee. By then, even some working level officers involved in this issue in the State Department, were convinced that either a compromise arrangement, or capitulation on the visit, was inevitable.

At the same time, some more senior officers in the State Department were convinced that Taiwan was deliberately opposing the Administration in ways harmful to U.S. interests. These concerns were in many cases exaggerated or beyond the control of the Taiwan side, but at the same time were not completely baseless. The Taiwan side was trying to handle two conflicting objectives. The diplomatic professionals were working to limit damage to the relationship. Others, some doubtless directed and some, especially among the Chinese-American community, wanted to make this first visit by a president from Taiwan a major event. Given the politics of Taiwan, and the politics among the many Chinese or Taiwanese organizations in the U.S., it was easy to believe whatever one wanted to believe.

In a meeting with a policy level official at the State Department during this time, I suggested that a visit to his alma mater by President Lee was the option that could most easily be rationalized. Further, if the Taiwan side was willing, a continuation of his journey after the visit to Cornell to Central America (several countries there recognize the Republic of China), would permit us to describe the visit as an elongated transit through America. It would at east save some face in Beijing even if they protested. Nothing came of it, however.

Some time later, at a meeting between some of the same policy officials, and visiting Taiwan officials who are among Taiwan's top American experts, there was some probing by the visitors on some form of compromise regarding the Lee visit, but nothing came of that as well. At that time our official position was to refuse granting a visa to President Lee. By then, even some working level officers involved in this issue in the State Department, were convinced that either a compromise arrangement, or capitulation on the visit, was inevitable.

In the end, the White House finally focused on the dilemma the U.S. President was being given—damned if he granted the visa to Lee with the harm this might bring to the PRC relationship, or damned if he didn't—arousing widespread congressional and public outrage. Inevitably he took the former course. Those that opposed that decision insisted Taiwan, (through the Cassidy lobbyists) had "bought," the visa.

Credit should be given to the Cassidy effort, there is no doubt it had contributed in achieving the final result. But it is too often overstated. The principle involved had much to do with it. How many members of Congress would vote to deny Lee a visa? How many editorials would support denial? At a time we were granting visas to the "terrorist" Gerry Adams of Northern Ireland, and Arafat from Palestine—it would have been almost impossible not to permit Lee a visit. It seemed clear when all was said and done, that the White House was not pleased with the State Department over the way the Lee visit had played out, with consequences on where policy decisions on China and Taiwan would be made in the future.

When the decision was made to grant a visa to Lee, the Taiwan Representative was briefed. It was an uncomfortable meeting. The State Department emphasized that U.S. policy toward Taiwan had not changed: our relationship remained "unofficial"; the visit was private in nature; aside from events connected with the Cornell reunion, there would be no public events, no comments that would embarrass the U.S.; contact with the press was strictly limited to the alumni events; and there was a need to work closely and keep each other informed.

Essentially, the talking points were: the Administration no longer objects to President Lee making a private visit to the US for the purpose of attending the Cornell University alumni reunion. The Clinton Administration has great respect for President Lee and what hw has accomplished for Taiwan and he will be treated with the courtesy appropriate to an unofficial, private visit. The basic tenants of our important relationship with Taiwan are, as the Administration has stated, and held by previous Administrations of both parties since 1979, a private visit by Taiwan's top leaders would not be consistent with the unofficial nature of our relationship, as set out by the Taiwan Relations Act. This is not a fundamental change to nature of US relations with Taiwan. The US will continue to maintain unofficial economic and cultural relations with Taiwan. We should work together closely to avoid any problems which could cause difficulty for either side. It will be important that the private nature of the trip be made clear in all public comments and all travel and other arrangement should be consistent with a private visit. The purpose of the visit is to attend the alumni reunion and deliver a lecture; there should not be any other public events. President Lee's public comments should not embarrass the United States or the President, or compromise our foreign policy objectives, and contact with the press should be strictly limited to the Cornell alumni events of media coverage. We will of course continue to entertain requests for transits to Taiwan's top leaders. We expect that requests for similar visits by other Taiwan leaders will be rare. We prefer President Lee inform Members of Congress that he does not intend to return to the US in the near future, and we would appreciate receiving your plans for carrying out the visit. The American Institute in Taiwan (AIT) should work closely with you to ensure that all appropriate arrangements are made. This matter should remain confidential until the White House makes an announcement

Not long before the visit, State made known its complaints about how our arrangements were proceeding: Taiwan was working with Congress against the Administration's policy; travel plans were released before agreement; Taiwan's "representatives" sought to have the ROC flag displayed, and a public reception arranged; they had encouraged other academic invitations and arranged caravans of Chinese Americans to go to Cornell; among many other transgressions. I do not believe these complaints could be verified one way or the other, and most never materialized. From my own observation, bonafide TECRO officials spent considerable energy preventing many of these activities from happening. But the atmosphere of distrust on the U.S. side, generated by having been publicly overruled by the White House, made an objective assessment very difficult. Beijing leaders were not the only ones who lost face over the decision.

During his four-day visit, I met with President Lee, Teng-hui both formally and informally, for about three hours. The President wanted my wife and me to share his limousine (except in Cornell), and formal sessions were with his delegation in the hotels in Los Angeles and Anchorage. I made clear my purpose was not to engage in a dialogue but to pass his thoughts about the U.S. relationship and cross-Straits relations on to those in Washington responsible for Taiwan policy decision-making. Before Ithaca, he spoke in English; afterwards in Mandarin. As usual, his conversations were disjointed as points he wanted to make came to mind. Also as usual, he ruminated on issues in a broad, long-term setting.

President Lee and his entourage arrived at Los Angeles on June 7th at the VIP terminal. There was no media present, no welcomers other than the staff of the Los Angeles TECRO office; the Taiwan representative and myself with our wives, and a representative from both the city and state governments. The State Department had agreed to assign several diplomatic security officers for the entire visit (because if they had not, the secret service, which protects visiting presidents, would have done so).

The motorcade with the city police escort took us to the hotel in the near suburbs of Los Angeles. As throughout the visit, except for the time spent in Cornell itself, the President and Mrs. Lee always asked us to join them in their limousine. Much to everyone's surprise, a small group of welcomers from the Taiwanese community, ROC flags and all, were waiting there. The President, now much more a politician than the academic he seemed a few years earlier, dove into the crowd with glee. The security people, both theirs and ours, blanched and dove in after him.

Having met so many of these people in my visits to the many Chinese and Tai-wanese organizations around the country, I knew the welcomers were not there because TECRO had encouraged them. On the contrary, they were organizations with whom at that time TECRO would have had little influence over.

Aside from that initial welcome, President Lee met discreetly with leaders of the more establishment Chinese-American organizations in the Los Angeles area, in the hotel. Then on the following morning, we left for the airport, to the special VIP terminal, and off to Syracuse, New York.

The airport there was not accustomed to handling 747 aircraft, and I was told the State Department security people had demanded the plane park some distance from the small terminal to avoid the small crowd that was gathering. The mayor of Syracuse was outraged and had overruled them. As we taxied toward the parking place, it was clear from our windows that a small welcoming group with flags were waiting—but so were Senators Helms, Murkowski, and D'Amato, who had flown up from Washington to meet him. The welcomers there were from the same type organizations I had seen in Los Angeles. After all the speeches of welcome were finished, President Rhodes of Cornell led the Lee entourage to the cars for the drive to Cornell.

The entourage went to a large tent on the campus for the welcoming speeches. Cornell students (and inevitably a few non-students) were lined up at the entrance to the tent, very emotionally waving flags and placards, to meet their president. One I recognized—a non-student and a Taiwan independence advocate who had used his radio station in Taipei to incite cabdrivers in the city to disrupt traffic as a protest against the Lee government. He was sought by the police there, had bolted to the U.S., and somehow was in the welcoming line with a large placard, cheering as loudly as any of the students in welcoming Lee, Teng-hui. The visit was launched and the entourage began two full days of meetings and speeches.

The only U.S. "official" presence at Cornell during the visit was the diplomatic security people, Ray Sanders, the Director of economic and trade issues in AIT, who worked with Cornell and Taiwan personnel at the visitor Control Center, and my wife and I who were a part Lee's entourage. The three senators who had greeted Lee had returned to Washington; but some members of Congress came up during the two days. The visit, rightly, was arranged and controlled by Cornell. Ray continuously kept the State department informed as the visit progressed.

One issue that was causing State much anxiety was scheduled press conference that traditionally followed the annual Olin lecture in that year being given by Lee. The Taiwan side would have liked to have it, and the media—both Taiwanese and U.S.—were expecting it. Cornell was insisting on it. The State Department wanted it scratched. Cornell as a compromise proposed having the Provost, diverting any political questions from the President. But the State Department continued to insist there should be no press conference. I talked with Lee's principal advisor who agreed to ask Cornell to cancel it. The media, needless to say, was very unhappy.

The Olin lecture was the high point of the visit. It was held in a gymnasium with a large attendance. Lee's speech was passed out just before he gave it (Ray faxed it to the State Department even as it was being given). He spoke in English, with excellent timing and pronunciation. For those of us witnessing the speech, with all the drama that had preceded it, the moment was memorable.

What impressed me most at that time, was that the speech—even the visit itself—could have, indeed should have, been so benign, not a tense issue between three governments.

But the speech became an event that the State Department and Secretary Christopher, in his memoirs, considered a pivotal issue. The Secretary's view was doubtless based on the analysis he received from his Department at that time, but it continues to be held by many of those then directing our policies toward China and Taiwan. Those in the State Department so inclined point to the generous use of the words "Republic of China", while Beijing criticized the absence of any reference to "one China". In my view, one might argue that the visit itself created the tensions that resulted (which I believe was only partially true), or perhaps how badly we managed the decision on whether or how to have the visit, but not the speech.

As soon as the speech was concluded, by phone I talked with the State Department, expressing my view that it had not been a "political" speech, and should not cause any additional problems. The officer told me that, in fact, it had been read and judged to be very "political". State was very unhappy. A few minutes later—I was still in the gymnasium—I received a call back: from State telling me that the State assessment should be retracted. The White House, I was told, did not find the speech "political". I thought, then, that would put to rest the speech and its impact. To my surprise, it seems, the view that the speech was a major irritant of the visit persists.

After several meetings and speeches, and a walk around the campus the next day, we went back to Syracuse and departed for Anchorage. Immediately after takeoff, we were fed with Chinese beef noodle soup—as much as we could eat—and the best relaxant one could have thought of. The stop in Anchorage overnight was to rest, and to permit the President's entourage to arrive in Taipei at a suitable time. The next morning my wife and I went on a private tour of Anchorage with President and Mrs. Lee. From Los Angeles to the return takeoff at Syracuse, we had used English (he wanted to practice). Thereafter, always in Chinese. Though aware of the problems this trip might bring, as usual he was looking far ahead of that. The world had been reminded of Taiwan—and that was the trip's ultimate purpose.

Back in Washington, in the weeks leading up to the visit, there had been several meetings I was asked to chair Representative Lu and our side. In addition to the strong messages to Lu regarding the State Department's opposition to the Lee visit, and complaints that Taiwan was ignoring these warnings, there were additional discussions about implementing the results of the Taiwan Policy Review. There were complaints here also, that Lu was pressing for more changes before the TPR changes had been put into operation. Lu, as always pleasant, kept pressing for more even after his proposals had been rejected. (I had explained to the State Department that Lu was under pressure from the Legislative Yuan in Taipei to show some accomplishment in his work). Even after the Lee visit, the meetings I chaired resulted in the same lack of agreement or useful communications.

There were two things that contributed to this lack of communications between Lu and senior policy officers that attended these meetings, Lu's style, and his lack of understanding on how to take part in the give-and-take of informal meetings dealing with foreign-policy matters; and after the decision on the Lee visit especially, the bruised feelings of those who had had a serious setback—or loss of face—in having to fold on the Lee request for a visit.

This eventually led to the periodic, informal meetings held in New York between a senior official from Taiwan and a counterpart from the NSC. These meetings were secret, but inevitably, after the fact, became public. They were meant to overcome the communications problem, but with time, and personnel changes on both sides, it seems to have become dormant.

In the post-visit period, there was two other issues that took up most of my time. First was to expedite the upgrading of the AIT financial system—a project that was requested when I first started in my position in AIT; and at the same time cope with the turmoil caused by the media publication and reactions connected with announcement of my replacement Chairman of AIT.

The most time-consuming problem was moving the changes needed in the AIT financial system. My initial report to the State Department in 1990 included this need to upgrade the AIT financial system. I laid out a plan to bring in a new Executive Officer with experience in State Department administration. This was approved but took two years to implement (because the replacement was to be done by attrition, and it included raising the rank of the position to assure professional capability). Over the five years in AIT, I worked closely with the State Department administrative offices in developing a far better, more open system. It was a long frustrating exercise that made headway but was still in progress when I left.

The complexities involved a recalcitrant AIT Taipei office; an inability, in my view, of the State Departments inspector general's office to understand AIT (it is legally a private corporation subject to private sector laws but required to abide by government regulations as well); an element of State Department administration that created unnecessary obstacles; a lack of support from the policy bureau; and, as usual, a number of personality differences. These were all frustrating and they slowed progress, but in the end, computers were already arriving as I left, and the plans for the new transparent and efficient financial system approved and being followed.

While these internal problems were going on, shortly after the Lee visit, I was informed that it had been decided I would, this time, be replaced. I agreed to stay until all the necessary processes were complete. I thought it would be at most a few weeks, but it was December before the replacement was approved. After the move was made public, the Washington-based Taiwan media had a field day throughout the several months the appointment was in process.

The board of Trustees of AIT has three members, one of which is the Chairman. The first AIT Chairman, David Dean, was still on the Board, and after writing to the Secretary advising him of the consequences of an inexperienced Chairman, he resigned in protest. The newest member, William Clark, also resigned. The bylaws of the AIT corporation required two votes to legally approve a new member of the Board, (although the Secretary officially selects each member). Thus, while a rather public process for approving the new Chairman was aired in the Taiwan press, the State Department was having difficulty finding two new members of the Board, to elect a new Chairman, partly because clearances (physical, financial, and security) took so long.

Mr. James Wood, an Arkansas lawyer with little background in the intricacies and nuances of one of Americas most important and sensitive relationships, was the replacement. This was in itself, grist for the media and Taiwan experts' mill. His past experiences, some real and some rumored, were publicly aired in great detail. His approval came as a surprise but was completed in mid-December. The State Department had succeeded in finding two new members of the Board, so I left the day before he officially assumed his appointment.

CHAPTER THIRTEEN
Final Thoughts

There were two other events started in 1995: the impact of the direct election of the president and the legislature, and an important result of the missile crisis. There were doubtless many reports from Taipei sent to Washington on these, but I continued my own trips to Taiwan informally. In 1994, after the National Assembly had voted in the law allowing the direct election of the President, I had reported to the State Department that since Lee, Teng-hui was very popular, he would very likely be elected again. As a president couldn't become more legitimate than a popularly elected one, I asked what were we to do then? I got no reply then, and would not if I were to ask today.

We did not know what to do, in other words, but China did. We heard about the missile exercises in the Taiwan Straits conducted by China in 1995. These were generated by the direct election of the Legislative Yuan, and presumably the forthcoming direct election of the President. The trip to Cornell by President Lee in June1995 had not been expected. In America, the experts still place the blame for the second missile crisis on their favorite troublemaker Lee, Teng-hui. It meshed nicely with the charge that the trip was "bought." Placing blame, however, on the direct elections of the President, was much more difficult as we support democracy.

The second event was an important result of the missile crisis. For years, American military aircraft, flying to-and-fro from countries in the area, flew through Taiwan airspace with no communications permitted, despite complaints from Taiwan. The risk of collision was high. It took the missile crisis of 1996 to finally address reality. In addition to the need for communications, the crisis made it clear that the requirement in the TRA that states the U.S. must maintain sufficient military capabilities in the area should the U.S. decide to help Taiwan from invasion from China, had to be observed. Congress subsequently passed legislation requiring annual reports on this and relevant PRC military capabilities.

Just recently a visitor to Taiwan, after describing Taiwan as having a "vibrant" democracy, asked me what that meant. The best description I could think of was the past election, where 80 percent of the eligible voters went to the polls. It is vibrant because such a large percentage of voters actually participate in the political process.

In the short span of a decade, Taiwan opened its society in what is often termed a peaceful revolution of its political system. Power is largely in the hands of a new generation, most of whom were born or raised on Taiwan. Power has been dispersed between the Executive Branch, the now more powerful Legislative Yuan, and local governments. There is oversight by the legislature and the open media. There are periodic open, vigorously contested, multiparty, direct elections at all levels of government. National priorities now more accurately reflect those of the electorate.

With the coming of a democratic system replacing an authoritarian one, the constitution has had to be revised, and the laws changed, to distribute political power differently, not only at the national level, but with local governments. The possibility of different political parties in control of different institutions and at different levels of government, have had to be addressed. As the country fashions its democratic government, it has introduced its own unique character by setting precedents for various activities as they take place. For example, the President, now participates in campaigns openly, and at the grass roots. Other national leaders of course follow. The National Affairs Conference of 1990 established, among many other issues, that consensus would be sought from all segments of society, not just the ruling party as in the past.

As a democracy, with political leaders competing for power, domestic concerns weigh more heavily on external matters than they did in the authoritarian past. Any policy or action which will at some point require legislative action, for example, must take the profile and the posture of the now empowered Legislative Yuan into account. In a democracy where the ruling party does not have a significant majority, issues become highly-politicized and progress is possible only with substantial compromise. These all apply to the domestic political scene on Taiwan.

No more so than on Cross-Straits relations. The practical economic need to expand the relationship with the PRC must be balanced not only by security interests but by the sentiments of a majority of the voters. The issue of national identity was not allowed to be discussed under the old regime but is now not only legal but vigorously debated. There are strong sentiments among people who would like independence, but relatively few who would press for it now. There are those who want or think it is best for Taiwan to unify with the PRC, but among them few who want it now. There is overwhelming agreement that any effort at resolution of the relationship with the PRC should be put off to a more propitious time well into the future. Whatever debate there is, therefore, is not how to resolve the issue now, but how best to assure the future outcome as they would like to see it. The over-arching need to maintain stability in this open and prosperous society, and the sensitivity of this relationship, places constraints on any bold initiatives by the leadership.

The highly competitive politics of Taiwan require the President to govern through a process of delicate balancing: first, between the increasingly evenly divided ruling and opposition party; secondly, in government, between what the Executive Branch wants and what the Legislative Branch will accept; and thirdly, on Cross-Straits matters, between moves toward improving relations with the mainland to satisfy some constituencies, and moves to demonstrate Taiwan's separate entity to satisfy others.

The most recent efforts to amend the constitution were an example of the checks and balances that are observed not only in the political arena but in government structure as well. The opposition gained a much sought after elimination of the provincial government in return for giving the president more power in dealing with the legislature. A proposal that was left for another day was a requirement for a majority vote to be elected president (something the KMT wanted), in exchange for the right of referendum (wanted by the DPP).

One of the fears many had with the coming of democracy to Taiwan is that the open advocacy of such sensitive subjects as independence would generate destabilizing actions if not outright military intervention by the PRC. There are several actions that have been taken that fall into this category. Yet one of the results of public discussion and debate inherent in the new democratic atmosphere, has been to actually lower the likelihood of such reaction.

When Hau, Pao-tsun was dismissed as premier, for example, there was concern that there would be a reaction from Beijing. There was none. When the proposal for the direct election of the president was being debated, the argument against it was that it favored Taiwanese nationalism and would draw a reaction from the PRC. It did not. (The missile "exercise" by the PRC was meant to curb nationalist sentiment on Taiwan). When the National Assembly voted to abolish (for all practical purposes) the provincial government, many predicted a strong reaction from Beijing. There was none.

Before any of these actions were taken, they were preceded by a substantial period of open, public debate. The result was that it became clear in each case that the purpose had more to do with domestic politics than with cross-strait relations. In an authoritarian regime, such actions could more likely be a part of some long term strategy; in a democracy they are more likely to be responsive to the domestic requirements of the present.

Some other changes that have resulted from democratization have had various degrees of influence on U.S.- Taiwan relations. The military, for example, has been taken out of politics. Their budget is submitted to the legislature and its defense committee. In the new, democratic Taiwan, oversight from there and the media now exist. This openness impacts on how the U.S. manages its arms sales program – a subject that has been especially sensitive in the past. In addition, the once feared Taiwan Garrison Command with its domestic political security apparatus, is gone.

In the past, a bureaucratic career through the ruling party was sought by the best and the brightest. It brought power, paid well, and one could rise to the top of government. With democracy and an open market economy, the status of a bureaucracy changed. A philosophy of control changes to one of service, for example. Many positions at the senior levels of government, such as cabinet ministers, are now not given to senior bureaucrats but to mainly leaders in other fields such as academia, business, or professionals. And when they leave the cabinet they return to the private sector. The transition at this senior level has begun, but the changes in attitude needed in the bureaucracy underneath it will take much longer.

Democracy in Taiwan has also brought with it the difficulty of coping with problems common to most democracies: law & order, money politics, and the power of the media. Corruption is another complaint that gnaws at the social fabric and undermines respect for political leaders and the bureaucracy. Democratization has eliminated the repressive laws of the past but has made abuse of those remaining easier.

What we have witnessed is a Taiwan that has gone through a peaceful revolution, and is very substantially different than the Taiwan that existed when the U.S. shaped its policies toward the island in 1979. It was clear that the extent of the changes would have an impact on Cross-Strait relations, and therefore on U.S. - Taiwan and U.S. – PRC relations. It took some time before the PRC and the U.S., each in its own way, have come to recognize the changed situation. Neither has developed an effective strategy to accommodate it, however.

The people of Taiwan, more conscious of their own identity, and now more able to express it, will continue to generate greater assertiveness on the part of their leaders. Democratization, in addition to opening the society to free speech and assembly, also has bestowed on the leadership, through open direct elections, a much greater legitimacy. It is not now adequate to dismiss initiatives made by the government in Taipei as merely strategic moves in a geopolitical game. They are just as often based on the mood, the attitudes, or the needs of a broad constituency.

In addition to the broad impact democratization has made, there is also the effect on the everyday conduct of the U.S. – Taiwan relationship. A fundamental understanding that existed for many years in this unofficial relationship was that Taiwan should maintain a low profile and avoid raising tensions with the PRC. Conventional wisdom was that this permitted the U.S. to improve its relationship with the PRC without the complication of the Taiwan "problem." "Low profile," however, and "democracy," are practically a contradiction in terms. With the now active oversight function of the Legislative Yuan, and the open media that ferrets out even the most sensitive of issues, low profile is no longer possible. Thus meetings with foreign countries that include officials from both sides are reported in the press. The sensitive subject of arms sales is now fair game not only for the Legislative Yuan through hearings in its Defense Committee, but by the media.

Some important restraints on senior official contacts remain. They were marginally relaxed by the policy review in 1994, permitting calls by Taiwan representatives on senior officials in U.S. Government buildings, except the State Department and the White House. Given the large number of issues that must be addressed between the two sides, the volume of business, both government and private sector, that must be conducted, the sensitivity of some of the issues, and the limited time busy senior officials have , even the remaining restraints hamper dialogue between the two sides.

The democratization of Taiwan as well as the larger changes taking place in the world – the globalization of economies, the effect on nations of the information and technological revolution – will continue to press the U.S. to do more in adapting present Taiwan policy to the new realities.

It will be difficult for history to assess if there was a broad strategy that brought about the democratization of Taiwan. CCK started a process of political reform, but it is not known what his long term vision for a political system for Taiwan really was. Realistically, it is unlikely that he had in mind establishing the system that has developed since his death. His roots were in the mainland, and his vision for Taiwan's future was shaped accordingly.

Lee, Teng-hui's presidency had steered Taiwan in a direction that it is unlikely CCK ever would have done. Lee had a broad vision of where he thinks Taiwan should go, but like any sitting leader, his actions often reflect the needs or the constraints of the moment. What is amazing is how quickly very fundamental changes were made, including a transfer of power from one community with a strong sense of mission, to another with a different perspective, peacefully. In the process, Lee, Teng-hui has thoroughly Taiwanized the politics of Taiwan.

Taiwan's democracy now faces its biggest threat ever, not from within, but from its giant neighbor and the increasing inability of the United States and its friends to defend Taiwan from a growing but no-less hostile China. President Lincoln at the Gettysburg battlefield once questioned whether the then experiment of American democracy, "whether … any nation so conceived and so dedicated, can long endure … it is for us to … highly resolve that these dead shall not have died in vain – that this nation, under God, shall have a new birth of freedom – and that the government of the people, by the people, for the people, shall not perish from the earth." It is my greatest hope that Taiwan's democracy does not perish from the earth, that it will persevere, and that the league of democracies in this world will endure to preserve it.

Acronyms

AIT	American Institute in Taiwan (set up by the U.S., under the Taiwan Relations Act to conduct unofficial diplomatic relations with Taiwan)
AIT/W	American Institute in Taiwan, Washington Office
AIT/T	American Institute in Taiwan, Taipei Office
ANC	African National Congress
ARATS	Association for Relations Across the Taiwan Straits
CCK	Chiang Ching-Kuo (President of the ROC)
CCNAA	Coordination Council for North American Affairs (counterpart to AIT, Taiwan's office in the U.S. handling unofficial diplomatic relations; later called TECRO)
CIA	Central Intelligence Agency
DAS	Deputy Assistant Secretary of State
DPP	Democratic Progressive Party
EAP	East Asia Bureau, U.S. Department of State
GATT	General Agreement on Tariffs & Trade (later re-established as the World Trade Organization (WTO))
ICAF	Industrial College of the Armed Forces
IO	International Organizations
INR	Intelligence and Research Bureau
KMT	Kuo-ming Tang Party (Nationalist Party)
MIG	Mikoyan-Gurevich fighter plane (Soviet-made)
PRC	People's Republic of China
ROC	Republic of China
TECRO	Taipei Economic and Cultural Representative Office
TRA	Taiwan Relations Act
UN	United Nations
USAID	U.S. Agency for International Development
USIA	U.S. Information Agency
WWII	World War 2

51859218R00125

Made in the USA
San Bernardino, CA
05 August 2017